THE
OBITUARY
RON FRANSCELL

WILDBLUE
PRESS

WildBluePress.com

THE OBITUARY published by:
WILDBLUE PRESS
1153 Bergen Pkwy Ste I #114
Evergreen, Colorado 80439

Copyright 1999, 2015 by Ron Franscell

All rights reserved. No part of this book may be reproduced in any form or by any means without the prior written consent of the Publisher, excepting brief quotes used in reviews.

WILDBLUE PRESS is registered at the U.S. Patent and Trademark Offices.

Cover Design and Interior Layout by Elijah Toten
www.totencreative.com

Art Director Carla Torrisi Jackson

978-1-942266-03-7   Trade Paperback ISBN
978-1-942266-04-4   eBook ISBN

This book is dedicated to Mom and Dad

You never know as you move through these labyrinths whether you are pursuing a goal or running from yourself, whether you are the hunter or his prey.

JOSEPH BRODSKY
Watermark

NIGHT PIRATES

Tuesday, June 3, 2003

Pearly Benson could have used a little more time. With a few more seconds, he might have been able to call for help on his cell phone. With a few more minutes, he might have prayed or pleaded for a few more minutes. With another hour, he might have made himself ready to die.

But it all happened too quickly.

While the Burlington, Iowa, truck driver, a single father of four, slept in an empty interstate rest area just outside Spearfish, South Dakota, three men crept into his Peterbilt sleeper cab a little after 3 a.m. One of them, wielding a small sledge hammer, pounded a sharpened railroad spike through Pearly's eye socket into his dreaming brain. He didn't even have time to hurt.

But pain was inefficient, and these pirates were nothing if not cold-bloodedly efficient.

They drove Pearly's truck west into Wyoming. Beneath a highway overpass at a dark little border town called Beulah, they dumped Pearly's still-warm body in the bed of a waiting pickup, which transported him to a secluded, lonely hole already custom-dug for him in the Wyoming prairie. Pearly would spend eternity in shallow, foreign earth far from his home and children, never found.

One hour later, right on schedule, they were met at a truck stop where three more men in rubber gloves swept the trailer for tracking devices; they found four, which were disarmed and dismantled on the spot, long before the truck or Pearly were ever missed. They also hacked into the QualComm satellite system from a laptop in their black van, and removed the tracking dish from the top of the rig. For anyone who cared, including the Feds, Pearly's stolen truck was rendered invisible from the protective satellites overhead.

And Pearly's load, a wide array of pharmaceuticals due to be dropped at a Wal-Mart warehouse in Minneapolis, Minnesota, was already sold. Broken up on the foreign and domestic black market, it would net more than three million dollars. The hijackers would eventually barter Pearly's repainted Peterbilt for a stolen rail shipment of military weapons and explosives in Mobile, Alabama. The brown stain in the sleeper was said to be spilled battery acid, but even the truth wouldn't have mattered much. In their world, battery acid was spilled everywhere.

And Pearly's four fatherless kids, their mother long dead, would be scattered by Iowa's overworked social services department to four different foster families, where they inevitably would come to hate the government for what it took from them.

All in all, it was a good night for the Fourth Sign.

CHAPTER ONE

Jefferson Morgan inhaled, wondering if particles of death floated on cemetery air.

After a night of rain, the graveyard smells like sweet resurrection. The morning sun draws out the damp, the dark and the ferment, and they mingle as they rise on the warming air.

The long-dead floated in the June morning, cleansed by both clay and concealment in Wyoming's ancient soil. He knew well that death in its various other forms was not so fragrant. He'd smelled most of them.

Morgan was sure even the stink of Laddie Granbouche had mellowed.

Laddie's tomb, a modest, above-ground chamber built of red sandstone from the fabled Hole in the Wall country, was disintegrating. Vandals, rigorous winters and riding lawn-mowers had taken their toll. Cracks spidered across the base — some wide enough for a man's fingers — and the mortar seal around the vault had dissolved. It was also sinking into the overwatered cemetery topsoil.

Ever the newspaperman, Morgan kneeled close for a photo. Only Laddie's epitaph remained intriguingly proud:

LADDIE GRANBOUCHE
1876-1969
Yesterday is history
Tomorrow is mystery

So before the tomb collapsed entirely, spilling what might be left of Laddie after thirty dead years, the Perry County commissioners decided to rebuild it in a new section of Winchester's Pine Lawn Cemetery. Besides, it didn't take much to qualify as a tourist attraction in any small town, and Laddie was the closest thing to a celebrity in Winchester, Wyoming.

It was a Saturday morning at the end of a long week. Morgan snapped a few pictures of her next-to-final resting place for next week's *Bullet* before the cemetery caretaker started dismantling it. This was big news in a small town where no news was nothing new. And the editor always worked harder on slow news weeks, which was most.

And although it was unlikely Laddie's bone dust would tell any new tales, a small cadre of curious forensic anthropologists under the renowned Dr. Shawn Cowper of the University of South Florida hovered around Laddie's grave that morning to take measure of the old gal. A surgical mask hung around each of their necks as they prepared for the exhumation of Laddie's husk.

Morgan zoomed in on a pretty grad student, one of Cowper's helpers. She seemed too young and full of life for the work of death. Under her Polar-Tec pullover, earmuffs and two pairs of rubber gloves, she resented the chill of Wyoming morning, even in June. Poor little Florida girl, Morgan thought. Her perky nose ran in the chilly morning, and she nibbled a glazed doughnut with the same ambivalent zeal the Donner Party approached lunch. Maybe it was her first exhumation, or maybe just her first Wyoming morning.

Laddie died in her sleep on a hot summer night in 1969, a natural and unremarkable end for a living mystery. She'd lived alone as long as anyone could remember, holed up in her riverstone mansion at La Plata Ranch beneath the sheltering, blood-red rimrock in the badlands north of Winchester. She wasn't a recluse, but she loved being alone. And if the myth she cultivated in the last half of her long life were authentic — and many people believed it was — she might have preferred the sanctuary of open spaces.

At any rate, she lay in her four-poster bed for two days before the county agent found her. If the truth be known, he never actually saw Laddie's putrefying remains; he merely smelled them from the front porch and radioed the sheriff from his truck.

Laddie was ninety-three years old, and her body just gave out. She had lived passionately and loved passionately, if the stories were true. She was one of the West's most legendary women, if the stories were true. Before she really died, she was fond of saying she'd already died six times, if the stories were true.

But nobody really knew if the stories were true.

Now, sanctioned by history and a country judge, Dr. Cowper and his forensic sleuths hoped to collect post-mortem evidence to prove (or disprove) the possibility that Laddie Granbouche was, as she long claimed, the infamous mistress of an equally infamous desperado.

Dawn unfolded warm. Morgan sipped tepid convenience-store coffee from a Styrofoam cup and watched Cowper's young scientists prepare the machinery of their curiosity: video and still cameras, high-wattage lights, a small gas-powered generator, mobile lab equipment, laptop computers, surgical instruments and garden tools. A lone gravedigger pounded his pry bar into the powdery mortar between

Laddie's sandstone blocks, peeling them away one by one, and setting them gently aside in the dewy grass. A plastic grocery sack fluttered in the highest branches of an old cottonwood, like a sentry angel keeping watch over the whole affair. The only sounds of the morning were the metallic clang of the gravedigger's pike, a meadowlark warbling somewhere in the cemetery, and the locust-click of laptop keyboards.

Laddie would have liked the attention, Morgan thought.

Some folks said she clutched an old photograph of her outlaw lover to her pale, naked breast. Others said it was his Colt revolver. All the sheriff ever said was that Laddie Granbouche seemed to be smiling when he found her.

In the end, nobody knew for certain whether her last pleasant expression was a smile or merely the rictus of death, but Laddie would have been happy to know people would always wonder. That's how mere mysteries became myths. Laddie always liked the idea of being a myth.

The gravedigger pried the lid off Laddie's cracked granite vault, exposing a simple oak casket.

Morgan took a few steps toward it and shot a few more photos, but he was also morbidly curious.

Would they still see Laddie Granbouche's last smile? Could they boot up their computers and electron microscopes to peer inside her withered brain and see that last dream, the one that made her smile?

And even if Laddie Granbouche had once been known as Etta Place, Morgan wondered, could they analyze the dust of her heart and know if she truly ever loved a common horse thief named Harry Longabaugh, aka the Sundance Kid?

THE OBITUARY

Etta Place was a ghost long before Laddie Granbouche fell asleep for the last time.

And she especially haunted Dr. Shawn Cowper.

Only 36, Cowper was a wunderkind, already one of the nation's leading historical detectives, using DNA, the latest computer technology and old-fashioned deduction to unravel some timeworn myths and dispel hoary hoaxes. His curiosity was romantic as well as scientific; he earned undergraduate degrees in literature and history.

In one of his first cases, he proved some old bones in a roadside museum shanty outside Richmond, Virginia, were not John Wilkes Booth's, as claimed. Later, after an exhaustive year's study of unearthed genetic material, he reported it was statistically likely that Lt. Col. George Armstrong Custer's body — or most of it — had actually been accurately (and miraculously) identified among the mingled remains at the Little Big Horn and reburied at West Point.

Even in the haze of the Buck Snort Tavern, a Highway 12 roadhouse thick with cigarette smoke and jukebox twang, his young eyes generated their own light when he talked about Etta Place, the enigmatic mistress of a legendary badman.

Cowper's char-broiled, hand-patted burger sat uneaten in its nest of curly fries and limp pickles as he explained her mystery to Morgan the night before the exhumation. His beer glass sweated in the vulgar ambience of the honky-tonk, and he traced his finger through the wet puddles on the table as he drifted through another life, not his own, long ago ended.

"If not for Butch and Sundance, Etta might have been no Place at all," Cowper said, relishing a cheap pun as only a scientist would. His eyes twinkled mischievously behind his studious, wire-rimmed glasses. "We don't even know her real name, and I've found credible evidence that at least five different women associated with the Wild Bunch used the alias 'Etta Place.'"

"What about Laddie Granbouche? How likely is it that she is the real Etta Place?" Morgan asked, swizzling a fry in a blob of ketchup.

Cowper clearly savored the puzzle.

"Well, she's the right age. We're trying to match some later photos of her to a 1901 picture of her with Sundance. We can analyze bone structure, facial symmetry and shape with a computer. We can even take a photo of an elderly woman and project her appearance into the past for a fairly good idea of how she appeared as a young woman. You gotta love computers."

"What about DNA?"

Cowper shook his head.

"Not much use in this case. We have nothing to compare it to. We'll harvest some tissue samples, but we'll mostly be looking for physical evidence to prove Laddie Granbouche was not Etta Place."

"Like what?"

"For instance, we'll be able to determine her living height within an inch. If Laddie was five-foot-one, we'll know she wasn't Etta Place, who was fairly tall, according to photos and the Pinkertons' description."

An Eagles song hung in the smoke, and drifted away. A drunken cowboy teetered on muddy boots at the jukebox until Patsy Cline began falling to pieces. He unhitched a cell phone from the hip of his Wranglers and dialed clumsily. He said something Morgan couldn't hear over the saloon's din then held the phone up to the jukebox speaker until the song was done. The whole of his life boiled down to three chords and a sad story. Then he sat down alone at a dark table and talked to his Budweiser.

"What else do you know for sure about Etta Place?" Morgan asked.

"Almost nothing. Maybe she was born Laura Etta

Ingerfield, the illegitimate daughter of a feckless British earl who sent her to be reared by Fannie Porter, a San Antonio madam. Or maybe she was Amy Parker, whose cousin was Robert Leroy Parker himself ..."

"Butch Cassidy?"

"One and the same. But I also think it's possible her real name has been lost altogether, like a shadow after the light is turned off."

"But she existed. You have photos. Nobody knew her?"

"Sure, but you know how people are. The stories all get embellished and romanticized, subjects lie, memories get foggy, secrets get carried to graves," Cowper ticked off all the reasons only good science was credible. "She might have been a teacher, with special talent for music. There's a little evidence she attended some of the swankiest schools in the East, all paid for by the sweat of Fannie Porter's girls. But there's equally compelling evidence she was a common prostitute in Texas. Take your pick."

"So, bottom line, you don't know much for sure," Morgan said. He was beginning to understand Cowper's fascination with secrets of the dead. But where Morgan's interest was sentimental, Cowper's was empirical.

"I know she was pretty, from her pictures. She was no Katharine Ross, but her face was quite attractive. I know she was adventurous. I know she was smart. I know she held her own in a very tough environment. Even the Pinkertons described her as 'refined' and beautiful. Who wouldn't love a woman like that?"

"Everybody loves a bad girl," Morgan joked.

"Those were different times, Jeff. Lots of people came West to forget old lives, including women. Everybody had a past. It was no sin for a woman to be unladylike, even to screw around a little bit. Her reputation rested solely on how she treated other people. Today, we might call Etta a bad girl, sure, but we've gotten harder to please."

"But not all frontier women holed up with bank robbers," Morgan said.

Cowper grinned.

"Okay, so Etta was a little wild. More than wild. One of my historians thinks she was married with two children when she deserted her family for Sundance. I've seen arguments that she was the Kid's cousin because both of their mothers' maiden names was Place, and they were childhood sweethearts. Others say Butch, not Sundance, was her cousin ... as well as her first outlaw lover."

"So she got around a little."

"She knew how to have a good time! We have some letters where they call themselves a 'family of three' and the possibility of a ménage a trois has entered a few of those dirty historians' minds."

"Makes good legend."

"And legends make good movies. But if she entertained both of them, it didn't last long. We know she and Sundance took a train to New Orleans in 1900 and probably got married. There's no public record to prove it, but soon after, they 'honeymooned' in Buffalo, New York."

"Outlaw romance," Morgan said. "How sentimental."

"Well maybe not. Their honeymoon suite was in a place called Dr. Pierce's Invalid Hotel. Back in those days, it was sort of a Betty Ford Center for syphilitics. It's very possible Etta was being treated for VD."

"Something borrowed ..." Morgan quipped.

Cowper smiled broadly and shook his finger at Morgan.

"You're bad, my friend," he said.

The jukebox belted out a spunky tune by a popular country girl group, one of those farmer-feminist protest songs that makes cowgirls put bumper-stickers on their boyfriends' pickup trucks. The lonely old cell-phone cowboy's brow furrowed, his mood suddenly as flat as his beer. He pushed his greasy Stetson back, exposing the white half of his forehead, and seemed to wonder where he went wrong.

How sad to want to make a connection with someone but never know if the message was getting through, Morgan thought. Ever since his mother had been diagnosed with Alzheimer's disease and gone to the Laurel Gardens Home in Winchester, he wondered about all the invisible barriers in life, from cells that had locked-in memories to the finite reach of a cell phone's signal on a summer night.

Morgan hankered to send a beer over to the old cowboy's table, for comfort, not entertainment. But he'd clearly had enough. Instead, Morgan decided to offer him a ride home at the end of the night.

Cowper wolfed some curly fries in the lull, and then continued his account of Etta Place's travels.

"Right after their pleasant tryst at the Invalid Hotel, she and Sundance boarded the SS Herminius for Argentina. And there, the cold trail of Etta Place freezes solid. We think she returned at least three times because she was homesick or needed medical attention, maybe an abortion. For every fact, we have a dozen rumors and two dozen myths."

"Like what?"

"One is that she was carrying a child — not Sundance's — and she came back to the States to give birth. Another is that she and Butch had a daughter in 1903. Personally, I think she just vanished after Sundance brought her back to Denver in 1908."

"Where?"

"If I knew, I wouldn't be here with you and the Dixie Chicks tonight. Nobody knows for sure. Some think she went to New York, some Texas. Maybe she went back to

South America. And there's a lot of territory in between ... and a lot of stories."

"For instance ... ?"

"Well, one historian claims she died with Butch and Sundance in the 1908 shootout in Bolivia. A Pinkerton agent swears he inspected the corpses of Butch, Sundance and Etta after a botched bank robbery down there in 1911. Some people say she committed suicide in the States in 1924, and others claim they can prove Etta, Butch and Sundance all fought with Pancho Villa in the Mexican Revolution. And then there's Laddic."

"So, just between us, what's your gut say?"

"My gut is pissed that I haven't eaten this burger because I'm talking too much," Cowper joked. "But we can't rule her out. We're still pulling together all the public records we can find. There's just not much out there. Not unusual for cases in that time period, especially for a woman in the West. Nobody really kept good records."

"So digging up Laddie is the beginning, not the end?"

"We had to move fast when the county decided to relocate the grave. Your county officials gave us a very small window of opportunity, so there are still lots of loose ends. We won't be doing a full autopsy. We'll open the casket, shoot some film with Kreskin, our portable X-ray machine. One of our people will inventory and photograph personal effects buried with Laddie, like jewelry and clothing. Then we'll take a few tissue samples like hair and skin, maybe some bone, quickly examine her body and do some measurements, then move Laddie to her next rest stop on the highway to Heaven."

"Then?"

"Then we go back to try to make sense of it. Maybe we'll never know, but at least we'll have evidence to prove our ignorance."

Morgan sat back in his honky-tonk chair, his green beer bottle stripped of its label.

"Gotta tell you, Shawn, this is the biggest thing to happen to a corpse in this town since Carter McWayne got drunk and rolled his hearse."

Cowper nearly passed a curly fry through his nose.

The lonesome cowboy gulped the piddling remnants of his beer and willed his loose-jointed knees toward the door. He slapped the leather cell-phone case on his belt, high noon at last call. Morgan briefly thought about excusing himself to drive the old boy home, but maybe the night air would be better for him. The rheumy-eyed cowboy pushed the tavern door wide and disappeared into the friendless night.

"What about Butch and Sundance?" Morgan asked, wondering what becomes of old men when they vanish into the dark. "Do you think they really survived and came home?"

Dr. Cowper turned his green beer bottle as if he were screwing it into the wooden tabletop.

"Oh, that's another project, my friend. Another dream."

"Why do you do this?"

"Are you kidding? We wouldn't have invented history if we didn't want to know what happened before us. But sometimes, history needs a little help. That's my job."

"You seem to enjoy it."

Dr. Cowper grew wistful.

"When I was a kid, I read Malory's King Arthur. The romance and the chivalry fascinated me, but I got this crazy idea that I could go to Avalon someday and find Arthur's bones, like it would prove the existence of Camelot and all it stood for."

Morgan recalled his own youthful visions, and even pondered Etta Place as a latter-day Guinevere, sharing her passions with two men. He lifted his beer bottle in a toast to dreams and to Dr. Cowper, who waved him off self-consciously.

"No, no," he said. "I think there's something perverse about a twelve-year-old kid contemplating a life of grave-robbing."

Morgan lifted his glass to Cowper, and they drank anyway.

"You have a family?"

Cowper shrugged. He studied the greasy burger between his long fingers for a long moment, as if looking for some clues to the life of the cow.

"My family is dead."

Morgan turned suddenly somber.

"I'm so sorry ..."

"No, no, I'm just goofing around. My 'family' is a bunch of ghosts and dried-out cadavers. I married my obsession. My children are old bones and computers. I spend all my holidays and weekends with them. The only bad thing is, I always have to visit them. They never travel."

A scientist with a sense of humor, Morgan thought. Then again, maybe it wasn't so rare among men and women who spent their days with customers who never laughed.

"Besides," Cowper continued, "what wife could compete with Etta Place?"

Laddie Granbouche's casket lid was already loose. Rather than lift it out of the vault, Cowper asked it be left where it was originally laid. He lifted the hefty top, blocking Morgan's view as he reeled off several photographs.

Flanked by several team members, surgical masks in place and cameras clicking, the young anthropologist visually examined whatever remained of Laddie Granbouche's mortal coil. From where he stood, Morgan couldn't see inside the casket, only Cowper's eyes as they methodically scanned the length of the box for a full minute.

Then, with a surgeon's grace and equanimity, Cowper gently closed the lid.

"Fellas," he said, stripping off his rubber gloves and mask, "we have a little problem."

CHAPTER TWO

Sheriff Highlander Goldsmith lingered around Laddie Granbouche's closed casket like a jumpy kid with a jack-in-the-box. The thick smear of Vicks Vapo-Rub on his upper lip, a cop's precaution against the stench of decaying flesh, looked silly.

Dr. Cowper lifted the lid, and Goldsmith leaned forward from a safe distance, as if ready to run. His nose was pinched like an earwig's tail and his Adam's apple bobbed in his scrawny neck as he craned to peek inside. The weight of his own badge threatened to unbalance him.

Morgan squelched the morbid urge to holler, "Boo!"

The sheriff was still examining the contents of Laddie's coffin when Carter McWayne, coroner by virtue of being Perry County's only mortician, jostled over the speed bump at the Pine Lawn Cemetery gate. His sleek black hearse throbbed with an old Three Dog Night song, "Mama Told Me Not to Come," and his tubby head bobbled to the cranked-up beat. Until that moment, it had never occurred to Morgan that a hearse would have — or need — a bass-boosted, Dolby-filtered stereo system.

"Yep, she looks dead to me," Goldsmith said, pulling a notepad and pencil from his neatly pressed uniform blouse.

Dr. Cowper glanced at Morgan, the shadow of a conspiratorial smile in his eyes.

"Mummification is a dead giveaway, Sheriff," Cowper said. "That, and the lack of a head."

Goldsmith nodded and made some notes as Coroner McWayne stepped out of his hearse. He clicked his key ring as he waddled up, and the hearse's door locks chirped. Who locked a hearse? Morgan thought. What's to steal?

Carter McWayne locked a hearse. He was only a mortician, but he considered himself a medical professional, and he ornamented his life accordingly with expensive possessions and habits. He even spoke expensively, always preferring clinical pedantry to much simpler expression, ten-dollar lexicology where penny words would do. His customers weren't just dead, they were deceased of myocardial infarctions (heart attacks), cerebral vascular accidents (strokes), metastatic and malignant neoplasms (cancers), acute inadvertent misadventures (accidental deaths) and multiple fatal transportational traumas (McWayne's own neologism for car-crash injuries).

Coroner McWayne's appetites were ambitious and legendary, especially for food. Only in his mid-40s, he was as fat and bug-eyed as his late mortician father, Derealous McWayne, so fat that the underarms of his short-sleeved white shirt were sopped with half-moons of sweat just from his short drive to the cemetery. His surplus flesh cascaded down his body like a fat-flavored ice cream cone. He was a walking billboard for atherosclerosis (clogged arteries).

"My dad told Laddie this lawn crypt memorialization wasn't a good idea. Folks around here prefer earth interment. And sandstone just isn't a good mausoleal stone. But Laddie was dead-set on a crypt. She always said, 'Every day I spend above ground is a good day.'"

But the architecture of Laddie's eternity was less momentous than Dr. Cowper's next news about the corpse in Laddie's casket.

"No apparent wounds other than the missing head, but it's a pretty good chance this is a murder victim," Dr. Cowper told the two local officials who were now in charge of this new mystery.

Goldsmith sighed. Murders were more troublesome than speed traps. Besides, he'd never handled a murder investigation in his six years as the law in Perry County, and he liked it that way.

"Great," he said, almost disappointed. "You sure she was murdered?"

"No, but somebody went to a lot of trouble here. This body was moved here from someplace else after the head was removed. People don't generally lose their heads over a natural death, if you'll pardon the pun."

Goldsmith made another note.

"She's all dried up. How can you tell?"

"Unless I miss my guess, Sheriff, this isn't a 'she.' It's a white male, possibly forty to sixty years old, dead at least a year. In my business, we call him 'desiccated,' but you'd just call him a mummy."

"Him?" Goldsmith asked. The normally verbose McWayne gandered down into the coffin and cocked his head sideways to study the headless corpse inside. The fleshy folds of the coroner's neck unfurled to reveal sweaty white pleats where the sun seldom shone. He breathed through his mouth, and the air droned in him like wasps in a wet-vac. He didn't even remove his wrap-around sunglasses, maybe because it required too much exertion.

"Yes, Sheriff," Dr. Cowper said. "This sure isn't Laddie Granbouche. No doubt in my mind."

Goldsmith lifted the bill of his official chocolate-brown, one-size-fits-all Perry County Sheriff's Office baseball cap and scratched his thin hairline. A fleck of Vapo-Rub clung to the tip of his beak-like nose.

"How do you figure?"

Dr. Cowper slipped a ballpoint pen from his breast pocket and kneeled beside the grim box. The sheriff and the coroner bent over for an anatomy lesson from one of America's most brilliant forensic anthropologists. Even Morgan leaned closer.

"Gentlemen," Dr. Cowper said, directing their rapt attention to a leathery flap near the corpse's pelvis, "this is a penis."

Dr. Cowper's handpicked forensic team became post-graduate pallbearers, hoisting the entire coffin onto Carter McWayne's morgue gurney and wheeling it to the hearse. Moving the fragile body itself would be too risky and might destroy clues.

Dr. Cowper himself checked the seals before closing the hearse's rear doors, then slapped the hot black roof twice. McWayne eased his wagon back onto the path and, for the first time in his life, carried a customer away from the cemetery.

Sheriff Goldsmith said his goodbyes and followed the coroner through the wrought-iron gates of Heaven toward McWayne and Sons Mortuary, only two blocks away. For good measure, he flipped on his red-and-blue vector lights, just so folks knew he had serious business.

"Think they'll ever find that head?" Dr. Cowper asked facetiously.

"Doc, those two guys couldn't find each other's asses with both hands," Morgan replied.

"Well, I can stay a day or two to help them find their asses, and maybe a few more things. We can use some of this portable equipment, and I can take some samples back to Florida for further testing. If nothing else, it will be good real-world practice for some of my interns."

The two of them stood silently at Laddie Granbouche's dismantled tomb for a moment while the team packed its gear back into its two green-and-yellow University of South Florida vans. A breeze rustled in the old cottonwoods overhead, but the hum of scientific machinery and anticipation was gone.

"Will you be able to identify him?" Morgan asked.

"Maybe," Dr. Cowper said. "We still have a few tricks. I'll help in any way I can, but it will take some time. All is not lost for your John Doe ... not yet anyway."

John Doe. Morgan thought of the drunken cowboy in the Buckhorn the night before. Anonymous. Alone. Unmissed.

Then Morgan asked what neither the coroner nor the sheriff had asked, nor perhaps even cared about. But he knew it was on Dr. Cowper's mind, which thrived on mysteries.

"Where do you think the ol' gal is?" the newspaperman asked as he snapped a photograph of the empty grave.

Dr. Cowper rubbed his tanned chin. His eyes were fixed on the empty vault where Laddie Granbouche should have been. Even if she was not the legendary lover of the Sundance Kid, another chapter in the enigmatic saga of Etta Place had been written. And if she was Etta Place, well, like her outlaw companions, she'd been larger than life; now, she might have outgrown death, too.

"Same place she always was," he said.

"Where's that?"

Dr. Cowper tapped his fingers on his chest and smiled.

The morning dee-jays at KROK-FM, Curtis and The Bug, were up to their usual ribaldry as Morgan drove back to the newspaper office. These clowns started their suggestive shtick at dawn and giggled at their own juvenile jokes until noon. They made Beavis and Butthead sound like Nobel laureates. Morgan imagined families all over town sitting down to their breakfast tables, tuned in to the farm report, the news (usually just headlines from the latest edition of *The Bullet*) or the school-lunch menus: *"Please pass the corn flakes,"* Father would say. *"Uh, honey, did The Bug just say 'tit'?"*

Morgan hated KROK, but the heart of the cassette player in his old Escort was sclerotic from eating too many tapes and KROK was Winchester's only radio station, a glorified garage with an Erector-Set tower on the edge of town. Its mix was eclectic, depending on the dee-jay; some days, it was country, some days heavy metal, some days Christian. Once, the afternoon jock locked himself in the booth with a pizza and a fifth of Wild Turkey, and played Frankie Yankovic's greatest accordion hits without commercial interruption — for sixteen hours. Inexplicably, Frankie Yankovic was the most popular artist on KROK's request line for the next two months.

"We've got a new Garth Brooks CD and an all-expense paid weekend with Brenda, our skanky but bodacious receptionist, for the ninth caller this morning," Curtis announced in a pukey impression of a real dee-jay. The Bug giggled in the background as they spun a Tracy Chapman song for the second time since their shift started.

"All Tracy Chapman, all the time," Morgan muttered to himself. Goddam small-town radio. He still missed Chicago's teeming airwaves, ripe with rock, talk and Cubs games. So he turned off the radio as he pulled into the Griddle's parking lot for a cup of real coffee, nothing more. Headless corpses tended to dampen his appetite.

A few ranchers bellied up to the Griddle's breakfast counter, the regulars. The radio was on in the kitchen, still thrumming with Tracy Chapman. Morgan plunked down next to Ray Pittman, a fourth-generation cattleman from up in the Black Thunder River breaks.

Ray Pittman believed state road signs bore secret codes to tell New World Order tank squadrons who owned guns. He believed jet contrails in the sky were secret government plots to control population and inoculate Americans against their wills with anthrax and other strange diseases. He believed, because he'd once heard it on Art Bell's late-night radio talk show, that Thomas Pynchon and J.D. Salinger were the same person, although he'd never read either author's books.

And every fencepost on his ranch was crowned with an old boot, but he didn't believe there was any good reason. He just liked the look.

"Hey, Ray," Morgan said.

"Hey," said Ray.

"What brings you to town?" Morgan asked.

"Boredom," the old cowboy said. "And dog food. Damned mutt eats like a horse, 'cept even a horse don't eat as much. I'd shoot the big, dumb fucker if he wasn't less valuable than a bullet."

Ranchers' casual attitudes about death always mystified Morgan. Unwanted kittens were piled in a burlap sack and tossed in the irrigation ditch. When beef prices were down, some thought killing the herd was better than selling it at a loss or allowing it to eat any more costly feed. City folk thought broken limbs were fixable, but a ranch horse with a broken leg was shot as useless.

Morgan had built a career, in part, by poking his nose into death, but not over breakfast. He changed the subject.

"I gotta a pair of old Tony Lamas I've been saving for you," Morgan said. "I should bring 'em out someday."

"Lamas look good on a post, yessirree."

Without asking, Suzie the waitress set a coffee-cup full of pink sweetener packets in front of Morgan, then poured hot coffee in a tall go-cup. She knew better than to put the plastic lid on it until Morgan had dumped four sugars in it.

"I heard on the radio where a body's chemistry turns that stuff into formaldehyde in your system and turns your skin gray like an embalmed corpse," she warned him.

"There goes your tip."

In truth, Morgan liked his coffee extra sweet. And his tea. And his oatmeal. Saccharin was merely the means to an end. He could quit any time, he told himself. Among his vices, it ranked among the most benign.

"If you wanna pickle yourself, you oughta just go get a direct IV of preservatives from Carter McWayne," she scoffed. "Wouldn't kill you any faster."

"We all gotta die of something, Suze," he teased as he stirred his coffee. "It's not so bad to die of sweetness, is it?"

Suzie squared off, hands on her slender hips. She looked like a woman who'd had more than her share of lines from men, and bought none of them.

"Sugar, you used up every last drop of your sweetness makin' that little boy of yours," she scolded. "He's so cute I don't know whether to breast-feed him or marry him."

The radio ran out of music, and the kitchen again echoed with the voices of Curtis and The Bug. Morgan gritted his teeth.

"Hey, dude, we got caller number nine on the line," The Bug chirped. "And you'll never guess who it is!"

"No!"

"Yeah, dude! It's that kid Grady! Dude's been caller number nine for, like, a month of Saturdays! How do you do it, man?"

A shy boy's voice came over the phone line softly.

"Just lucky, I guess."

"Lucky? Dude, you got nothin' better to do with your Saturdays than sit around and call the radio station?" The Bug said. "You're what, thirteen? Haven't heard of masturbation? Can I say masturbation on the air?"

"You just did."

"Cool."

"So, Grady," Curtis piped up, "If you're only thirteen, you might need some, like, pointers on what to do with Brenda, your prize for being caller number nine today. I personally know she likes to be licked ..."

"In Yahtzee!" The Bug yelped.

They cackled salaciously. Dead air was more entertaining than these two boobs, Morgan thought. He was certain Ray Pittman, the laconic and paranoid rancher with a boot fetish who sat beside him, would get higher ratings.

"Awesome, now I know why my mom makes my dad play Yahtzee," The Bug said. "Hey, Grady dude, does your mom play Yahtzee? ... dude, you there?"

Grady had hung up.

The kid's timing truly was flawless.

The Bullet newsroom was empty, as it was most Saturday afternoons. Morgan souped his film, emptied the wastepaper baskets, propped open the back door to air out the pressroom, and sat down to contemplate the blinking cursor on his word processor.

Soon, it would be five years since he left the cop beat at the Chicago Tribune and came back to Winchester, his childhood home, to pursue the elusive dream of running his own newspaper.

Winchester wasn't perfect, it was just home. Morgan could overlook the town's peccadilloes and idiosyncrasies because, to him, they were part of the natural order of things. All the locals — and none of the tourists — knew about the hornet's nest under the toilet seat at the town park. Ranchers stopped their pickups in the middle of Main Street to shoot the breeze. The gas station on the far edge of town had a live-bait vending machine. The hardware store closed on Sunday. Everybody believed the shopping was better in the next town, but nobody wanted to be seen shopping there. A "formal" occasion merely called for a new pair of jeans. The fluctuation of beef prices was more important than the Dow Jones Industrial Average.

These were all a part of Morgan's expectation from life: It goes at its own pace.

But, in truth, after twenty years of covering big-city crime, he also came home looking for something he'd lost along the way, some reaffirmation that newspapering had a purpose, and that news wasn't just a summary of the various and sundry ways humans imitated animals.

His cynicism consumed him after Bridger died. His son was only eight when his own blood poisoned him. Leukemia killed Bridger, much too slowly and painfully for a child, and it killed something inside Morgan, too. So it was easy for him and Claire, to leave Chicago after that, because they were already lost. Maybe even dead.

Things had started out rough at *The Bullet*, but he worked hard and slowly proved himself to his readers as fair, plucky and guile-less. Now, he'd survived a few hundred weekly deadlines, a couple dozen green reporters always looking for the next biggest paper, and even watched one press burn down. But *The Bullet* always came out.

Every week went long. He missed too many family dinners, too many Saturday picnics. Although he'd grown more comfortable as the *Bullet* editor, the hours seem to have grown longer.

And now, Colter. He made it all make sense. This six-year-old boy was the key to everything in Morgan's life. When he was born, Morgan knew what the purpose of his life should be, a bundle of clarity in baby powder and poopy diapers. Some mornings, he would creep into Colter's room to kiss him goodbye, and he'd smell his second son's sweet, dreaming breath. It filled him.

Morgan traced his finger around the picture of Colter and Claire on his cluttered desk, but his mind drifted to Laddie Granbouche. He mused on how she had slipped out of history's grasp again, but caught himself: Again? He smiled and admitted secretly that maybe, yes, he wanted Laddie and Etta to be the same woman. It wasn't just a good story. To Morgan, it would be the final stroke on a magnificent, almost artistic life. Etta Place, and maybe Laddie Granbouche, had been her own work of art.

Two greasy little hands covered Morgan's eyes.

"Bet you can't guess me, Daddy," a little voice said.

"Hmmm," Morgan said. "Let me see. It's somebody who likes salty french fries."

"Yeah."

"And I think it's somebody who isn't ... wearing any shoes."

"Yeah."

"And ... let's see ... it's a little boy who just got done with swimming lessons."

Colter hugged his father's neck as Morgan wheeled around to scoop him into his lap. Colter's swimming trunks and hair were still damp, and Morgan caught the sweet odor of chlorine on his skin, the smell of a thousand summer memories.

"How do you know?" Colter asked him.

"Lucky guess."

Claire breezed in from the pressroom. She carried a couple of oily Rocket Burger sacks, some napkins and two tall fast-food sodas. Her long, blond hair was tied back under a floppy summer hat, and her bare shoulders had been reddened by the morning sun as she sat at the town pool while Colter earned his guppy badge.

"The back door was open," she said. "We thought you might like some lunch. You still eat lunch, don't you?"

Morgan cleared a corner of his desk and Claire handed him an oozing Monster Rocket in its oleaginous wrapper. The Rocket Burger drive-in billed it as a half-pound hamburger, but Morgan was certain much of that vaunted poundage had soaked into its paper packaging. And his envelope of greasy fries was already half-empty.

"Uh-oh, I think a hungry puppy got into my French fries," Morgan said, feigning surprise.

"Mommy ate them," Colter said, pointing a suspiciously salty finger at Claire, who rolled her eyes. At 42, she hadn't kept her appealing figure by filching French fries. Colter, on the other hand, was a serial filcher. If stealing French fries was a crime, his sunny little face would be on every Post Office wall.

"Hmmm, what should we do to Mommy for eating all my fries?"

"Tickle her!"

Morgan smiled at Claire.

"Any last requests before we carry out the sentence?"

"Not the feet."

Morgan looked at Colter, who crinkled his little nose and shook his head devilishly. Together, they leapt on Claire, who was laughing too hard to fight them both off.

"Stop! Can't we make a plea bargain?" she begged.

Morgan and Colter stopped.

"What kind of bargain?"

"I'll give each of you a kiss if you stop tickling me."

Colter thought hard.

"A kiss and a hug," he bartered.

Morgan waggled his hand, unimpressed with the new offer. He was holding out for something more.

"Don't push it, buster," Claire warned playfully.

"Okay, okay. For a kiss and a hug, you get parole," he said.

Claire embraced Colter tightly, and kissed each chubby cheek. Morgan leaned down and kissed his wife's forehead, smelling suntan oil and her vanilla shampoo.

He combed his fingers through her thick hair and felt grateful for her. And for Colter.

Somewhere under the mess of press releases, books, ledger sheets, wedding announcements, phone messages, old pop cans, unpaid bills, letters to the editor, notes, candy wrappers, magazines, clippings, empty sweetener packets and coffee-stained photographs on Morgan's desk, a phone rang.

"*Bullet.* Jeff here."

The voice sounded distant and raspy, likely a cell phone.

"Jeff, this is Shawn Cowper."

"Any news on your John Doe?"

"Nothing yet. We posted him, but couldn't find any evidence of heart attack, cancers or any other natural death. No major scars, no hidden bullets or blades. We certainly can't find any mortal wounds ... well, other than decapitation."

"Oh, that."

"He bled out, but not in Laddie's crypt. He drained dry. That's to be expected when you pop the top off, even post-mortem. It was a pretty clean cut, maybe a chainsaw. It might be the cause of death, or it might just be the killer's way of making my job harder than it needs to be."

"No teeth, no face, no marks, no telltale wounds ..."

"Well, not exactly."

"What do you mean?"

"Two things," Dr. Cowper said. "John Doe had a crown of thorns tattooed on his upper arm. It's still there."

"And the other thing?"

"He was crucified."

"No shit?" Out of the corner of his eye, Morgan saw his six-year-old son cover his mouth in surprise, and Claire gave him the evil eye.

"Found gashes in his palms and feet. Probably railroad spikes or tent stakes. Lots of tearing from his weight hanging against them."

"Jesus."

"Yes, exactly like Jesus."

"No, I didn't mean ..."

"Just a quick question: Any missing-persons cases around here from the last few years?"

"I don't know of any. None accidental, anyway."

Dr. Cowper exhaled over the phone. Or maybe it was a passing truck. Morgan couldn't tell. Cell phone service in this part of Wyoming was poor, but only when it wasn't awful.

"The sheriff is checking the computer for Montana, South Dakota and surrounding counties. There's a slim chance somebody somewhere is missing this fella. But the sheriff seems sure our guy isn't local."

"How about a story in the paper? Maybe somebody will come forward with something."

"Good idea. Officially, you'll want to get all this from the sheriff, but we're looking for information about an adult white male, thirty to sixty years old, medium build, 150 to 180 pounds ..."

"Height?"

"Shorter now."

The two men needn't have snickered to know they were both jaded, but they did.

"Sorry," Cowper said. "Make that five-foot-seven to five-foot-nine ... give or take a head."

"Jesus, Doc," Morgan said, smiling. "How long do you think he's been dead?"

"At least a year," Dr. Cowper said. "The mummification stumps me. If the body is exposed, the climate must be very dry and shielded from bugs and animals. If he was killed in summer in Wyoming, the dry heat would have mummified him pretty fast, but there'd be lots of bugs. So, he died in spring or fall maybe, when the bugs aren't around. I just don't know. I can't be sure without more sophisticated tests."

Morgan knew DNA was useless without comparative tissues from known descendants or the corpse himself before he was a corpse.

"So is it unlikely you'll ID this guy?"

"It'll be tough, but not impossible ... if we get lucky. I might be able to bring up some fingerprint fragments, but who knows? If he was ever fingerprinted, we might find a match, but then again, we might not. We'll certainly take some tissue samples to test any future possibilities, but right now, he's still John Doe."

"Any foreign substance in his system?"

"Off the record? Toxicology is iffy on old remains. We'll look for drugs and poisons in the skin and body hair. We can spot some toxins that stay in the body, like arsenic, but I'm not holding my breath. My gut tells me this wasn't a pleasantly poisonous death. There are deep ligature marks on his ankles, and his lower leg bones were all smashed. From the look of it, I'd guess he was hog-tied upside down at some point. But we found something else."

"What?"

The cell phone crackled with electric fuzz.

"Damn phone. Anyway ... we found some greasy dirt under his fingernails. His hands were big and tough, too. It might mean nothing, or it might help us place this guy someplace before he died. More tests, I'm afraid."

Dr. Cowper sounded less intrigued, more frustrated at the moment, but Morgan sensed he was on the scent.

"Well, look on the bright side, Doc, at least you know it isn't Laddie Granbouche. So ... one corpse down, a few million to go."

"That's why I'm calling, Jeff. You might be able to help."

That's a new one, Morgan thought, somebody asking a newspaperman for help in a death investigation. Most cops and prosecutors preferred to keep their secrets in the family. It was neater and cleaner that way. Reporters always mucked things up. What the public didn't know about cops' foul-ups wouldn't hurt.

"Sure, anything," Morgan said. "But you've got McWayne and Goldsmith. That better than Jack Klugman and ... well, I don't know. Who else could you possibly need?"

"Not who, Jeff. What. I'd like to borrow your darkroom to develop some film we shot this morning. There are a couple things I want to look at, things we missed on video."

"Something important?"

"Honest, I don't know what I don't know, Jeff. I simply want to take another look at some little details that didn't seem significant when we thought we were just copping a quick peep at Laddie."

"No problem. Anytime."

"Good. I'll send one of my tech guys right over. And thanks, Jeff. I owe you one."

At dusk, while the forensic team's photographer developed his film in *The Bullet*'s darkroom, Morgan surfed the Internet for morsels of information about Etta

Place and her outlaw lore. He found hundreds of articles about the Wild Bunch, but his interest was most piqued by a 1901 honeymoon photograph of Etta and Sundance taken by a New York photographer who later sent a copy to the Pinkerton Agency.

In it, she and Sundance wore sober, even melancholy expressions, although both were elegantly dressed. The frock-coated Sundance carried a top hat and shiny black shoes, every bit the wealthy Wyoming cattle buyer he pretended to be. Etta wore a high-collared dress, tight at her slim waist. Her dark hair was swept up on her head in a Gibson Girl style, the way a stylish, nineteenth-century woman of means might wear it, but one rebellious strand slipped down her neck, a subtle, sensual clue to her less civilized nature.

One more thing caught Morgan's eye. He magnified the electronic image for a closer look.

Over her left breast, Etta had pinned a man's pocketwatch. Its fob chain disappeared in a graceful loop beneath her decorative ruffle.

Had it been a wedding gift from her outlaw groom, a bauble snatched from a startled train passenger or a petrified bank clerk? Or had he bought it for her at Tiffany's, a fresh, never-possessed object for the love of his life?

Or was it something more, a memory saved from a past that would be utterly forgotten in her distant future? Could she have known that time would erase almost every detail from her portrait and leave only the mystery?

Maybe she had. At the very moment the photographer's flashpowder flared, maybe she knew. Time was her hiding place, her refuge.

Morgan saved the image. The ghost of Etta Place had begun to haunt him, too.

CHAPTER THREE

Apple-wood smoke wafted over their Sunday afternoon barbecue. Jeff Morgan spiced his low fire with green, finger-thick sticks pruned from the orchard in spring, letting their sweet smoke embrace his thick steaks.

Dr. Shawn Cowper sipped unsweetened tea and absorbed the friendly June sun while Morgan cooked. The secret garden behind the Morgans' magnificent house at Mount Eden was in full bloom, with bees busily floating on the still, warm air. Still, Morgan knew, if not for a special guest, he'd likely be down at the newspaper, working.

"I can't get over the quiet," Cowper said as Morgan tenderly checked his three juicy, fawn-colored steaks. The fire hissed as he lifted them slightly and beads of fat dripped through the grill.

"The man who owned this house was a dear friend," Morgan said. "He edited *The Bullet* and made me want to be a newspaperman when I was a kid. This whole place, the garden and the trees all around, was sort of a personal shrine that was built for his mother and a retreat at the same time. I come here for perspective."

Claire brought a bowl of fresh strawberries and cream from the house, setting them on the garden bench between her and Cowper. Colter tagged along, distracted by an earthworm among the peach iris.

"Just picked these a few minutes ago," she said.

Cowper smiled and chose a fat, ripe one. As he sunk his teeth into it, its juice trickled down his lip and chin.

"Oh my," he said, cupping his hand beneath his face.

"All that April rain," Claire said, giggling like a little girl as she unconsciously dabbed the juice away with a napkin, just like the mother of a small boy. When she caught her husband's eye, she quickly handed the napkin to the handsome young scientist and turned to look for Colter among the sunny flowers, hiding her blush.

"Colter, baby," she called softly as she tucked a strand of blond hair behind her ear, "come sit on Momma's lap."

Morgan knew Claire was understimulated by Winchester. She'd grown up among the neatly trimmed lawns and shaded lanes of Winnetka, Illinois, the middle daughter of a corporate-accountant father and an artist mother. She had attended a private prep school and held degrees in art and history from Millikin University, a prominent liberal arts college in Decatur where she graduated magna cum laude. Morgan met her at the Chicago *Tribune* when he was a stripling cop-beat reporter and she was a newsroom librarian. She had loved the choices Chicago laid before her. Had the great city not come to represent Bridger's death place, she'd have stayed forever.

She had embraced their escape to Winchester, but it was Jeff's home, not hers. She felt safe with Jeff, but this place had often seemed alien and impenetrable to her. They visited Chicago often, but leaving seemed harder every time. She had few friends in Winchester who stirred her mind, mostly just the happily unemployed and equally understimulated mothers of other pre-schoolers who never knew — and so never missed — the choices Claire now missed.

Colter clambered into his mother's lap, a worm

dangling from his fingers.

"He was eating the flowers," he explained.

"No, baby, he helps the flowers grow," Claire said.

Colter held the earthworm close and examined it.

"Bad breath," he said, tossing it into the nearest flower bed.

Cowper laughed as Colter wiped dirt and worm slime from his curious fingers onto his little polo shirt.

"I sometimes play with worms myself, Colter," he said. "Did you know worms don't have ears?"

Colter grabbed his own ears, and his eyes grew wide.

"How can they talk to each other?"

"They don't. They can only feel the ground move. That's how they hear. They don't have eyes, either."

Colter was clearly fascinated by these worm facts. He closed his eyes tightly and covered them with his dirty hands.

"But here's something very interesting, Colter," Cowper said, tousling the boy's wheat-blond hair, nearly the color of his mother's. "Worms have hair!"

"No way!"

"Yes way! That's why robins have a hard time getting them out of the ground!"

Inspired, Colter suddenly slid off his mother's lap and ran off down a garden path in search of a hairy worm.

"Gee, Doc, Arthurian legend, outlaw history, country music, forensic medicine, old bones, and now worms ..." Morgan said. He flipped the steaks over, careful not to pierce their seared, apple-infused surfaces and allow their juices to drain away. "Remind me not to challenge you to a game of Trivial Pursuit."

Cowper smiled abashedly.

"Oh, I suck at the sports and movie questions," he said, sipping his tea. "I don't get out much."

Over dinner, they talked about all manner of trivia, except the cases of Laddie Granbouche and her intimate squatter, John Doe. Headless corpses, murder and human tissue sampling weren't exactly appetizing topics, even for a hardened veteran cop reporter and his anthropologist dinner guest. But as soon as the dishes were cleared and Claire had taken Colter upstairs for his Sunday bath, the talk came naturally around to the mystery that intrigued them both.

"Your sheriff," Cowper said, sipping a jelly glass of Bailey's Irish Cream, "he hasn't led many murder investigations, has he?"

Morgan smiled. He had little regard for Goldsmith, and not just because he was elected only after the real sheriff, his childhood friend Trey Kerrigan, had flamed out on the politics of the job. Goldsmith was, plain and simple, a tinhorn poser. Trey Kerrigan ends up selling insurance, and Goldsmith gets a real-life, honest-to-God mystery dropped in his lap.

"Doc, he hasn't even led many felony investigations," Morgan said, his lack of respect barely checked. "His biggest case so far was a rape."

"That's no small thing."

"No, a rape is a rape," Morgan said. "In this case, a young Mormon missionary came to a woman's door and ..."

"And forced his way in?"

"Not exactly. She was an oilfield roughneck. She allowed him inside, subdued him, and then tied him to her bed, where she had her way with him ... for several hours. Let's just say she didn't spare the rod."

"Oh my."

"The worst part is, Hi Goldsmith got cold feet. He couldn't see how it was rape if the Mormon kid got a stiffy."

"Well, his feet aren't just cold this time," Cowper said. "They are Size 9E popsicles, frozen solid."

"That chickenshit geek. What now?"

"He called the state police this morning. They're coming up to take over the case."

"Dammit."

"Not good?"

"Definitely not good," Morgan said gravely. "Those guys are just politicians with badges. They answer only to the governor, and I'm sure even he doesn't get all the answers."

Of all the government agencies Morgan had the pleasure of mistrusting — from the simply fatuous to the supremely imperious — the Wyoming Division of Criminal Investigation was the worst. Its mission wasn't entirely clear to him, and that's the way DCI liked it. It investigated high-level government misdeeds and political crimes, and occasionally loaned its considerable resources to local lawmen who found themselves in over their heads, or who were trying to avoid a nasty political debacle. It accumulated favors, skulked around freely in any jurisdiction, observed only the laws it liked, rebuffed any outside examination, and enforced a strict code of silence — like some government-sanctioned crime family. To Morgan, they were simply the "secret police."

"A little stingy with information, are they?" Cowper asked.

"A little stingy? By comparison, the KGB is downright chatty. Once DCI gloms onto this case, we'll never hear another word about it ... until they put out a press release announcing they have solved the crime of the century with their usual brilliance."

"Good cops?"

"How would we know?"

"Good point."

"So what else can you tell me?"

"State investigators will be here in the morning. The sheriff has asked me to give them a tour of John Doe, from missing-head to toe. They want all my photos and videotapes, notes from the examination, statements from my team, even John Doe himself. The whole nine yards."

"Can they just grab it like that?"

"Jesus, Jeff, it's a murder. You know the drill. I can fight them off while they get a court order, but I might as well save myself the trouble and give them what they want now."

"And it will all disappear forever into the black hole of DCI, goddammit."

"Maybe not."

"What have you got in mind?"

"We've got all night to make copies of everything. You got a couple VCRs?"

Morgan nodded.

"Darkroom?"

Again, Morgan nodded.

"Copy machine?"

"Yeah."

"Excellent," Cowper said as he rose to leave. "Meet me at the funeral home in thirty minutes. You won't believe this, but he leaves the back door unlocked."

Morgan smiled.

"It's a small town," he said. "The only time we lock our cars around here is zucchini season. If you don't, somebody will stick a box of squash in your front seat."

"I'll keep that in mind. You up for this?"

"I was born up," Morgan said.

"Good. Maybe Claire could help?" Cowper suggested, patting his pockets for the keys to the USF van he drove to Mount Eden.

"I'm not sure she's up to seeing ..."

"No, no, no, I mean with the copying at the office. We have several dozen documents already, and she could transcribe some tapes, if she has time. If not, we'll just dub them on your stereo."

"Okay. Anything else you'll need?"
"Yeah. Coffee. Hot and black."

In his shroud of clear plastic, John Doe was packaged like anonymous meat in a supermarket cooler. Cowper untaped it under the fierce light that illuminated Carter McWayne's embalming table. Aside from the astringent odor of mortuary chemicals and the lingering pong of urine, ammonia or both, Morgan caught only a faint whiff of stale leather as the old corpse was exposed.

John Doe's torso was split from crotch to collarbone with a Y-incision, but it looked more like a cardboard cutout than a surgical slit. His vital organs, which merely looked like various dark cuts of beef jerky, had been examined and placed in evidence bags, then stuffed back into his body cavity.

Looking close, Morgan saw the ragged black gashes in John Doe's hands and feet where he'd been spiked by his likely killers, but without blood or even viable flesh, they were no more gruesome than torn leather.

Morgan had seen worse. In twenty years on the Chicago police beat, he'd seen infants whose heads had been splashed against cinder-block walls, naked women fished from Lake Michigan after months on the bottom, homeless men whose entrails had fed rats and stray dogs. The Des Plaines, Illinois, police allowed him to watch the post-mortem examination of John Wayne Gacy's young victims, some still rotting after they were scraped out of his Summerdale Avenue crawl space. And he couldn't erase the dead face of Sandra Tarrant from his mind. A human animal named P.D. Comeaux had strangled the former homecoming queen, eaten her sexual parts raw and left her in a South Dakota dumpster.

Death saddened Morgan, but it didn't sicken him. When he first started on the beat, he vomited once, he stopped eating for a few days. The corpses haunted him, but he got past it. He awoke one morning in those days and smelled a dead woman's perfume on his jacket, so he stuffed it in the building's incinerator and went to breakfast. He got no thrill from visiting the dead. It was just his job.

John Doe looked pitifully withered on the stainless steel embalming table. Minus sixty or eighty pounds of fat, muscle, blood and the other effluvium of life, he was little more than a leather-upholstered skeleton.

Minus his head, he was hardly even human, for the substance of a face was incorporeal. Minus a soul, he was just an empty husk labeled John Doe for the convenience of the living.

But he was missing something else: his fingertips. Or, more specifically, the skin that covered the last carpal on each of his fingers.

"Back in 1921, somebody developed a solution to rehydrate an Egyptian mummy's tissues, but formaldehyde or Photoflo work just as well," Cowper said. He gently swirled a small jar labeled "left index" and held it up to the light. A fat brown nubbin circled and tumbled in it. "It's not the most reliable technique, sort of a last resort thing. But in a very few cases, we can saturate a desiccated corpse's fingers and get some identifiable prints."

"So we're here to fingerprint John Doe?" Morgan asked.

"That's one thing, yes. When these tips are rehydrated, I'll just slip them over my own and make a set of prints, just like they do down at the cop shop. Then I'll ship them off to a buddy of mine in the FBI's IAFIS unit and see if they have any matches in their magic computer."

"That's it?"

"No. We're also going to harvest some tissue samples. Your state investigators will never miss them.

You don't trust your state cops, and I don't trust Sheriff Heckle and Coroner Jeckle. This way, John Doe won't disappear down the black hole."

"But this isn't your case. You can just hand it over and move on to some other unsolved historical puzzle. Why get involved?"

"Did you ever feel like you were the only one who could make a difference?" Cowper asked him, without seeming immodest.

Morgan knew the feeling well. He nodded.

"It's arrogant and maybe even a little stupid," the anthropologist continued, "but I can't just walk away. We can't always choose our obsessions. Sometimes they choose us."

Shawn Cowper watched John Doe's fingertip eddy around the jar, like some macabre snow-globe.

"So we make our own case file?" Morgan asked.

"Exactly."

"Isn't that withholding evidence?"

"Not at all. We'll keep nothing from the investigation except a few superfluous snips from John Doe. We'll want a copy of everything, but they'll get the originals. So we'd best get moving. We've only got a few hours."

Later, back at *The Bullet*, Colter slept on a Spongebob Squarepants slumber bag he dragged under a reporter's desk, his fortress against imaginary shadow warriors and spiky-haired skater boys. Claire fed page after page into the Xerox machine, creating two photocopies from each original. Intensely and naturally curious, she read each one.

Fueled by coffee and a brown bag of assorted candy bars from the MotorTown Truck Stop's all-night convenience store, Morgan scanned the pathology team's photographic negatives one by one into the computer, burning them at high resolution onto writable compact discs, while Cowper duplicated videotapes and transcribed his tape-recorded autopsy narrative.

His incidental "snips" of John Doe sat in evidence bags among the fast-food condiments and forgotten lunches in the kitchenette refrigerator. And three reasonably clear sets of fingerprints were sheathed separately in plastic liners in Cowper's briefcase. Everything else would be surrendered to the DCI investigators when they arrived ... everything but the copies.

Sometime after two-thirty in the morning, Claire lugged Colter out to the car and drove him home. An hour later, when the coffee ran out, Morgan and Cowper drove the USF van down to MotorTown for refills.

The night was windless and moonless. Three hours before dawn, the yellow-blue halide light in the truck stop's parking lot provided both false daylight and false security to sleeping truckers in their idling rigs. Ranks of them sat side by side across the blacktop, droning like snoring steel beasts.

Nobody was moving around, but a bad bulb guttered in a Winnebago on the edge of the lot. As Morgan and Cowper got out of the van, a frowzy man in greasy cargo pants and a wool jacket slammed the Winnebago's thin aluminum door and walked toward them, steam purling from a Styrofoam coffee cup in his hand. When he came within hailing distance, his thin lips curled into a smile.

"The Lord give us another day, amen," he said, his eyes brighter than the morning that hadn't yet broken.

"Yes, He did," Morgan replied.

The man, in his fifties, seemed far too perky — and holy — for the hour. His graying hair sprouted like weeds beneath his Cubs ball cap. *An admirer of underdogs*, Morgan thought. The fellow with a slight Texas twang extended a smudged hand to them and just kept smiling.

"Pridrick Leighton," he introduced himself. "On the

road for Jesus. Takin' to the highway for the *high* way. Get it? Savin' souls and wastin' gas!"

The Reverend Leighton was a truck-stop evangelist, one of those pavement preachers who prayed and proselytized without the overhead and boredom of an immobile sanctuary, just a holy Winnebago and a plastic Jesus on the dashboard, baptismal water from a radiator and communion wafers from a café cracker basket.

The preacher reached into the inner breast pocket of his jacket and handed Morgan his business card:

REV. PRIDRICK LEIGHTON
Tabernacle of the Transaxle
Sunday School and
Strong Coffee for the Soul
www.crossroads.com

Endless hours on endless roads made the Reverend Leighton long on conviviality but short on small talk.

"Do you know your personal Savior?" he asked Cowper, who must have seemed more in need of a savior at this moment than Morgan. After three in the morning, in a truck stop parking lot, beneath the counterfeit light of man-made moons, Pridrick Leighton was a missionary with a mission and a transmission, high on Jesus, caffeine and probably some whites dropped in his collection plate by grateful drivers.

"Right now, Reverend, my personal Savior is the guy who invented the mattress," Cowper joked.

"There's plenty of time to sleep after we die, my friend," the preacher said, "but if you'd like to unload some of that mental freight you're haulin', maybe you'd like to hear my testimony . . ."

Cowper raised his hands, not in a hallelujah, but in defense.

"Sorry, Rev," he said. "Just coffee."

"Peace be with you, my son," Reverend Leighton said, backing off. He shook both Morgan and Cowper's hands again and disappeared into the men's room for his morning constitutional.

Unsaved for the moment, Morgan and Cowper lingered in front of the pre-split and shrink-wrapped fire logs and newspaper stands in front of the convenience store.

"Not a religious fella, huh?" Morgan asked.

"Nope, I got plenty of religion as a kid," Cowper said. "Did you ever wonder why all of man's problems started when Adam and Eve found the Tree of Knowledge? God says the fruit is forbidden, but Eve eats it anyway and all Hell breaks loose. Seems like God intended that we keep our mouths shut and not ask any questions. So I became a godless scientist."

Morgan couldn't argue, and wouldn't. It was too early and too logical.

Inside, the little store smelled like sweat, spilled gasoline, overboiled coffee, toilet disinfectant and stale doughnuts.

The clerk, a local girl who never saw the point of college if she could get a good-paying truck-stop job without a degree, was reading "The Delta of Venus" by Anaïs Nin and absently toying with the tiny gold ring in her eyebrow. With her face buried in her book, Morgan saw only her short, dark mane of tousled hair and the swale of her smooth shoulder where the scoop of her loose, gray sweater pulled away.

Her name, according to the tag dangling from her tight blouse, was Robin. Her delicate nose and sleek jaw contained a few hundred years of Tolbert genes, and Morgan knew she must have been born into the old family that homesteaded the badlands west of town. Out there, where the Earth's crust was thicker and more stubborn, the oil wasn't as easy to drill, the coal not as easy to dig, so for decades the Tolberts had only enjoyed meager, fluctuating earnings produced by sunshine, spring snows and grass. And out there, every muddy county lane was named for one of the historic Tolbert women, all dead and gone now: Arabella, Frances, Virginia, Evangeline and so on, as if each led her man from the main road of life to an inevitable dead end. Maybe someday, one of the rutted gravel sideroads would be named Robin.

Cowper filled his Big Swig cup with Mountain Dew while Morgan emptied the coffee urn and snatched some pink sugar packets from the basket by the microwave pastries. On the bakery shelf, a few packages of chocolate-covered donut-gems sat forlornly until the next delivery truck arrived. Morgan picked one up.

Cowper leaned casually against the counter, but the clerk kept reading.

"'I only believe in fire. Life. Fire. Being myself on fire I set others on fire. Never death. Fire and life,'" he said in a smooth romantic voice.

The young woman looked up, her big, dark eyes tired and cynical, though she was no more than twenty-five. Even from the donut rack, Morgan could see she was uncommonly pretty for a truck-stop girl, her lips full and bare, turned down a little at the corners. And she wasn't soft under the chin, like most of the small-town girls who never left.

Her hair was the color of French roast coffee, and on her tiny island amid cigarettes, breath mints and jackalope keychains, she likely must have appeared as an enchanting Calypso to every lonely, long-haul trucker who drifted in on the asphalt current.

That she read Anaïs Nin and not Danielle Steel made her even more attractive to Morgan, who found a smart woman as sexy as a beautiful one.

"Excuse me?" she asked.

"Anaïs Nin," the doctor said, pointing to her book.

"She said that."

The young clerk suspiciously scanned the back of the book to see if the quote had been printed there.

"Yeah? Lucky guess," she said wearily.

Cowper turned briefly to Morgan and smiled confidently, then leaned closer to her.

"'And the day came when the risk it took to remain tight in the bud was more painful than the risk it took to blossom,'" he quoted Nin once more, almost in a whisper.

The clerk's eyes widened.

"Wow," she said, clearly aroused. She inclined her head close enough that Cowper must have smelled her warm, wintergreen breath. "That's really amazing."

"Well," he said, suavely peeling the paper sheath from his straw, "I happen to be very familiar with the erotica of Anaïs Nin."

"No, it's really amazing that yet another allegedly grown man has no life," she murmured in a good imitation of a sultry-sexy sigh. "That'll be a dollar ninety-six on the Big Swig."

Morgan laughed out loud. He couldn't help himself. He was sure Shawn Cowper didn't strike out very often, much less go down in flames. After he paid for his coffee and donuts, the two men slumped in the van outside.

"I dunno about her, Doc," Morgan said, dumping four packets of fake sugar in his hot-and-cold Big Swig, "but you were making *me* horny."

Cowper, a middle-aged professor at a distant college, smiled his frat-boy smile.

"Just trying to sow my wild oats," he said.

As impressed as a married man can be with a bachelor's romantic menu, Morgan shook his head.

"Yeah, Doc, but you're supposed to do it before you look like the guy on the box."

Cowper turned the key and the road-worn university

van growled under the hum of incandescent parking-lot lights. He watched an eighteen-wheeler ease into the dark highway's westbound lane, its running lights as luminous as the skyline of a small city. Cowper turned the opposite direction on the state road, toward the dim glow of the sleeping town. He didn't look at Morgan, but spoke into the vacant, lukewarm pre-dawn as he flicked on his bright lights.

"Anybody ever tell you that pink stuff will petrify your pancreas?"

The two DCI agents glided into the Perry County Courthouse parking lot a little after ten in the morning in their unmarked, government-issue Crown Victoria. They pulled into the space beside Morgan's cranky, insecure Ford Escort, where he and Cowper sipped coffee and hoped the caffeine would soon kick in.

Unlike their brethren in the FBI, the DCI agents affected a casual-cop flair, crime and punishment Calvin Klein-style: razor cuts, aviator sunglasses, sporty polo shirts, jeweled watches, khaki chinos and twill trousers, dun walking shoes and urban hikers, accessorized with gleaming badges, leatherette cell-phone cases and holsters on stylish canvas belts they probably laundered regularly. They were among the new wave of frat-boy fuzz: hip, cocky and well-groomed, more "Jump Street" than J. Edgar Hoover.

As the two thirty-something agents stepped out of their polished ride, Morgan caught a stiff whiff of air-conditioned after-shave and checked his six-dollar Kmart sports watch.

Cowper got out of the Escort to meet them.

"Shawn Cowper," he said, extending his hand to the agent on the driver's side. "I found the body."

The DCI agent shook his hand perfunctorily. He was

all business.

"Eric Halstead, DCI. This is my partner, Scott Pickard."

Though he wasn't tall, Halstead bent gracefully at his trim waist to peek inside the puny hatchback where Morgan still sat in the driver's seat, feeling woefully under-dressed for a police action.

"Sheriff's waiting inside for us," Cowper continued. "My team has gathered everything related to this case, and I assume you've made some arrangements to take possession of our friend, John Doe?"

"What kind of a doctor are you?" Halstead asked, making a note on a palm organizer that magically appeared from one of his fashionable pockets.

"Anthropologist, forensic style."

"In Wyoming?"

"No, Florida. But I ..."

"Okay, that's fine. We'll get all the particulars later. Right now, we need to talk to Sheriff Goldsmith privately. Where can you be reached?"

"I'm not invited to this meeting?"

"No. You're a witness."

"But I performed the post-mortem on your victim."

"Yes, Mr. Cooper, I know ..."

"Doctor Cowper. And wouldn't it be easier to let me work with you on this?"

"We can handle it from here."

Cowper took a breath to quell his rising anger.

"So you will take all my data and recordings without so much as a thank-you?"

"It's not yours anymore, Mr. Cooper. It's evidence. And any evidence in this case is ours. In fact, I think it'd be wise to have Agent Pickard go with you right now to make the transfer, just to ensure nothing gets ... lost."

Pickard, a tall, blond agent who might have been a golf pro in another life, was talking quietly on his cell phone on the other side of the Crown Vic, but snapped it shut when he heard his name.

"I don't understand," Cowper confessed. "You've got the expense-paid help of a top-flight forensic anthropologist and you're blowing me off. Is that it?"

Agent Halstead took off his sunglasses and hung them from the open collar of his saffron polo shirt, making it easier to look directly into Cowper's eyes with the commanding presence he likely learned by watching Ricky Schroder on "NYPD Blue."

"Fact is, you aren't a duly sworn law enforcement official in the State of Wyoming and regardless of your work in Florida, you were allowed improper access to evidence in a criminal case. That's just one of the many issues we have with the sheriff's handling of this investigation so far."

"Agent Halstead, I assure you I am eminently qualified in forensic pathology, and I have been involved in hundreds of death cases in an official scientific capacity. This is just asinine."

"Yeah, well, right now you're just an overqualified witness. And unless you want to have a little chat about the consequences of tampering with evidence, I'd suggest you cool your jets, all right?"

"Are you shitting me?"

"Mr. Cooper, I don't shit."

Doctor Cowper bit his tongue.

"No," he said with remarkable restraint, "I don't suppose you do."

Morgan leaned across the passenger seat of his Escort and spoke through the open window.

"So is DCI taking over this investigation?"

"Who are you?"

"Jeff Morgan, editor of *The Bullet*."

Halstead made another memo in his PDA.

"We can't comment on that," he said without looking

up.

"Can't ... or won't?"

"Morgan. Common spelling?" Halstead asked, stylus ready.

"Sorry," Morgan said. "I can't comment on that."

Halstead glared. Morgan just grinned as the agent turned to Cowper.

"Mr. Cooper, given the delicacy of your situation as a witness in a presumptive murder case, it'd be wise not to talk to the media. Are we singing from the same sheet of music here?"

Cowper smirked as he poured the cold dregs of his convenience-store coffee on the parking-lot pavement, splattering Halstead's newish Rockports.

"Loud and clear, maestro."

DCI Agent Scott Pickard followed them back to the Arrowhead Motel, a dowdy motor-lodge out by the highway where Cowper's team shared four queen-size rooms. Most of them had spent Sunday watching bugs-and-bones shows on The Learning Channel, recovering from a honky-tonk Saturday night at the Buck Snort, or both. By the time Cowper arrived with Morgan and Pickard, they had meticulously stowed all their scientific gear in the vans for the long trip home to Florida and were sitting on the Arrowhead's mostly ceremonial lawn awaiting check-out time, more than ready to be gone.

Cowper stood over three cardboard boxes left on the cracked sidewalk in front of Room Nine.

"Here you go, Agent Pickard," he said. "This is John Doe."

Pickard suddenly looked like he might be sick.

"Well, not John Doe himself," Cowper said. "Just everything we know about John Doe. Reports, video and voice tapes, photos, preliminary analysis, turn-ons, turn-offs ..."

Pickard apparently didn't catch the joke, and if he did, he decided it wasn't officially funny. The DCI's official handbook discouraged humor. He opened the boxes, inventoried the contents and wrote out an official receipt for Cowper. Then he loaded them in the Crown Vic's official trunk and left, slurring his official tires in the Arrowhead's crushed gravel lot, like Steve McGarrett.

"You'll never see him or those boxes again," Morgan said.

Cowper winked.

"One can only hope," he said.

Matt, a lanky grad student in a "Don't Bug Me" sweatshirt, flicked his cigarette into the gravel. He was the team's photographer, and when he was developing film at *The Bullet*'s darkroom, Morgan learned Matt had a grim but passionate fascination with forensic entomology — the relatively new medico-legal study of the insects that attend human mortality and how they can help pinpoint the time and place of death.

"We're all mounted up, Shawn," he said. "Any time you're ready to split, we're outta here. If we get moving now, we can make Sioux Falls before dark. I already signed us out."

Cowper tossed him the extra set of van keys.

"Take my stuff out of the back, would you?" he asked. "And leave me one of the laptops. I'm gonna stick around here for a while."

Matt asked the question on Morgan's mind: "Why?"

"A few loose ends," he said. "I'll fly back to Tampa when I get them all tied up. I'll e-mail. And do me a favor: When you get back, call Gettysburg College about that field-hospital excavation. Tell them we had a little delay up here, but we'll be there by the end of September, long before the ground freezes."

"What'll we do in the meantime?"

"It's summer vacation, for god sakes. Take the week off and go see what normal people do for fun. It might surprise you, but it almost never involves flesh-eating bugs."

Matt shrugged and shook Cowper's hand as the rest of the team loaded up.

"You're the boss," he said. "I'll just tell Gettysburg we encountered grave problems."

The anthropologist's blue eyes sparkled with mischief.

"No, Matt," he said, clapping his helper's bony shoulder, "tell them I'm just trying to get a head."

The team never got as far as Sioux Falls.

But they got to the western bank of the Missouri River, which bisects South Dakota, dividing the western badlands from the agrarian east, the dark frontier from the refulgence of civilization. At twilight, before they'd even crossed the Big Muddy, they were flagged down by a frantic woman carrying a baby. Fumes belched from the open hood of her broken-down Chevy Impala.

Both vans pulled off the highway just beyond the smoking car, in a turn-out that overlooked the Missouri below. Very soon, another Samaritan in a white Suburban came to the rescue, too, quickly pulling off the highway just in front of Matt's lead van.

But the small group of eight young scientists and grad students was in far greater danger than the woman and her child, which was in fact a gas mask swaddled in a white towel.

Within a few seconds, three men from the white Suburban and the woman surrounded them. Their faces were hidden by gas masks. The women in the vans screamed.

It was finished within two minutes.

Into each closed van, the attackers dropped a canister of tabun gas, a deadly nerve agent. The bitter gas paralyzed their lungs in the first few seconds. Within thirty seconds, the eight people trapped in the vans had lost control of their bodily functions entirely, vomiting through blue lips, defecating and urinating all over themselves. In sixty seconds, the convulsions began. By the time the twitching and jerking ended, the hijackers had emptied the vans of their medical and scientific gear, as well as some of the team's luggage, purses and backpacks, which were all loaded into the white Suburban.

One of the men, his face still protected by a gas mask, shoved Matt's shit-stained body aside and started the first van. Shifting it into drive, he steered it around the guardrail and stepped away as it rolled down the embankment into the muddy river. The second van soon followed, also sinking beneath the water.

As that last van hit the water, a minivan with Minnesota plates passed the killing spot. The bored children inside waved at the three nice men who had stopped to help a young mother whose radiator had overheated.

Four minutes, forty-three seconds.

Dying was fast.

Being dead took longer.

CHAPTER FOUR

A tart rain fell before dawn on Tuesday, obscuring the sunrise.

The narrow trail meandering up the steep side of Saddlestring Mountain circumscribed secret, unvisited places where lupine and wild mountain strawberries flourished, and no man ever saw. Up higher, where the air was thinned of civilization's heavy stink, the virgin woodlands had known only the touch of wind, snow, rain and hawks, never an axe.

Morgan kept to the path because he seldom ran in the morning, or in the rain, or up Saddlestring. His breath was hot and his legs heavy, but he scrambled farther up the foggy hogback through the mist-scent of pine and banking fog. His lungs ached for oxygen, his ankles whined with every rugged step, and sweaty rain trickled down his back, but he was alone.

Except for the thought of two sons. Morgan had kissed Colter in the dark that morning, as light as the dust on a butterfly's wing. The boy didn't stir from his dreams, but his tiny hand rose to his father's cheek. So Morgan kissed his moist little palm and tucked it beneath the blanket.

Back in the trees, a red-daubed flicker laughed its wick-wick giggle, then swooped across Morgan's path. He stopped, hands on his knees, grateful for a bit of color in the slate morning. The trail ahead dropped over the crest into a cloud-filled ravine. Morgan wondered if he might just descend into the vapor and find all the lost ones gathered where no man could see, as if Heaven might be no more than a deep, cloudy cleft beyond where the trail just ends. He imagined Laddie Granbouche puzzling over life, death and country music with the attentive but disembodied head of John Doe, or the Sundance Kid sharing a cigar with King Arthur.

And Bridger. His memory would never fade, any more than a morning could be bereft of light.

The drizzle continued, but Morgan did not. He sat on a rain-slick boulder and thought about his two sons, so close now. He wished they could meet, right here, right at this rock, and go play in the secret woods, where they'd roll in grass that had never known a little boy's laughter, or chase butterflies where no trail had ever gone. He wished they could challenge each other to climb the highest tree, or throw the farthest stone, or make the loudest echo. They were brothers, after all.

And his mother was alive, but her mind functioned only beyond some invisible boundary, deep inside her distance. Rachel Morgan was a silhouette of herself. Every time he saw her, three or four times a week when he walked through the ammonia-scented hallways at Laurel Gardens, she was meeting him for the first time.

He was a new friend she met every day, not the baby she bore nearly fifty years before, raised through Cub Scouts, Little League and high school graduation. She'd held Bridger before he died and Colter in the minutes after he was born. The memories, Morgan had to believe, were still in there someplace, caged in brain cells to which the key had been lost.

He missed her. For all the reminders of what had passed away, he had her and he could hold her, even if he couldn't be sure that she understood when he told her he loved her. When he would come home from the nursing home and Claire would ask how he was doing, he'd just say he was fine, and sometimes he'd take a shower. Nobody could hear him cry there.

On the mountain, Morgan studied his own two hands. The same but different. Each carried its own scars, its own stains. They were starting to look like his father's hands, he thought. Creased, tired, practiced and patient. His fingers felt thick and cold, but alive, each with its own memories.

He knew he was working too hard, and too much. He had trouble sleeping most nights, skimming just below the surface of waking. Too many things to think about. Maybe they'd take a weekend soon, drive someplace, maybe Montana. He'd always enjoyed being in the car with Claire. They talked, and they saw things together at the same time.

He started back when he knew the sun wouldn't show. He looked back, just once, at the gully of Heaven and followed the trail away from it. On the mountain, in this diffuse light, it was nearly impossible to tell the difference between sweat, rain or tears.

Sheriff Goldsmith's white Bronco was parked on the county road outside Mount Eden. He was checking his teeth in his sun-visor's vanity mirror when Morgan jogged up and rapped the fender.

"Stick 'em up!" he hollered.

Startled, Hi Goldsmith splashed the crotch of his crisp new county uniform with hot coffee.

"Goddammit, Jeff," he snarled as he tried to hold his butt off the puddle of coffee in his seat. "Can't you just quit the grab-ass for once?"

Morgan suppressed a smile.

"Oh, man, you can't go back to town like that," he

said. "C'mon inside, and Claire can throw those trousers in the wash."

Goldsmith tried to sop some of the coffee with some blank incident reports, but he was far more absorbent than government paperwork.

"Today of all days," Goldsmith said, exasperated.

"Forgot your underwear again, didn't you? Tsk, tsk."

"I'm wearing underwear!"

"I got some clean undies inside if you..."

"Goddammit, I'm wearing underwear!"

"So why's today worse than any other day to spill coffee on your wee-wee?"

Goldsmith cursed under his breath.

"Them DCI boys are all over my ass," the sheriff said. "They're pissed off about this John Doe case. They come up here from Cheyenne in their fancy Sophia Loren duds and they treat us like a bunch of hicks who don't know shit from granola."

"Ralph."

"What?"

"Ralph Lauren," Morgan said. "He makes the duds. Not Sophia."

"Then who was Jackie Gleason?"

Morgan didn't want to laugh at the sheriff. It would only add insult to a hot-coffee injury.

"That was Ralph Cramden," he said. "Different Ralph."

"So is Ralph related to Sophia?"

"Hi, did you need to see me about something so early on a Tuesday morning?"

The sheriff cleared his throat.

"Jeff, them DCI guys want me to make sure you aren't gonna print nothin' about John Doe. They say it's still under investigation, and if it was public, the case would be in jeopardy."

Morgan shook his head.

"Bullshit."

"C'mon, Jeff. I've already got my tit in the wringer with these guys. That short, cocky one called me Barney Fife. The little fucker."

"Well, Hi, you just go back and tell them you're the sheriff, not the newspaper editor. The story will run. I don't owe those guys any favors."

"It ain't a favor they're askin', Jeff."

"What's that supposed to mean?"

Sheriff Goldsmith leaned across the seat and fetched some coffee-stained papers, which he handed to Morgan.

"Court order, Jeff. Judge will hear your arguments Friday."

"He can't do that!" Morgan said, scanning the legal document in his hand. "And I can't wait until Friday. The paper goes to bed tomorrow."

"Those DCI kids play hardball, Jeff. Sorry."

"But they can't keep me from printing this story!"

"No, but the judge can."

"But he can't! It's not against any law to print the truth, and for god's sake, those bastards can't just stop the presses like that. It's called prior restraint."

"I don't make the laws, Jeff. Hell, I don't even know what half of 'em are. Damn legislature. Is that one of the new ones?"

"The government can't decide what a newspaper can't print before it prints it. That's censorship."

"Well, I wish I could tell you to take it to the next highest court, but all Their Honors left this morning for the state bar convention in Jackson. You could try to get one of the district judges to set this injunction aside over the phone, but I reckon you won't find 'em real handy ... unless you call over to the Cowboy Bar after dinner. Won't be a sober judge anywhere in the Hole by 10 o'clock."

"You guys are supposed to uphold the law, not piss

on it."

"The judge is the law, as far as I'm concerned. And he says no news is good news."

"This is just bullshit, Hi," Morgan protested, tossing the injunction into the sheriff's humid lap. "I won't obey it."

Goldsmith shrugged as he started his Bronco.

"In that case, I'll have one of my deputies tidy up a cell at Chez Goldsmith. We'll leave the light on for ya!"

A weekly paper's newsroom is anything but symphonic, but as deadline approaches, it at least rises to the dissonance of the orchestral tune-up before a concert.

Morgan paced. His young reporters — and they were always young — avoided his eye and hunkered down behind their computer screens, trying to look small and busy. But Morgan wasn't prowling for stories.

A lawyer friend in Laramie who relished media cases but couldn't build a practice on them advised Morgan to print the story and face the music, which he presumed would be furious but short-lived. "Those peckerheads are just trying to make you blink," he said. He even offered to defend Morgan at half his usual hourly rate if he were found in contempt of court.

But Morgan wasn't worried about jail. He'd already decided to hand-deliver this week's *Bullet* personally to the sheriff and offer to be handcuffed on the spot. He was certain Hi Goldsmith didn't have the balls to lock him up.

No, Morgan worried more about the lead for his story, which must prove to be worth all the fuss. Two entwined mysteries in one grave. A puzzle where they had expected to find an enigma. A grave that wasn't even qualified to be a hole in the ground. A missing woman without a history replaced by a man without a head. Where had Laddie Granbouche gone, and where did John Doe come from?

The bell over *The Bullet*'s front door chimed as Dr. Cowper strode in off Main Street. He'd slept late for the first time in several days, and he looked rested.

"You walked over here?" Morgan asked. "You should have called and I'd have picked you up."

Dr. Cowper shook his head and plopped in the thinly padded chair beside Morgan's desk.

"Thanks, but I needed the exercise. This dry air clears the head."

"Well, you might want to make yourself scarce around here after today. DCI got a court order to stop me from printing anything about John Doe, but I'm doing it anyway."

"No shit?"

"Yeah, and these twerps are as serious as a heart attack. They might barge in here guns blazing when they read tomorrow's paper."

"I wouldn't worry too much about it," Dr. Cowper said, wiping the Wyoming road-dust from his shoe. "They might storm the newspaper and shoot everybody, but they'll sure look snappy doing it. Just wear something nice for your shooting tomorrow, huh?"

"So what are you up to today? A little cow-tipping?"

"I was wondering if I could see your morgue."

"You could if we had one. It burned up about five years ago. We have everything since then, and the state archives sent us microfilmed papers dating back to about 1895, but all the old papers and subject files are ashes."

"There goes that."

"Did you need something specific?"

"Yeah. Laddie's obituary, to start."

Morgan rummaged through the papers on his desk and produced a small tube of curled pages.

"Way ahead of you, Doc. And here's the story that

went with it."

Dr. Cowper spread the thermal copies from *The Bullet*'s microfilm reader on the desk. Laddie's death earned her a full story across the top of the front page under an ironic banner headline, Professed Outlaw Bride Dies, and her Page Two obit was unusually long, at least twenty-four column inches. Inside, *The Bullet*'s late and legendary editor Bell Cockins wrote one of the most startlingly eloquent tributes a small-town newspaperman ever committed to paper, not just about the passing of Laddie, but the passing of time, too:

The infinite moment of Laddie Granbouche

"Where do we begin to explain a life and a legacy? Every death needs meaning, just as every life needs meaning ...

"History is a wide, profound river. In time, nearly everything of the past is lost in the deep end of this river. Some of history's flotsam is washed ashore on the far bank, but we can only see it through the spyglass of memory, which distorts what is true. In the end, we leave the river to the scholars of future generations to navigate and map, to interpret our perceptions and help us understand them. So we make a deal with these wise men: They promise they will reconstruct the past as faithfully and as accurately as they are able, and we trust they are telling us the truth ...

"Will we ever know the truth about Laddie Granbouche? Did she truly ride with and love mythic outlaws ... or was she merely a lonely woman who yearned for a history more romantic than her own?

Have we missed our chance to know her?
To know ourselves?
"The river flows on."

"He was good," Dr. Cowper said reverently as he finished Old Bell's elegy for Laddie.

"The best," Morgan said.

Dr. Cowper scanned the obituary.

"Not the same," he said. "The words, the phrasing, the thought process ... well, it lacks the same fluency."

"Yeah," Morgan agreed. "It looks to me like Laddie wrote her own obituary before she died. Pretty common."

"She wrote this?"

"That's my best guess."

"Would it have been changed at all? Anything taken out?"

Morgan thought briefly.

"Maybe spelling or basic grammar, but probably not much more. Old Bell once told me some people only get their names in the paper when they are born, get married and die. He would have been generous on a self-written obit. I suppose he would have added the time and date of death, and all the funeral information, and left the rest as Laddie originally wrote it."

Dr. Cowper studied the obituary more closely.

"This might be the only thing we have in her own words. If she wrote this, it's her story, unfiltered by historians and reporters. Just her words. Sorta like the DNA of her thoughts."

"But maybe it isn't true," Morgan said.

"It doesn't matter if it's true or not ... this is what she wanted us to know. Would there be an original anywhere?"

"Not here."

"Where does an obituary normally come from?"

"Usually the funeral home."

Dr. Cowper bolted from his chair and headed for the front door.

"Plan on lunch," he said, not looking back.

Morgan swiveled around in his chair and stared at the guileless cursor blinking on his empty computer screen. It offered no reassurance. Not for Laddie's story, not for John Doe, not for deadline.

"You're either in deep thought or deep shit," a voice behind him said.

It was Cal Nussbaum, *The Bullet*'s hangdog pressman. Even in his late seventies, his ink-black glower could spot-weld a green reporter's rectum. God knows, it had certainly warmed Morgan's on occasion. Cal's compulsion was punctuality, and he had an uncanny sixth sense that anticipated missed deadlines. That's why he set his own clocks ahead ten minutes. Just to be sure.

"Both," Morgan said.

"I'm holding six pages right now, and three of 'em should already be locked up. Still ain't got the main sports photo or any of the lifestyle section, and the Town Hall's public notices are a day late. Maybe we should just close up shop and try again next week, huh?"

In fact, Cal would rather die — and take several laggard reporters with him — than miss a paper. In his almost fifty-five years on the job, every week had a *Bullet*, even after a fire-bombing had gutted the newspaper office and pressroom six years before. Once, in a fit of pique, Cal even started the press at the appointed moment, even though only half the plates were ready. He met his deadline, even if nobody else did.

"I think we'll be okay, Cal," Morgan assured him.

Cal harumphed and disappeared into the pressroom, his mythic realm where deadlines were never missed.

Morgan wandered to the front desk where Crystal Sandoval, his receptionist, was stuffing the week's advertising invoices in envelopes.

"Crystal, any idea why the Town Hall's public notices are late?" he asked.

"Hacker," she said without looking up.

"What happened?"

"Beats me," she shrugged. "They just said somebody broke into their server last night and erased a lot of stuff."

"Like what?"

Crystal cocked her head.

"Public notices, for one, geez."

"What else?"

"Parking tickets, dog licenses, sewer bills, that kind of stuff. The clerk's gals gotta key it all back in, but they don't have anything else to do."

"Sounds like a story. Would you call and ask them to send over their hard copies of this week's public notices and ... well, is it possible for you to stay late and typeset them tonight? Pretty please?"

Crystal rolled her eyes and picked up the phone. Morgan button-holed one of his two reporters, a lumpy kid from Rocky Mountain College in Montana who'd decided even journalism was better than running his dad's ranch. Certainly the manure couldn't be any deeper.

"Josh, I need a story about the Town Hall computer getting hacked. They apparently lost a lot of stuff. Let's find out what. I need fifteen inches max, maybe with a sidebar on how regular folks can protect their computers from hackers. By three o'clock, no later. Call the mayor and the town clerk and see what they know. Avoid the techno-geek jargon. Who, what, when, where, why, how ... and who cares? Got it?"

Josh nodded meekly. Morgan started back to his desk, but turned in the narrow aisle between his reporters' desks.

"And, guys, please try to get your other stories done right away. We gotta have 'em ASAP. If you don't, I'm gonna let Cal have his way with you. And I'm warning you, he likes it rough."

The unctuous odor of chicken-fried steak and viscous coffee congealed in The Griddle's dining room. Even the windows were greasy with it.

Dr. Shawn Cowper sat in the corner booth. He'd shoved the sticky syrup carousel, Tabasco and ketchup bottles, a crusty bowl of sugar, a couple of humidity-clotted salt and pepper shakers — all the epicurean enhancements a small-town bon vivant could possibly slurry on his fine cuisine — to the far side of his broad table. Several photocopies were arrayed in front of him.

"So what did you find?" Morgan asked as he sat at the edge of the booth. Without asking, Suzie, the waitress, delivered a tall glass of iced tea and a handful of pink packets as she flitted from table to table like a pork chop-scented bumblebee.

Dr. Cowper didn't even look up.

"The mother lode," he said, sliding several handwritten pages toward Morgan. "You were right about one thing: Laddie wrote her own obituary. That's a copy of her original, and it's just the same as in the paper. But she also gave the mortician some very detailed instructions about her funeral and burial, including directions to a remote spot in the Hole in the Wall where a particular color of sandstone for her crypt was to be quarried. And she paid cash up front for everything."

"Sounds like Laddie, all right."

"So did you ever wonder where she got her money?"

Morgan shrugged and stirred four packets of fake sugar into his glass.

"She was always a very old woman to me. I never thought about it, I guess. I thought all old people had money."

"Well, Laddie had money. Lots of it."

"How do you know?"

Dr. Cowper shuffled through his papers and produced a sheaf of stapled pages.

"Laddie's will and probate records from the courthouse."

Morgan skimmed. After twenty-five years of breathing the stale air in courthouse vaults, he'd become efficient about reading documents written by lawyers. His eyes naturally skipped the boilerplate legalese and landed on the meatiest passages.

"Jesus Christ ..."

"Jesus had nothing to do with it. With her La Plata Ranch and investments, Laddie's estate was worth more than thirty-seven million dollars. The old gal was sharp. She liked her blue-chips, and she held onto them for a long, long time."

Morgan scanned Laddie's portfolio.

"Coca-Cola, AT&T, General Electric, Trimark Pictures, Ford Motor Company, Union Pacific Railroad, Eastman Kodak, Wells Fargo ... Wells Fargo? That would be ironic, wouldn't it?"

"Maybe it was just a 're-investment,'" Dr. Cowper quipped. "Worse, take a look at the tax bill on her estate."

"Well, she wasn't hurting for money," Morgan said, flipping through pages.

"Good God, twelve million bucks to Uncle Sam," he said, astonished "If she wasn't already dead, that would have killed her. She hated the government."

"And where did it all come from, you think? She wrote a lot of things about herself in her obituary, but not a word about even a part-time job, much less any lucrative career ... except ranching the Pampas in Argentina."

"Inheritance maybe?"

Dr. Cowper looked dubious.

"The foster daughter of a Texas madam?"

"But we don't know that for sure," Morgan said.

"It's just a story. For all we know, she could be Daddy Warbucks's love-child. You're starting to believe the legends, my friend."

"Yeah, yeah, I know. Sorry. But what else do we have? Nothing here disproves her story."

"C'mon, Doc. Nothing here proves Laddie's story, either. Besides, crime doesn't really pay, and criminals aren't exactly patient investors. They crave instant gratification. Even the greatest outlaws don't die multi-millionaires ... well, okay, except for those savings and loan creeps."

Dr. Cowper seemed to know he was on thin scientific ice, but Laddie's legend appealed to his heart.

"Point taken," he said to Morgan. "So ... what do you make of this?"

Dr. Cowper pushed another piece of paper in front of Morgan. It was a copy of an invoice.

"Greenbrier Crematory, Billings, Montana, for services rendered, August twelve, 1969 ..."

"Two days after Laddie died and two days before her funeral," Dr. Cowper said.

"You don't think ...?"

"Why else would it be in her mortuary file?"

"A filing error? Her name isn't on it."

"Unlikely. The dates fit too perfectly. And this town doesn't seem big enough to have a confusing traffic jam at the funeral home."

"Okay, so what if Laddie were cremated? It doesn't prove anything one way or the other. It just means you came out here on a wild-goose chase."

"Maybe not. Did you say Bell Cockins was a good reporter?"

"No," Morgan asserted. "I said he was the best."

Dr. Cowper read from *The Bullet*'s front-page story about Laddie's funeral.

"Listen to this: 'Eight pallbearers lifted her casket

off the horse-drawn caisson beside the crypt and, after some strain, lowered it into the vault.'

"Okay. What's your point?"

"C'mon, a caisson? Eight pallbearers? Eight *strained* pallbearers? At first, I just figured maybe Laddie had put on some matronly weight, but now ... if she was cremated, what made that box so heavy?"

Morgan said nothing. The siren song of Laddie's mystery was too seductive. He grasped for logical explanations, but his mind was vacant.

"I don't know, Doc. But I suppose you have a hypothesis."

"Promise you won't laugh?"

"No. But go ahead."

Dr. Cowper spread his hands over the pile of papers in front of him and formed his words carefully.

"What if ... Laddie truly was Etta Place? What if ... some part of her myth was actually true? What if ... all this was an elaborate scheme to keep a secret, not reveal it?"

"And you see evidence of that in all these papers?"

Dr. Cowper pursed his lips.

"Hey, it's just a theory, okay? Science works the same way your buddies here buy pickup trucks: We find a theory we like, drive it hard, rip out the oil pan, burn up the engine, toss out the girlfriend, add a gunrack ... then go buy a new theory."

"Science ... like a rock."

"Well, my point is, theories are disposable, but they can get you where you want to go."

"Yeah, but they're supposed to be educated guesses, not frothy fantasies."

"All right," Dr. Cowper said defensively, "I'm educated and it's a guess. Satisfied?"

Morgan shook his head. "I can't win. What's your grand theory?"

Before Dr. Cowper could begin, Suzie arrived at their table.

"What'll it be?" she asked.

"What's today's special?" Dr. Cowper asked.

Suzie whiffed the fatty air. "Smells like chicken-fried steak, mashed potatoes and one-hour green beans."

The anthropologist wrinkled his nose.

"I'll just have a salad. Oil and vinegar on the side."

"I'll have the special," Morgan said, handing Suzie the gravy-stained menus as she flew to the next lunch order.

"Think Mexican," Dr. Cowper said.

"Not for lunch," Morgan answered. "Too heavy. Makes me fart."

"No, no," Dr. Cowper waved him off. "My theory, think Mexican."

"Jesus, Doc ..."

"Okay, hang with me for a few minutes. Keep an open mind. I'm kinda thinking out loud here."

Morgan checked his watch. "You've got til lunch arrives."

"Matt, my bug guy? Last summer, the Mexican government hired him to excavate some sites on a ranch in Chihuahua. Ever hear of Doroteo Arango?"

"No, should I?"

"You probably know him better as Pancho Villa. Anyway, Matt was hired to poke around in a small family cemetery on Villa's ranch for a cache of stolen silver."

"Find it?"

"Nah, but that's what's interesting. Seems that in 1913, Villa's rebels robbed a Wells Fargo train of a thousand bars of near-pure silver bullion, worth well over a million dollars at the time."

Morgan stirred his tea.

"Is this train going someplace, Doc?"

"Yeah, just chill, my anal retentive friend. Wells

Fargo didn't waste a minute alerting the authorities, and soon there was no way Villa was going to be able to unload the silver for cash-money. So there he is, sitting on a magnificent treasure that's worth nothing to him. Zip."

"Doc ...."

"So Wells Fargo brokers a deal with Villa. In exchange for a quarter-million in pesos from the mining companies who owned the bullion, Villa agrees to return the silver and to stop robbing Wells Fargo shipments. The ransom fuels Villa's Revolution, the mining companies recover their precious metal, and Wells Fargo has bought protection. Everybody's happy. No harm, no foul."

"Tell me this has a point."

"Well, when the exchange happens, Villa only gives back two-thirds of the silver. He tells Wells Fargo that his merry men stole the rest: Almost three hundred bars of pure silver, worth about $300,000 at the time."

"Sounds about par for the course with a bunch of hungry renegades. But how do you know all this?"

"In 1999, some researchers at Berkeley found all the correspondence in Wells Fargo's archives. At the time of the robbery, Wells Fargo refused to publicly acknowledge the ransom for fear it'd look like they were helping the bad-guys. They also worried about copycats. The internal papers were buried for almost ninety years. The Mexicans now say the silver wasn't pilfered by Villa's men, but that he kept it. It never turned up."

"Well, it's a jim-dandy story, Doc, but I don't see what it has to do with Laddie."

"What if the rumors about Butch and Sundance and Etta riding with Pancho Villa were true? What if they masterminded the Wells Fargo train robbery? After all, trains and banks were their specialty ..."

"And their cut just happened to be 300 bars of silver?"

"Hey, they were professionals. Villa was a thug.

One-third of the heist as a fee? Most lawyers charge more."

"And how much is it worth today?"

"Over a million, easy," Cowper smiled.

"Just for yucks, Doc, how long a shot is this?"

"Define long."

"A million-to-one?"

"Well, okay, even a million-to-one pays off once every million times."

"Don't look now, but your theory has a flat."

"Enlighten me."

"The silver itself. They could have melted it down and sold it off piecemeal. They sure as hell wouldn't sit on it forever. A sombrero is a cute souvenir from a Mexican vacation, not a half-million dollars worth of silver bullion."

"Unless they couldn't unload it. Maybe it was still too hot. Maybe they couldn't get a good price. Maybe they lost it. Maybe they got separated."

"You need to stop sniffing formaldehyde, Doc."

"Hey, it's possible. Not probable maybe, but possible."

"You think that Laddie Granbouche, aka Etta Place, ended up with it all? You think what she couldn't spend was buried with her? And now you think we're on the trail of a missing treasure?"

Dr. Cowper looked sheepish.

"Who knows?"

"We don't. You're dreaming."

"A lack of knowledge is temporary, my friend. A lack of dreams is forever."

"So how do we gain knowledge, Master Yoda?"

"We dream."

"That's it? Just fantasize until we're smart, huh? If that were the case, I'd have been a genius when I was thirteen and had a crush on Debbie Mahaffey."

"OK, well, maybe it takes a little more."

"Like what?"

"Oh, not much," Dr. Cowper said. "Just an open mind, some cotton swabs, a flashlight, a few drops of nitric acid, and an atomic absorption device. That's all."

Whether it was the lateness of lunch or just a bad chemistry-class flashback, Morgan's stomach clenched.

"By the way," Dr. Cowper added, "you know what La Plata means?"

Morgan shook his head. "The name of Laddie's ranch? I don't have a clue."

Dr. Cowper smiled.

"La plata is Spanish for 'the silver.'"

After midnight, a dog barked as Morgan and Dr. Cowper crept down the alley behind McWayne and Son Funeral Home. As usual, the mortician's door was unlocked.

"He stuck the coffin in his display room after we lifted John Doe out," Dr. Cowper whispered.

Morgan didn't relish the idea of walking around a funeral home in the dark, much less the prospect of opening strange doors there.

"God, I still hate the smell of ether," Dr. Cowper said, his nose crinkled like foil. "You take that side of the hall."

After poking his head in a few dark visitation rooms and jiggling a few locked doors, Dr. Cowper found the casket repository on his own. Laddie's old coffin was still on the gurney, pushed to one side among the shiny, floor-model caskets. How odd, Morgan thought, that Carter McWayne didn't display the cheaper cardboard boxes that a family could buy for cremating a loved one.

Morgan held the flashlight while Dr. Cowper opened the coffin. He swabbed several surfaces of the unlined interior with Claire's borrowed Q-tips, placing each in its own plastic sandwich bag. He labeled the location on each baggie with a black marker. When he finished, he closed the lid and the two men left the way they came, quietly down the back alley.

This time, the dog didn't bark.

On Wednesday morning, press day, the first *Bullet* was for Sheriff Highlander Goldsmith.

The ink was still damp on the entwined stories of John Doe and Laddie Granbouche. Morgan snatched the new edition off the conveyor belt before stuffers bundled the papers for the post office. It would be Morgan's declaration of independence ... or his arrest warrant.

Either way, he'd deliver it himself.

The sheriff's dispatcher said Goldsmith hadn't checked in yet this morning and was likely still at home, so Morgan planned a social call.

Unlike the old days, when the sheriff lived in or behind the jail and his wife cooked meals for inmates, Highlander Goldsmith was a bachelor and lived on the far edge of town. His spacious ranch villa sat on a bluff overlooking the confluence of the Black Thunder River and Little Poison Creek. The stone-and-cedar homestead had once been the main house for a sprawling cattle ranch, but the surrounding land had long ago been subdivided into twenty-acre "ranchettes" where accountants and lawyers could drive big trucks, wear cowboy boots and play at animal husbandry without the hardships of real agriculture. Cowboy posers, every one, Morgan thought.

The county graveled Goldsmith's long drive every year, a perk the commissioners rationalized as an aid to public safety, but the county graveled the commissioners' driveways, too. Grade A, government-approved pea-sized pebbles crunched under the Escort's tires as Morgan turned off the pavement at Goldsmith's cottonwood-lined lane. It was marked by an ornate, black ranch portal that arched over the road, with a lawman's star welded to its apex.

The sheriff's white Bronco was parked next to the house. An overfed blue heeler yipped nervously as Morgan stopped near the sheriff's front porch, but nobody came out to shush him.

"Relax, Cujo," he said as he knocked on the front door. The dog barked more insistently, although from a safe distance. Funny how some dogs assumed the personalities of their owners, he mused.

He knocked again.

The porch was a narrow, open-air walkway, lined with flagstone. Weeds poked up through bark mulch around the pavers and snaked their tendrils as far as they would reach. A breadloaf-sized UPS package, its brown wrap weathered, was beneath a spidery ragosa rose bush, unpruned for at least a season. Above Morgan, a strand of Christmas lights looped across the portico to the porch light, sagging in the June heat like rural electric wires in an ice storm.

Morgan pounded on the sheriff's big wooden door again. Chips of brown paint fluttered onto the unworn welcome mat.

When Morgan left Winchester for college at Northwestern University in Chicago in the fall of 1975, he hauled one suitcase and a dream to become a newspaperman. His father, a hardware store owner, had hoped he'd pursue a more practical career, so Morgan took a few architecture classes to please him. But at the time, after the fall of Nixon and Vietnam, changing the world seemed like a reasonable design, even for a kid from an end-of-the-road Wyoming town where nothing, including the architecture, had changed in a hundred years. Still, the study of building design had added an abstract element to his perceptive skills: Morgan saw human frailties and virtues reflected in the walls that surrounded the lives he covered.

In High Goldsmith's house, he saw a country manor with the heart of a homesteader's shack, a place that had not so much been built as evolved season after season. A room would be added here in years when the beef brought top dollar, a pantry there when it looked like a hard winter ahead. With each new growth spurt, stones would be brought from the river below for the walls.

But it was not High Goldsmith's house. He owned it, sure enough, but everyone knew it as Vernie Kilpatrick's place. When Vernie died a few years before, without any heirs, the sheriff auctioned off most of the land to pay her property taxes, holding back the main house for himself. He paid a decent price, but it was still wrong. It was only fitting that it had not yet become his in the community's conscience.

Still no answer. Morgan wandered to the side of the house, trailed at a secure distance by the suspicious blue heeler. The kitchen windows were open, and Morgan called inside, but no answer.

The back storm door was propped open with a rusted pipe, although it seemed ridiculous: the screen had long ago been shredded by the anxious little whelp. Morgan stepped inside.

"High, you here?"

Nothing.

Mindful that this jumpy sheriff carried a gun, Morgan stepped carefully into the breakfast nook and hollered again, a little louder.

"High, it's Jeff Morgan. I came to surrender. You gonna arrest me or what?"

The refrigerator purred, but there was no sign of Highlander Goldsmith. Some dirty dishes languished in the sink. A revolver lay on the kitchen table, its cylinder out, amid a clutter of blackened patches and cleaning rods. Morgan could smell the gun oil.

"Extra, extra," he said loudly. "Read all about it: Headless corpse found in unlikely spot ... a cemetery."

The living room was spare, but in order. Magazines were scattered across the redwood burl coffee table, a blanket draped over one arm of the leather sofa. The VCR blinked perpetual midnight.

"Goddammit, High. What does a guy have to do to get arrested around here?"

Goldsmith's nervous little dog suddenly dashed through the room, his unclipped nails clattering on the hardwood floor as he careened down a dark hallway. He leapt against a bedroom door and as it slowly swung open, slipped inside.

Morgan plucked his notebook from his shirt pocket and sat down to write a note to Goldsmith. Something glib. Something unthreatening but firm. Something that would twist the DCI agents' tails without being a rant. Something, of course, that pointedly wouldn't mention lost silver or Pancho Villa or breaking into the funeral home in the dead of night.

As he pondered the wording, he glanced down the hall where the dog had disappeared, likely cowering beneath a bed, Morgan guessed. The back-bedroom door had yawned wide on its arthritic hinges, and a shaft of sunlight spilled into the hallway.

Through the bedroom window, across the lane, Morgan saw High Goldsmith's brilliant red horse barn bathed in morning light. From where he sat it would have been possible to see right through the barn itself, since two thick-paned windows aligned perfectly with the sheriff's back-bedroom and the sofa where he sat.

But a peculiar shadow blocked Morgan's view of the new summer pastures beyond the barn.

It might have been a saddle or an oiled duster hanging

from a stable rafter, except for the distinct silhouette of a dead man's hand.

CHAPTER FIVE

Highlander Goldsmith died naked, all white and trussed up like a raw turkey.
Except for the red teddy.

Morgan found him hanging by his neck, dangling from a rope attached to the raised bucket of his John Deere Model 410E, the gentleman-farmer's distinctive green, diesel-powered backhoe tractor. He was suspended cross-legged, neither sitting nor standing, by a canvas safety harness strapped around his neck and grafted to a rope tied to the shovel. Goldsmith had wrapped a terry-cloth towel around the strap to protect the fragile skin of his neck.

The tractor had run itself out of gas, and the hydraulics were slowly relaxing.

A length of white PVC tubing was duct-taped to the backhoe's hydraulic control lever in the driver's cubicle. A broom stick was taped to the other end of the pipe, tucked under Goldsmith's buttocks. His slightest movement would easily raise or lower the shovel; up, he could pinch his own airway, and down, he could relax his noose ... as long as he could stand on his feet.

His dead hands splayed out from his sides like Frankenstein's monster, already blackening with the blood curdled in them. His tongue was swollen, his eyes half-open. His feet coiled beneath him, lifeless toes scrawling grotesque pinwheels in the barn's hard-packed manure. The filmy red nightie around his chest fluttered in the soft morning breeze that drifted through the open barn door.

The ambulance arrived first, after Morgan called 911.

Then came Undersheriff Willis Luckett, Goldsmith's second-in-command whose main job for the past six years had been to oversee the jail menu and promulgate daily memoranda to the department's ten jailers, dispatchers and deputies.

Carter McWayne was next, in his tricked-out black hearse, first in his role as Perry County Coroner and second as the funeral director. Such built-in efficiency left him more time for eating. In fact, the spot of egg yolk on his tie suggested he'd been called from breakfast.

And right behind McWayne, the officious DCI agents Eric Halstead and Scott Pickard rolled up in their sleek Crown Vic. They wasted no time commandeering the crime scene from Willis Luckett, who seemed genuinely relieved to be marginalized.

Almost like good cops, they quickly surveyed the scene and took Morgan, their main eyewitness, aside. They stood outside the red barn in the full morning light, on the rutted path to the empty horse corrals. The barnyard was pocked with horse manure, some dried, some big and wet. Hi Goldsmith had apparently been lax about shoveling shit.

Morgan walked with them, his hands in his pockets, side-stepping the fresh chips, awaiting the agents' first question. They stopped a proper distance from the barn's gaping door, where Carter McWayne was still examining the sheriff's suspended corpse.

Somewhere up the lane, a meadowlark sang its euphoric little song, undaunted by death within a stone's throw.

"Deputy," Agent Halstead snapped at the hapless

Luckett, "arrest this man."

Morgan expected to be grilled, but now he was being handcuffed.

"What the hell ...?"

"You violated a court order."

"You can't throw me in jail for that!"

"No? Well, then maybe we can rustle up a charge of evidence tampering."

"Bullshit."

Pickard came out of Goldsmith's house. He was carrying the new *Bullet* edition and Morgan's reporter notebook, which had his name and address on the cover. He'd left both on the sheriff's coffee table when he raced to the barn.

"How about breaking and entering?"

"The door was open. I brought the paper to Hi. I was writing him a note when I saw ... him."

"From inside? You saw a dead man in the barn while you were inside the house? You see through walls?"

Morgan said nothing. He knew how close he was coming to sounding suspicious.

"Careful with your privates, Scott," Agent Halstead said facetiously to his partner, "This paperboy's got X-ray eyes. Maybe he's a perv like our Barney Fife-on-the-flying trapeze here. Read him his rights, deputy, and take him back to town."

"Hell, let's just hang his nosey little ass from the nearest cottonwood and be done with him," a man's voice echoed across the yard.

While Willis Luckett fumbled with the pair of handcuffs he'd never used, the two DCI agents and Morgan turned toward the sound.

Morgan knew the loping walk, the tight Wrangler fit of his jeans and the grin under a prodigious mustache that would have made Wild Bill Hickok himself proud. Only the Stetson was new ... well, not new, but not worn for almost five years.

"Hold it right there," Agent Halstead barked. "This is a crime scene. Please stop where you are and go back to your car."

"Crime scene? Then I'm damn sure at the right place. Thought maybe I'd just walked in on a random lynching. I hate it when that happens."

"Sir, I'm not going to ask you again," Agent Halstead warned, discreetly unsnapping the safety strap on his stylish black leather holster. "You're interfering with a criminal investigation here. So get back to your car. Now."

The cowboy just kept coming, stepping casually through the horse-dung minefield. When he got within ten yards, Agent Halstead drew his weapon, a Glock semi-auto that could fire an extra two bullets – 19 instead of the usual 17. Morgan most certainly felt safer. He also knew the interloper was unarmed.

"Whoa, hold on there, Dirty Harry!" the cowboy said, his open hands in the air, but still walking deliberately at the locked-and-loaded DCI agent. "You don't wanna go shooting the new sheriff so soon after the old one got all choked up."

"You got some ID?"

"Kerrigan," the cowboy said, a big grin spilling across his face. "Trey Kerrigan."

When Agent Halstead holstered his weapon, Trey Kerrigan yanked a tarnished badge, a five-pointed star, from his back pocket. It just said Perry County Sheriff. His father, the legendary Deuce Kerrigan, had worn it proudly for forty years. Trey himself had worn it for eight years before he abandoned his last campaign in midstream, too cynical and too political to do justice for Perry County or to his father's memory.

"Funny thing about small towns," Trey told Agent Halstead, "nobody can keep a secret for shit. Within thirty minutes after Mr. Morgan's 911 call, the dispatcher had called her sister, whose husband is a volunteer firefighter who leases some pasture from a rancher who wants a new county road paved up to his place. So's he called a county commissioner to deliver the sad news about Hi, and the commissioners decided over the phone that they were gonna need a new sheriff, pronto. Seein's how I already owned a badge and a gun, they reckoned I already had the outfit, and things've been pretty slow in the insurance business, so's I took the job. You might wanna just give 'em a jingle just to confirm."

Trey winked at Morgan, his old high school buddy, as Agent Pickard whipped out his cell phone and wandered off across the drive where he couldn't be heard.

"Fine, you can play sheriff," Agent Halstead said, "but we've got this case under control. We won't be needing your assistance."

"Willis, you can take the cuffs off my good buddy Jeff now," Trey told the deputy he'd hired almost fifteen years before. "Whatever he did, I'm sure he won't do it again. We can let him off with a warning this time."

Agent Halstead held up his hand, like a traffic cop halting oncoming traffic.

"Hold it. You didn't seem to hear me, sheriff," he said. "We're in charge here. This is our case. This man is under arrest."

Trey looked at the ground and booted a small rock toward the corrals. Morgan knew his aw-shucks routine by heart.

"Aw shucks," Trey said. "You musta been shopping for Tommy Hill-*finger* slacks that day at the Academy when they explained that DCI can't take over any investigations. You can be here only at my invitation, and I gotta say, you're wearin' out your welcome."

"Sheriff Goldsmith invited us," Agent Halstead growled.

"Well, Hi's a little tied up right now," Trey said calmly. "So I'm un-inviting you."

"Fuck you, Kerrigan."

"Hey, now that might be fun ... as long as I'm on top and there's no kissin'," Trey said, arching his eyebrows flirtatiously. "But I like it long and slow ... and you're just leaving. Maybe next time."

Agent Halstead stepped so close to Trey, their noses almost touched. Morgan could see only a sliver of light between them, but the chasm that separated these two lawmen was vast and barren. Neither blinked.

"You better watch your ass, cowboy," Halstead seethed, "because I damn sure will."

Trey stared him down.

"You might wanna *keep* your eyes on my ass, kid," Trey said. "Then maybe you won't notice you just stepped in a big pile of horse shit."

Agent Halstead looked down. He'd landed his right foot in one of the fresher piles, and his Rockport was smeared with muddy green manure that looked like a rotten spinach experiment gone badly wrong.

"Oh man," Trey added, holding his nose. "I think that horse is sick."

Agent Halstead lifted his skanky-swanky shoe from the splatter and tried to scrape it on the dirt, but that only spread the crap around more evenly. He glowered at Trey, then walked away. After a few steps, he stopped and turned toward Trey and Morgan one last time.

He aimed his thumb and forefinger like a gun and let the hammer fall. Then he smiled a cold smile and headed for the car with the grim-faced Agent Pickard, who snapped his cell phone shut petulantly. Whatever he had learned didn't please him.

"You know, Jeff," Trey confided as he watched the

DCI agents stalk back to their Crown Vic in a huff. "I could never be a state cop."

"Why's that?"

"My ass just don't look right in khakis."

"What do we got here, Carter?" Trey asked the coroner as they both stood before Highlander Goldsmith's sagging corpse. The barn was foul with rotting dung and death. McWayne was sketching the body and its deadly apparatus, minus the tractor.

"Probably strangulation caused by autoerotic asphyxiation. I guess he's been dead less than twenty-four hours, judging by the epidermal color and rigor mortis. He'll clean up real good for the funeral."

"Oh, for crying out loud, you still looking at dirty pictures in the Journal of the American Medical Association? Jesus, just say it in English, Carter."

"That is English. Autoerotic asphyxia is a method of producing sexual excitement. The subject mechanically or chemically asphyxiates himself while, you know ... masturbating," McWayne explained, stroking the air lewdly. "The theory is that cerebral hypoxia ..."

Trey kicked the dirt.

"Okay, the theory is that a lack of oxygen to the brain will heighten the orgasm by altering perceptions or inducing transitory anoxia."

"I'm gonna do somethin' to you, Carter," Trey bristled. "Somethin' bad."

"Well, the danger of transitory anoxia ... okay, okay, temporary suffocation ... is that even a brief miscalculation can cause the subject to lose consciousness and ..." Coroner McWayne lolled his tongue, emitted a throttled gag, and rolled his bug-eyes back in their sockets, mimicking a strangling man.

"So this is an accident?"

"Not exactly. Barring any evidence to the contrary, I'd call it suicide."

"But he didn't mean to die, did he?" Trey asked.

"Well, no," McWayne said. "The intention is not to die, but to produce heightened sexual gratification. But the hanging part was intentional. The key to my diagnosis of this specific sexual entity is the presence of the towel between the noose and Hi's neck. A fella doesn't much worry about rope burns if he's committing *real* suicide. Hi just wanted to get his rocks off ... which didn't happen, by the way. I always knew there was something queer about that guy."

Deputy Willis Luckett stood in the open barn door, listening and watching, his beefy arms crossed over his chest. Trey said nothing but chucked his head sideways in a silent suggestion to move along. The deputy saluted with one finger to the brim of his white straw cowboy hat and left.

"Any way this is a murder?" Trey asked McWayne.

"Hey, I just tag 'em and bag 'em," he said. "But I've heard about this type of pervert-o stuff. And a killer would have had to go to a lot a trouble just to rig this up. Nah, it's not murder."

"Okay, so we could say it was an accident," Trey said in a low voice to the coroner.

"Well, Trey, I just ..."

"Dammit, Carter, it was an accident. Don't go getting self-righteous. It's bad enough he got caught wearin' a teddy while spankin' Elvis. That's just peculiar. But suicide is what crazy people do, and Hi wasn't crazy. Okay, maybe really lonely, but he wasn't crazy. Do we need to kick the man while he's dead?"

"He hanged himself on purpose, Trey," McWayne argued. "It just wasn't as fun as he thought it was gonna be. He knew the risks."

Trey twisted his big mustache between his fingers,

thinking hard.

"So you're sayin' if a man walks behind a rank horse and the horse kicks his lights out, it's suicide because he knew the risk of walkin' behind a mean-assed horse?"

"I can't just put 'accident' down," McWayne said. "I gotta be more specific. State law."

Trey tilted his Stetson and scratched his head.

"You know, Carter," he said, barely concealing his frustration and his thinning hairline. "Right now, the state law has a shoeful of horse shit."

"What about Jeff? He saw all this. How are you gonna keep it out of the paper?"

"I've known Jeff since we were kids," Trey said. "He'll be honest, and he'll do what's right. But ain't you got enough chores without trying to be the newspaper editor, too?"

The pleats of fat under the coroner's chin shimmied as he huffed.

"And you think I won't do what's right, is that it?"

"Look, Carter, I ain't askin' you to lie. I'm askin' you to find a discreet way to report this as an accidental death. With all your fancy-assed vernacular, that shouldn't be too hard, should it?"

Carter McWayne screwed the pale, manicured sausage of his forefinger deep into his itchy ear and shrugged petulantly.

"Whatever you say, Trey. You're the new sheriff in town," the coroner grumbled. "You'll notify his next of kin?"

"Know anybody?"

McWayne smirked.

"Willis might know somebody, but looks to me like Hi's closest friend was John Deere."

The ink was still damp on the newest edition of *The*

Bullet, but the biggest news of the week ... of the year ... wasn't in it.

Morgan needed a phone, fast. He never carried his own cell phone, mostly because he always forgot where he put it. Anyway, it was a meaningless appliance in the dead zone called Winchester, Wyoming.

McWayne's hearse was locked. Hi Goldsmith's house was now a crime scene. Trey Kerrigan had arrived in his shitheap Willys Jeep, whose primitive electronics fried before man landed on the moon.

Morgan ducked quickly into Deputy Willis Luckett's cruiser, parked politely in the shade of a primeval cottonwood. He dialed *The Bullet*'s main number on the handset. Receptionist Crystal Sandoval answered.

"*The Bullet*," she said, "Coming at you every week."

"What?"

"What yourself?"

"Crystal, this is Jeff. Just say, '*The Bullet*. Can I help you?' That's less ... menacing."

"I thought it was cute."

"It scares people," Morgan said. "Look, tell Cal to keep all the papers in the pressroom 'til I get back. Shouldn't be long. Just don't put any out, okay?"

A long pause on the other end.

"Don't put out the papers? You sure?"

"I'm sure. And tell him to get the press ready to print a one-sheet extra. We'll wrap it around the papers we already printed. If we don't, the story will be a week old when we tell it."

"An extra. Cool," Crystal chirped. "Just like a real newspaper."

A *real* newspaper? Morgan almost growled, but there wasn't time.

"Send Josh out here to Hi Goldsmith's house on the Little Poison bench right away. Tell him to bring a camera and two notebooks. And no farting around. I want to see him within ten minutes."

"He's gone."

"Where?"

"I dunno. Lunch? Or maybe a nap in his car."

"Find him. Ten minutes."

"Yeah, yeah," she said. "So is it true?"

"Is what true?"

"About the sheriff ... you know ... flogging the bishop on a tractor? Sounds kinky to me."

"Jesus, how'd you hear about that already?"

"He was so straight," Crystal clipped along, not missing a beat. "I mean, like Opie Taylor in Mayberry. I guess Opie's gone bad."

Crystal popped her gum.

"Dammit, Crystal ..."

"My sister works over at the Kurl Up and Dye Salon, and my nephew's girlfriend who keeps books for the feed store came in, and she said she heard it from Arnella Bagwell, the fill-in clerk over't the video store, and she was ..."

"Goddammit," Jeff barked, "just send Josh."

Morgan slid the deputy's phone back into its cradle and slid against the half-open driver-side door. It wouldn't budge.

"Dammit, Jeff," Trey Kerrigan said, "one of these times I'm gonna have to arrest you on general principle."

The new sheriff of Perry County had his big paw on the cruiser's door, preventing it from opening or closing any further. Morgan was a captive audience.

"Trey, I was just using the phone."

"That ain't just a phone, Jeff," Kerrigan said calmly, staring off in some philosophical direction. His eyes were hidden by his dark glasses. "That there is a county phone, which means it's for the exclusive use of *county* employees on *county* time for *county* business. I think it's a felony or some such to steal county services."

"Aw, bullshit, Trey. I was just making a call."

"Yeah, I heard."

Kerrigan leaned close and took off his glasses. His eyes were dark, like a distant thunderstorm boiling to violent ripeness over the mountains.

"Jeff, you're like a cat with nine lives," he said, low and angry. "That was Number Nine."

The late Highlander Goldsmith's entire ranchette became an official crime scene when Trey Kerrigan escorted Morgan to the end of the driveway and slammed the gate behind him.

"Step one foot on this property before I say you can," the sheriff warned him, "and I promise you'll go to lock-up. Interfere with any police investigation ... lock-up."

"C'mon, Trey ..."

The sheriff raised his hand, stopping Morgan in mid-sentence.

"Whine about a free press ... lock-up."

Kerrigan shook a frustrated finger at his old friend, lifelong ties strained to their limit.

"I have half a mind to feed you to those DCI snakes," he snarled. "You're just pissin' me off, and I ain't even been sheriff for two hours yet!"

The one-sheet extra edition about Highlander Goldsmith's death was written, pasted up and printed in less than three hours.

It contained Morgan's first-hand account of the death scene, a couple of general photos of the house and barn, file mugs of the main players, "no comments" from everyone involved in the investigation, a G-rated sidebar explaining autoerotic asphyxiation in terms suitable for Puritan children, a brief story about the return of Trey Kerrigan to Perry County law enforcement, and a slender profile of Highlander Goldsmith culled from his campaign flyers.

The late sheriff's public life was only a small part of him, and a small part of his private life was now public, but nobody knew much about Highlander Goldsmith, the man. Whatever was in his heart was, in the end, as mysterious as the contents of Laddie Granbouche's heart ... or her coffin, for that matter. Morgan promised himself to do more next week, to find someone who'd laughed or cried with Highlander Goldsmith, to make a meager attempt to give his death a meaning.

For the moment, all it meant was that Hi Goldsmith was dead, and the entwined mysteries of Laddie Granbouche and John Doe were Page Three news.

All available hands, even Claire and Colter, helped wrap one freshly printed sheet around every copy of the week's *Bullet*. The lazy union twerps down at the Post Office had closed up early, but Cal pounded on the loading-dock door until somebody answered, and he forced them to take his papers for tomorrow's delivery. They grumbled and swore, but Cal just smiled. For all the abuse they'd heaped on him in *The Bullet*'s darkest days, he delighted in their displeasure.

When *The Bullet* hit mailboxes the next day, it merely added detail to the stories already flying back and forth over Winchester's back fences. Small-town readers are seldom surprised by what they see in the local paper, since they've usually heard the genuine news — or a version of it — in the coffee shop or the beauty parlor long before the paper arrives.

It just makes them feel better to know the paper knows, too.

CHAPTER SIX

"Jesus, this town is a theme park for forensic anthropologists. The Disneyland of Death."

Dr. Shawn Cowper plopped in the chair beside Jeff Morgan's cluttered desk, the latest *Bullet* under his arm. He smelled smug, like suntan oil.

"Well, you sure don't see a high-ranking public official cinched to a backhoe wearing nothing but a red nightie every day," Morgan said. "Or do you?"

"You'd be surprised what I see, my allegedly jaded friend," Dr. Cowper said. "People can be very creative when it comes to dying. Makes my job fun."

"What do you make of this one?"

"Probably just what they say. Accidental. Killers usually don't cover their tracks so elaborately. Besides, sexual hypoxia is more commonly practiced than you might think. But the tractor ... well, that was a new one for me."

"Where the hell were you anyway?"

"Funny you should ask. I drove over to Blackwater and found a little environmental testing lab with an atomic absorption device."

Morgan leaned back in his creaky chair, vaguely troubled by the idea of anything "atomic" in the hands of the typical Wyoming citizen.

"Laddie's silver?" he asked.

"Right."

That was it. Nothing more. Morgan sat forward again, a new trouble on his mind.

"Well ... are you gonna tell me?"

"Did you know rich people once stored their food in silver vessels to keep bacteria from growing?"

"No."

"Oh yeah. And it worked. You've heard of 'blue bloods'? They call 'em that because they ate from silver plates with silver forks and spoons, and people believed the silver got into their veins and protected them from illness. But it wasn't just queens and kings and dukes and stuff. American settlers often dropped silver dollars in their milk cans to make the milk last a little longer. Silver was thought to be a powerful antibiotic until the drug companies got involved."

"Is there a point to this fascinating little biochemical history lesson?"

"The human body naturally contains tiny traces of silver and a lot of other metals, such as tungsten, vanadium, nickel, molybdenum, tin, aluminum, uranium, mercury, even gold. Sorta makes you feel like that liquid metal guy in *Terminator* ..."

"Or the Tin Man. Doc, really. I flunked biology, and I still have bad dreams about it. Humor me: was there silver in Laddie's casket or not?"

Dr. Cowper plucked a small notebook from his shirt pocket and leafed through it.

"Yes."

"Yes? That's it? A lot? A little?"

"I was trying to tell you."

Morgan rubbed his tired eyes and spread his arms in surrender.

"You media guys always want to cut to the chase," Dr. Cowper chided. "No appreciation for foreplay."

"Yeah, yeah. By all means, let's postpone the chase

while we cop a feel of the endlessly wonderful delights of biochemistry."

Dr. Cowper shook his head and continued.

"The human body contains only a trace of silver, about two milligrams," the anthropologist said. "But that's not much. If I could smelt all the silver from your body, I'd need about forty guys just like you just to gather a penny's worth at today's prices. So you're safe ... unless, of course, the price of silver rises."

"The casket?"

"Well, that's the kicker: My swabs gathered more than six milligrams of silver, *three times* what a normal human body would contain."

Morgan sat up. "No shit?"

"Bottom line: Laddie's box once contained an enormous amount of silver, and it wasn't part of her anatomy," Dr Cowper said. "The swabs showed traces of silver on every interior surface of the coffin except the lid. Basically, we have a microscopic layer of silver dust throughout the coffin."

"So how much?"

"I'd guess a few hundred pounds. Not much more if Laddie was trying to fool her pallbearers."

Morgan was jangled by the leap from chemistry to conspiracy.

"Hold on. You think this was some last big joke by a dead woman?"

Leafing through equations scribbled in his notebook, Dr. Cowper smiled and shrugged like a little boy with a frog in his pocket, but said nothing. Morgan tested him.

"Okay, let's play this out. If the casket contained a mother lode of silver, somebody else had to put it there. Laddie was dead and, if your theory is correct, was already reduced to ashes."

Dr. Cowper shrugged again, unfazed by the challenge.

"Sure. It seems obvious to me the mortician was in

on it."

"Derealous McWayne?"

"Is that how you say it? I was way off. Does it mean something?"

"What?"

"Derealous."

"Goddammit, I don't know. I'm still trying to figure out this whole wacky plot you've hatched out of thin air."

"It's not wacky," Dr. Cowper smiled. "I'm a scientist. And it's not a wild-assed, paranoid conspiracy theory. It's a ... a hypothesis."

Morgan threw up his hands.

"Fine. A scientist's gotta have a hypothesis. And a hypothesis is never weird, right? If a scientist thinks he can prove JFK is living as a vegetable on a Caribbean island, he's got a hypothesis. If a cabbie says it, he's just paranoid."

"It's possible."

"Laddie's silver?"

"No, JFK. See, the path of the bullet was ..."

"Look, doc, I'm up to my ass in rattlesnakes here. The old sheriff is dead, the new sheriff is pissed. I have bodies in the wrong place and bodies that are NO place. I almost went to jail for printing a newspaper. State cops would love a bite of my ass. I broke into a mortuary and helped you steal evidence, which largely consists of fillets from a headless corpse stored in Tupperware in my goddamned refrigerator! What the fuck is going on?"

Dr. Cowper calmly leaned forward.

"Breathe."

"I'll breathe. You explain."

Dr. Cowper put away his scientific notations. From here on, his mind and heart were in charge.

"Let's say Laddie ends up with some of Pancho Villa's silver. I don't know how. She can't or won't unload it. She literally wants to take it to her grave, the one place nobody will ever look. It'll be hidden forever. She makes elaborate plans to have it entombed in her place. The one problem: she needs help."

"McWayne."

"Right. So she pays him handsomely to cremate her secretly and to bury her cache of silver bullion in her crypt ... in place of her body."

"Okay, that's such a great theory, it leaves only about, oh, a hundred or so questions. Like, why wouldn't she just bury the silver in the hills? Nobody'd find it there, either, and she'd never have to let anybody in on her secret."

"I don't know."

"And if Laddie was Etta Place, you gotta think she didn't trust many people. She wouldn't just trust Derealous McWayne to seal her crypt with a fortune inside, would she?"

"I don't know."

"And let's say there were three or four hundred pounds of silver in that casket. That'd be only a small part of Butch and Sundance's Wells Fargo booty. Where's the rest?"

"I just don't know," Dr. Cowper admitted. "But I know one thing."

"What's that?"

"Laddie's casket was full of pure silver. We don't know where it came from or where it went ... or why ... but we know it was there. Doesn't that make you the tiniest bit curious about a lot of things?"

Now Morgan was the one without an answer.

The repulsive morning dee-jays at KROK-FM swooped upon Highlander Goldsmith's bizarre death like vultures on roadkill. No, Morgan thought, vultures chewing rancid carrion were funnier.

"Man, I've heard of choking the chicken," the Bug said, "but *CHOKING* the chicken?"

"You think a guy would take a few precautions, you know," Curtis said. "But I guess when you're boinking a tractor, you don't really think about safe sex, huh?"

The Bug snorted.

"You know, I'm sprouting a woody just thinkin' about bumpin' uglies with farm implements. And let's face it, even a ditch-witch is cuter than the girls around here!"

"Dude, you got a tractor at home, doncha?" Curtis asked, ever the twisted straight man.

"Yeah, but it's a Tonka tractor!"

"Cool! Perfect size for your ..."

"Dick is on the line right now," the Bug hollered. "What's up, Dick?"

The two pinheads laughed, but a distant, metallic voice hummed like evil electricity over the radio, some guy on a party line out past the Highline, possibly from Hell itself. Morgan reached across his desk and turned up the volume a little.

"God punishes the sinner who spills his seed for wicked and iniquitous purposes," the growling voice said. "The seed is life, and when this man disobeyed God, he was punished. In the end, he squeezed his own life out of his pathetic little root, and he died before it seeped into the dirt. God saw. He is first but not last."

Click.

Curtis said the first thing that occurred to his limited vocabulary and even more limited intellect:

"Cool."

But it wasn't cool. Morgan pondered how such pure malevolence might drift on the electric airwaves, not just a tiny echo that bounced off a small Wyoming town and disappeared, but a sound-pulse that would resonate through space and time, beyond the gravitational pull of Earth, past the moons and stars and the emptiness beyond, the way they broadcast Hitler's voice as a message from a tiny, allegedly harmless planet, to the ear of God Himself.

In the small galaxy called Winchester, Wyoming, only one man denied space to unbelievers, doubters and sinners. Only one man believed in a special Hell for anyone who crossed him, and most did. Only one man used free speech as a sword, never a shield. Only one man would let loose the hate others kept chained in the darkest parts of their souls, like a mad dog.

Morgan knew the voice almost as well as his own, and it twisted his gut.

Malachi Pierce.

"Dude's harsh," The Bug said. "Bet he eats his dead, huh? Raw. No sauce."

"You're on Curtis and The Bug's restaurant and kinky sex review show, caller," Curtis said.

A smaller voice came over the air. A child's voice.

"It's not right to say those things about the man," the boy said. "He's dead."

"Wussie!" The Bug hollered. "Dead guys can't call the FCC!"

"I'm no wussie," the child said, his voice a little shaky. But he stood his ground, tenuous as it was.

"Hey, is this Grady? Sounds like the Grady-meister," Curtis said. "Dude, you definitely got the magic vibe on the touchtone."

An uncomfortable silence.

"Take it back," the boy said.

"Take what back?" The Bug asked.

"What you said."

"Yo, Grady, chill. We're in the media. We don't take nothin' back. It's our mike, not yours."

"Take it back."

The boy was slightly more insistent, but Curtis and

The Bug just chortled, as if they were bullet-proof as well as sound-proof in their soft-sided little box on the edge of town.

"What's the 4-1-1, Grady dude?" Curtis asked. His faux street-jive grated on Morgan's ear, another small-town white kid trying to sound like the hip-hop music he hides from his parents.

"Just take it back."

"No, you little shit!" The Bug yapped without even his usual lame attempt at humor.

The air went dead with an electric pop. In a moment, it surged back to life in a vortex of sound: advertising jingles, country music, overlapping voices from public radio and Hitler rallies, sound effects from distant galaxies, a child laughing. Every fifteen seconds or so, a voice that sounded like Homer Simpson's intoned: *the mayor is a dorkface.*

Morgan rolled the radio dial up and down through the babble of frequencies, a single voice in a thousand places. But the electronic space occupied by 99.9 KROK-FM was a thousand voices in one place, and it was deafening to hear.

But Curtis and The Bug were silenced, and Morgan smiled.

Morgan got home late, past sunset in places farther west than Winchester, Wyoming. Past the time the road to Mount Eden was passable without headlights, when deer lingered in the barrow pit. Past the moment when the warm orange had bled out and turned blue.

It was dark.

The house was dark, too. And empty. Nothing on the stove. No night lights. No notes. No children laughing. He tossed his Colorado Rockies cap on the table and snooped around his own kitchen, hunting for signs of Claire and Colter, and scavenging for chocolate chip cookies or chips or beer or anything to distract him from an early bed. He hadn't eaten all day.

In the cold glow of the open refrigerator, nothing looked good. He took a bite of some cold pizza, but the cheese was as hard as garlic-flavored marzipan, the sauce cold and clumpy. A ring had congealed around the inside of a glass of undrunk milk. He found a plastic tub of French onion dip in the back, but it was splotched with mold. A foil-covered plate contained some noodle salad, which he hated, and some grilled chicken, which he didn't, so he took a bite from a drumstick and crimped the foil back. Claire had split a fresh melon and some peaches, but late-night fruit never seemed right to him. Too responsible. Animals that foraged at twilight ate lower on the food chain.

Then he heard Claire laughing out in the gardens. From the back porch, he could see almost nothing. An incandescent purple bug light over the back door crackled, one more insect soul dispatched to bug heaven on a wisp of ozone and moth dust. Then silence.

Old Bell Cockins had called the magnificent garden a "pleasance," his British-born mother's word for the magnificent gardens at Mount Eden, and he tended it gently until he died. It spread over nearly an acre, encircled by tall pines, and he'd left it all in the care of his best journalistic pupil, Jeff Morgan.

In the dark warmth of a summer night, Morgan couldn't see beyond the trees, but tonight he could hear voices. His wife's was among them, and she was laughing.

Morgan picked his way along the path toward a flickering citronella candle in the clearing. The canopy was too thick for moonlight. Midges swarmed inside the woodland, where a stream trickled. On hot nights like this, he would walk into the grove and pass through cool puddles of air suspended there, invisible globes of air much cooler than the air around it. He figured it was a trick of evaporation or humidity, a microclimate the size of a child, no more ... but he allowed for spirits, too. When he felt the coolness of these night-wraith pools of air on his cheek, he thought of Bridger and felt him close.

But other spirits haunted him now. Laddie Granbouche was his most persistent ghost. And John Doe was his most perplexing. But the freshly minted ghost of Highlander Goldsmith literally hung in his forebrain, a grotesque marionette whose shadow fell against a blank canvas. A blank canvas Morgan felt compelled to fill with words and color and compassion for the guy.

The candle flickered in the garden.

Colter slept on a bench, his skinned knees drawn up beside him. Claire said something he couldn't understand, then giggled, and a male voice followed from the shadows. Morgan recognized it.

"What's up, Doc?" Morgan said, stepping into the small circle of light thrown by the bug candle.

"Jeff," Claire said, a little surprised. "What time is it?"

"Late."

"Gotta try this stuff," Dr. Cowper said. "The perfect muscle relaxant."

Dr. Shawn Cowper pulled an odd bottle from its hiding spot in the iris bed and poured Morgan a tiny glass. He sniffed and got a whiff of something intense, more than moonshine, less than kerosene.

"Jesus," Morgan said, "is this flammable?"

"Grappa," Dr. Cowper said. "Used to be poor man's brandy, but now it's the rage. Even the bad stuff goes for twenty-five bucks a bottle. Don't swig. Maybe just sort of dip your tongue in it at first."

Morgan did. The grappa curdled the lining of his

mouth. It had a vile bite.

"My god," Morgan said.

"Yeah, it's an acquired taste. They say Hemingway drank it at Harry's Bar in Venice. No wonder he had hair on his chest, huh?"

Claire brushed her hair back and a primrose petal fluttered to the path at her feet. She looked down and said nothing, but not in a guilty way. Nonetheless, Morgan thought she seemed a little uncomfortable, especially since she'd been laughing only a moment before. But now wasn't the time to press.

"Sorry about dinner," he said as he sat beside her on the garden bench. "Film processor broke down and ruined the Class of 1960 reunion photos. Had to go shoot new stuff."

"No problem," Claire said. "I made a plate for you."

"I saw it. Thanks."

After a moment's pause, Dr. Cowper squinted close at his watch in the dark.

"Man, I gotta run. Early morning tomorrow."

"What's up?"

"Nothing, just dead-guy stuff," the anthropologist said. Morgan felt brushed off.

Dr. Cowper leaned over and kissed Claire on the cheek, then clapped Morgan on the shoulder. He walked a few steps down the path toward the house and disappeared into the dark.

Claire gathered Colter in her arms as Morgan squinted to see if Dr. Cowper was out of earshot.

"What was that?" he whispered, a little peevish.

"What?"

"That kiss."

"What kiss?"

"He kissed you."

Even in the guttering citronella light, he saw Claire roll her eyes.

"On the cheek."

"A kiss is a kiss."

"Yeah, Jeff, I saw that movie."

"C'mon. I get home late, there's a guy here, you're having a grand time, and as soon as I show up, the party's over and a guy kisses my wife. Goddammit, and howdy-do to you, too."

"You're kidding, right?"

"Why is he even here?"

"Shawn brought something for you."

"Shawn? Shawn? That's a little familiar, isn't it?"

"For god sakes, Jeff, it's his name," Claire said. "You're overreacting. You've got yourself all worked up over nothing."

"Bullshit. I've seen Doc at work. He's smooth. He quotes books of erotica ... from memory!"

Claire fixed him in her sights. The air around them was pungent, but only part of the bitterness was citronella.

"And you think he's hitting on me, is that it? I mean, he's so smooth he'd do it right in front of you, is that it?"

Morgan weighed his words carefully.

"A single guy. A *smart* single guy. A pretty woman who's maybe a little, I dunno, understimulated. A warm night in the dark. A few high-octane cocktails. Husband's not around. Kid's asleep. A ... single guy ..."

Claire cocked her head as if he were speaking a foreign language, but she *still* didn't like what he was saying.

"Blow out the light. Dinner's in the fridge. Good night."

As she carried their sleeping son back to the house in the dark, Morgan heard the bug-zapper sizzle.

Claire slept on the far side of the bed that night, still and cold as death, cast-off sheets crumpled like a range of mountains between them.

Morgan lay awake most of the night. He watched a

gibbous June moon transit the open bedroom window. A distant train mourned as it crossed the grasslands below. The summer night exhaled through the lace curtains. Drifting toward sleep, he half-dreamed, half-imagined a train to the prairie moon, a poetic image of absolutely no use to him. He was where he wanted to be, and he desperately wanted to apologize, but couldn't, partly from fear of saying the wrong thing again. He'd spoken from the heart, yes, but he knew it came from one of the shameful chambers deep in the heart of his heart.

He turned the pillow, seeking the coolest part. Then turned it again. No part of him was comforted.

Sleep took him unwilling before the right words drifted through his troubled mind. Somewhere in the night, he waved goodbye to a train carrying Claire and Doc and Colter and all his ghosts to the moon, issuing a meteoric silver tail of primrose petals on its way to its last stop on the other side of the mountains.

And the porter served grappa.

A crow caviled through the open window as the sun rose above the trees. Jeff awoke no more comforted than when he fell asleep, and a whole lot more ashamed.

He reached across the bed to touch Claire, but she was already gone. It was a summer Saturday morning, already nine o'clock, and he expected to hear the clangor of pots and pans in the kitchen, or a door slamming, or a vacuum-cleaner humming, or Claire in the shower, or the blip-bloop of cartoons on the television, or Colter giggling or singing or talking earnestly about anything that captured his boundless imagination.

But the morning was deathly quiet, except for the crow.

The house was empty. Still in his boxers, Morgan padded barefoot from room to room, like a lonely puppy.

The coffee in the pot was cold, and the leaky faucet dripped into a bowl of soggy cereal. Colter's bed was made, and Claire's Volvo was gone.

A fat FedEx envelope sat on the breakfast table. It had already been opened. The invoice behind the plastic sleeve came from a lab in Denver, and a yellow stickie note was pasted to its front: *Jeff — John Doe tox — Shawn.*

"Fuck," was all Morgan could say.

The phone echoed in the vacuum his morning had become.

"Jeff, it's Shawn. I get you up?"

"No, I've been up."

"You looked at the John Doe tox screen yet?"

"Just the envelope."

"I can summarize," Dr. Cowper said. "Mr. Doe is saltier than a nut roll."

"Salt?"

"Packed in it, like a ham. The salt leached him dry and preserved his skin. He's more pickled than a pickle."

"But why?"

"I don't know, Jeff. For some reason, his killers held on to him for a while. Wyoming must have sixty billion square miles of earth untouched by man. They could have driven twenty miles out of town and buried his corpse in a gully, and it would never be found. They could have chopped him up and fed him to coyotes, hawks and badgers. They could have rolled him over a cliff into an inaccessible canyon. Why didn't they? That's just one of the unanswered questions I have."

"What's another?"

"Why put him in Laddie's crypt?"

"You gotta admit, the cemetery is a pretty good hiding place for a corpse."

"Good point," Dr. Cowper admitted, "but were they trying to hide him, or did they want him to be found?"

Second-guessing killers was fruitless, Morgan knew. Every scenario prompted a dozen more questions. Mob hits often followed a certain logic, but serial killers might see a falling leaf and interpret it as a message from their twisted, personal gods. The rituals of murder ran the whole blood-colored spectrum from efficiently businesslike to fanatically bizarre. On the crime beat in Chicago, he learned fast not to dismiss any peculiarity as impossible, no matter how illogical it might sound. Morgan knew logic could be a help or a hindrance when trying to understand murder, but it was the only tool he had.

"Okay, but if they wanted him to be found, why pack him in salt for God knows how long?" Morgan asked. "Why not dump him on Main Street? None of that makes any sense if his killers intended for John Doe's corpse to be discovered. And if they wanted him to be found, they'd want him to be identified, so why cut off his head?"

"Shock value. Souvenir. Ritual. I don't know exactly, but they weren't trying real hard to obscure his identity by whacking off his head. If they were, they'd have cut of his hands, too."

"Have you heard anything from the FBI on the fingerprints?"

"No, I was hoping to hear yesterday. Once they digitize the prints, it only takes a couple hours to find a match. Not likely to hear anything today because it's Saturday. Maybe Monday."

Patience wasn't Morgan's strong suit, but he decided to wait ... at least on particulars about John Doe. Not on Claire.

"Doc, about last night ..." he started.

"You golf?"

"Golf?"

"Yeah, you know, it's a game just like marbles,

except you use a stick."

Morgan huffed impatiently.

"Yeah, I've heard of it. And yeah, I've golfed, but I wouldn't say I'm a golfer."

"Let's play."

"Now?"

"It's Saturday, it's sunny, and you might be in jail on Monday, so why not?"

"Doc, I don't know," Morgan said. "Claire isn't here and I just ... don't know."

"We have some things to talk about."

"Like what?"

"I think maybe you got the wrong impression about some things."

"Like what?"

"C'mon, Jeff. Claire told me."

"When?"

"She called this morning. I'm really sorry. I didn't mean ..."

"Goddammit. This is starting to piss me off, Doc."

"Yeah, yeah, I know. Let's go golfing and breathe a little fresh air and talk. My treat."

Morgan agreed, reluctantly. Claire still hadn't returned by the time he showered and dressed, so he left a note on the kitchen table.

"I'm sorry" was all it said.

The nine-hole Squaw Nob Country Club was known locally as The Weed.

It passed for a golf course in the same way Winchester's hackers passed for golfers. In a loathsome landscape where the golf season was shorter than the hunting season, where citizens worked doubly hard to disguise their material ambitions, and where the word "par" sounded suspiciously foreign, golf could never be a profound pursuit.

On The Weed, divots went unrepaired simply because nobody knew any better, so fairways tended to resemble test ranges for cluster bombs.

The greens were worse. In fact, they were actually several dozen shades of green, an optical (and horticultural) illusion that psychologically damaged long-putters.

The rough was very rough. Knee-high buffalo grass concealed those errant drives not gobbled up by cactus and sagebrush. Prairie washes split slopes like raggedy gashes. Barbed-wire fences, grasshoppers and blood-sucking ticks proved the rough wasn't truly barren, but it was certainly inhospitable enough that almost nobody looked for lost balls.

And The Weed's hazards made it more obstacle course than golf course: Pronghorn antelope grazed on the fairways, sage grouse flocked unruffled in the tee boxes, badgers burrowed in the margins, and rattlesnakes lounged in the cool, watered grass. When the course was built, monstrous boulders were simply left where they sat — even in the middle of fairways. And sand traps were not sand at all, but pea-gravel from the river bottom, quarried and dumped by the county's road crews far more cheaply than imported sand.

The only water feature on The Weed — apart from the alkali-crusted cow wallows dating back to Squaw Nob's days as a pasture — was a stock pond beyond the seventh green, which could be reached only by driving over a working cattle ranch. It was America's only Par 9 hole.

Suffice it to say, good shots generally went unrewarded, while bad shots were punished severely. But since nobody in Winchester golfed well enough to be disappointed, the course's sadistic peculiarities were never fully appreciated.

Still, The Weed had its rewards: any golfer who survived all nine holes with the same ball earned a bottle of Moose Drool Ale for half price in the "clubhouse," which was, in fact, a Tuff Shed and an ice-filled Igloo cooler. But since country clubs elsewhere were known to cater to the affluent, Squaw Nob Country Club charged double for beer, so the big prize was a wash.

Dr. Cowper wouldn't be drinking any half-price beer. He lost three balls on the first two holes; one extraordinarily true, two hundred fifty-yard drive ricocheted off a sandstone boulder into the malpais, where it would likely rot before it was found. Morgan whacked a worm-burner into the dense brush and scared up a covey of quail.

"About this stuff with Claire," Dr. Cowper finally said as they milled around in the third tee-box. "I'm really sorry. I was too familiar."

Morgan traced a gash in his rented driver with the sharp end of a wooden tee, and said nothing.

"You and I hit it off as friends, and I guess I just naturally included Claire in the little circle," Dr. Cowper continued as he chose his next club. "She said you were a little jealous, and I just wanted to clear the air right away ..."

"I figured a smart, single guy like you would have no trouble finding admirers," Morgan snipped. "*Single* admirers."

Cowper sighted off about a thousand yards to where he imagined the next green should be. He shielded his eyes against the sun, but saw nothing.

"Well, I suppose I do, and single ones are the only kind, I assure you. A friend of mine once said a cowboy's gotta have a few different ponies in the remuda: an easy rider, a sporting mount, one with a little sass, a cutter, and one to eat."

Morgan managed a thin smile of forgiveness,

although a wicked image flickered through his dirty mind.

"Friends, huh?" Morgan asked.

"Yeah, I thought so."

"So how come you never kissed me?"

Cowper shook his head and squinted down the fairway to a ragged flag poked in a circular patch of green four hundred yards away. Maybe five hundred.

"You know, your humor pops up at the oddest moments," he observed.

At the fifth tee, they caught up to the rag-tag foursome ahead. Morgan recognized them all: Duncan and Angus McBeth, two brothers who ran cattle on a modest spread south of town; bank president Hamilton Tasker, to whom Morgan owed nothing; and Ben Pomeroy, the mercurial owner of KROK-FM who hated Morgan simply because they competed for the same advertising dollars. They weren't golfing at the moment, just standing around drinking beer.

Cowper nudged Morgan and pointed at one of the golf bags propped against a buckrail fence. A holstered pistol, presumably loaded, was strapped to it.

"Snakes," Morgan murmured.

Ben Pomeroy tipped a beer bottle up and swigged the last of it.

"One more dead Indian," he said. He winged the brown bottle into the rough, where it shattered with a sharp, distant chink.

"Hey, Ben, in California they'd give you a nickel for that bottle," Morgan said, wiping antelope shit off his running shoe.

"Yeah? Well, maybe you oughta go out there and glue all them pieces back together, then drive out to La-La-Land to get your nickel," Pomeroy sniped. The McBeth brothers thought it was funny.

Morgan smiled.

"I might," he said. "Say, you been able to get back on the air since that weird outage yesterday?"

Pomeroy stared at Morgan.

"Wasn't an outage," he seethed. "Fuckin' computer network went haywire. You guys gonna golf or circle-jerk?"

Tasker sliced his ball far into no-man's-land, eager to move on. He didn't even bother to take the mulligan, just picked up his tee and his bag, and hustled Pomeroy and the McBeth brothers down the fairway.

Morgan and Cowper watched them fan out across the fairway in almost every direction, looking for wayward balls.

"I thought small-town folks were supposed to be friendly," Cowper said.

"Most are," Morgan admitted, "but there's always one turd in the punch."

Cowper's cell phone chirped and he plucked it off his belt.

"Cowper," he said.

A meadowlark trilled somewhere in the domestic wilderness call Squaw Nob Country Club. Morgan swung his driver idly.

"You're shitting me, right?" Cowper said, a finger in his open ear. "How sure? ... Jesus. Okay, hold on, let me get this down ..."

Cowper unfolded their scorecard and scribbled with his dwarf pencil. He glanced at Morgan, his face drawn as if a ghost had appeared before him on the fifth tee of The Weed.

"Gabriel Antonio Rodríguez ... thirty-two ... July, nineteen-ninety-eight ... when will your guys be here? Know anything else? Yeah, yeah, fine. That's plenty. Dave, I am really grateful, and, well, I'm sorry, too. Thanks, I'll call you when I get to the file. See ya."

Cowper stood looking at his notes in the margin of

the scorecard for a long time. Morgan's curiosity got the best of him.

"Well ... what?" he asked.

Cowper looked up.

"John Doe isn't John Doe anymore," he said. "He's Gabriel Antonio Rodriguez, age thirty-two, reported missing sometime in July 'Ninety-eight. The FBI matched his prints."

"So he had a criminal record?"

Cowper laughed weakly.

"No."

"Military?"

"No."

"Then how'd the FBI have his prints?"

"Gabriel Antonio Rodriguez," Cowper said as he picked up his golf bag and started across the badlands toward the parking lot, "was an undercover ATF agent."

CHAPTER SEVEN

Gabe Rodriguez suffered, and that was precisely his killers' intention. He died in pain, spiked and splayed like a flensed coyote, smelling his own blood.

While Cowper searched for lost pieces of the late agent's mutilated body, Morgan hunted for his interrupted soul. But the secrets of Gabe Rodriguez's shadowy life as an undercover federal agent were harder to kill than he was.

The Bureau of Alcohol, Tobacco and Firearms wasn't any help. Two days had passed since the FBI's fingerprint lab identified Rodriguez, but the ATF's media affairs office in Washington, D.C., was apparently clueless about the case and promised to call back after making a few inquiries.

The FBI wasn't talking, on or off the record, but the Bureau's media spokeswoman was unctuously gracious in her rebuff. A decade of FBI embarrassments — such public contretemps as Waco, Wen Ho Lee, Olympic bombing, Whitey Bulger, Robert Hansen and more — had resulted in better phone manners if not more openness. But the ingratiating FBI spokeswoman also promised to call back after making a few inquiries.

The secretary who answered the phone at the Wyoming Division of Criminal Investigation, which had no need for a media spokesman because it never revealed anything, made no promises to call back and no effort to make any inquiries. With a petulant sigh, she took Morgan's name and telephone number, and said she'd pass it to the Director if she saw him. Then she hung up.

Morgan didn't wait for calls that might never come. Cops didn't respect newspapermen's deadlines unless it made cops look good, and he had two days to flesh out Gabe Rodriguez, aka John Doe, for *The Bullet*. Who was he? What mission sent him undercover? Did he have a family? Who saw him last? What kind of man was he? Is there anyone out there missing him?

For now, all he had was a name. He needed more, and he needed it fast.

Morgan spun his Rolodex and plucked a smudged card from the O's.

Jerry Overton had just retired from the ATF after 30 years in the Chicago office. He'd been the bureau's point man on radical religious extremists, white supremacists and dozens of underground militia groups. It was the perfect job for the former Methodist seminary student who quit school to serve two tours with the Marines in Vietnam. After he got back to the World, he eventually earned a master's degree in forensic psychology from the University of Illinois.

He'd once risked his career helping Morgan, then a cop reporter at the Chicago Tribune, link the vicious serial killer P.D. Comeaux to a little-known group of violent Christian fundamentalists known as the Fourth Sign. But that's the kind of passionate cop he was: a workaholic who owed the rules but didn't play political games. So he never got a cushy headquarters job, but he got respect.

Overton never wanted to leave Chicago anyway, and not just because he was a hopelessly hopeful Cubs fan. Almost every Saturday, he walked up Mount Prospect

Road to visit his son's grave in Mount Emblem Cemetery. The boy had died almost twenty years ago in a prom-night car crash, and even before the mourning was over, so was his marriage. So the routine of his grief, amid all the violent colors of death in summer and the white-on-white bunting of winter, was his solace. He never spoke to the grave, like some people did, because he didn't think anyone was listening. Instead, he went there to be close to someone.

Dead sons connected Overton and Morgan. Neither of them had ever stopped grieving, but after a long time of crying when they thought nobody else could hear, they'd found a place for the pain, then moved on.

Morgan dialed the number scribbled at the edge of the Rolodex card, Overton's home in Elmhurst, where he now spent his days cataloging his collection of rare books on crime and theology, jogging on his treadmill two or three times a day, obsessively watching the History Channel, and experimenting with bagel recipes. It rang several times, then the answering machine clicked.

"You've reached the home of Jerry Overton ..." the fuzzy taped announcement said, but suddenly there was a live voice on the line, too. "Dammit ... hold on ... *not here at the moment* ... don't hang up ... *just leave a number after the beep and* ... shit, hold on ... *as soon as I return ..."*

But before the machine beeped, the line frizzed and popped. After a second of silence, the live voice came back. "Damned machine. Hello? Still there?"

"Jerry, this is Jeff Morgan. Is this you or is it Memorex?"

"Hey, Jeff. Had to unplug the sonofabitch to shut it up. Don't know why I even have it. Nobody calls and I never leave. Still winter out there in Montana?"

"Wyoming. And it's June here, just like there."

"Isn't that still winter in Wyoming?"

"Only in odd years."

"They're all odd years in Wyoming," Overton said. "So what's up? How's that little boy of yours?"

"Everybody's good," Morgan said. "Colter is learning to swim and doesn't have a care in the world."

"How's your mom?"

"Still the same. She doesn't know me anymore, but that's what the Alzheimer's does. She's here and I can kiss her every day. That's better than the alternative."

"And you?"

"Busy," Morgan said, "and that's why I called. I have a case ..."

"Hell, Jeff, I'll do what I can, but I've been out of the loop nearly a year."

"Thanks. You know anything about an ATF agent named Gabriel Rodriguez? Undercover guy went missing in July of 'Ninety-eight?"

Overton said nothing for a moment.

"Why?"

"He might have turned up," Morgan said.

"Alive?"

"No."

"Where?"

"Here. It's a long story, but we've got a headless, mummified corpse and the fingerprints match."

"No dental?"

"No head."

"No DNA?"

"No comparables yet."

"Nothing else?"

"Only a tattoo. A ring of brambles on his upper arm."

"Goddammit." Morgan sensed Overton's anguish over a thousand miles, and it seemed to confirm John Doe's true identity.

"So you know him?"

Overton took a long time answering. Morgan could

hear a television in the background, a grave narrator describing the carnage on Omaha Beach.

"Yeah. Good cop. College kid, but you'd never know ... hold it, are we on the record here?"

"Background," Morgan assured his friend. "I need to make him human. Family. History. What he was doing. I've got nothing at this point."

"Call the media guys."

"I did. Nothing."

Overton huffed. "Figures."

"You can't help?"

"Nope. Sorry."

"Can you point me in the right direction?"

"Nope."

"Why?"

"You put me in a real pinch here, my friend. I can't say anything without saying too much."

"Okay, off the record. I won't print it unless somebody else confirms it. Deal?"

Overton contemplated the deal for a moment, then spoke.

"Rodriguez was undercover, way deep. He was wading in shit up to his neck. I'm surprised you know as much as you do."

"What was he into? Butts, bullets or bombs?"

"Nice try, kid, but I didn't just fall off the turnip truck. That's all I can say, and it's totally off the record."

"Who or what was he investigating?"

"You don't want to know."

"Yes, I do."

"Bad guys. Old friends of yours. I wouldn't be surprised if they weren't watching you right now."

Morgan had lots of old friends who were anything but friends. Many of them were on Death Row in a dozen states, but many more weren't in jail at all. His stories at the Chicago Tribune had exposed organized crime, radical movements, terrorist cells, drug cartels, neo-Nazis, street gangs, serial killers, bad cops, the Klan, gun runners, corrupt politicians, white slavers, desperate fugitives, child pornography rings, and suicidal cults — all friends who called on him from time to time with tender and affectionate messages about revenge and disembowelment.

"Well, that could be anyone. I've got lots of friends. Give me a clue. Is this 'friend' on my Christmas card list?"

"Not likely," Overton said. "Just watch your ass."

"Who was watching Rodriguez's ass? Isn't there somebody out there who'd like to know what happened to him? A wife? A kid? Parents?"

"They'll be told," Overton said.

"So he had family, right?"

Overton paused.

"We all have family, kid. I can't tell you anything more."

Overton's unusual reticence frustrated Morgan.

"Rodriguez is dead. Murdered, in fact. Kinda late to get anal about policy, don't you think? Besides, if you can't give out classified stuff, just say so. I only need biographical details. You don't even work for ATF anymore. What would they do ... fire you?"

Overton always knew the rules. He bent them, but never broke them. For some reason, they weren't bending now.

"Listen, and listen close," Overton growled. "It's not about policy. It's not about me. It's not even about Rodriguez. It's about you. The more you know, the more danger you're in. Whoever killed Rodriguez is still out there. Just let our guys handle it."

"But I've got a murder here!" Morgan snapped. "Somebody's dead, and somebody else did it. I can't ignore it any more than you could ignore it. It's a story.

A big story."

"I hate to offend your journalistic sensibilities, but if you know what's good for you, you'll butt out."

"Just ignore the fact that while a dozen people watch, the headless corpse of a federal agent turns up in somebody else's grave in a small town?"

"You don't even know for sure if your stiff was an agent. You're speculating. What if you're wrong?"

"FBI is pretty sure it's him."

"Yeah, and the FBI *never* screws the pooch." Overton seeped venom.

"Are you saying it can't be Rodriguez? Or are you saying there is no Rodriguez?"

"Don't fuck with me, Jeff."

Morgan breathed deeply and sat back in his chair. Even if he wouldn't be completely candid, he knew Overton wouldn't lie.

"Jerry, if you were me, what would you do?"

"I'd let this one go. For your own good."

"No way, Jerry. You know me better than that."

"Fine," Overton said. "Then I'd go home tonight, kiss and hug my little boy, and tell him how much I love him. Just in case I don't get the chance to do it again tomorrow."

Nothing historic had ever happened in the Perry County Courthouse.

No famous outlaw ever stood trial there. No American president ever stumped from its six pathetic granite steps. No great idea was ever launched from its fescue-infested lawn. And no great leaders had ascended from its halls since Sputnik, even though Perry County was constitutionally obliged to send three legislators to Cheyenne every year.

But the old courthouse was a proud landmark in the

county seat of Winchester, a town where the only other tourist attraction was the decrepit grave of a woman who claimed to have slept with Old West bandits. The fact that the old building was slowly disintegrating only made it seem more historic.

The worst effect of its decomposition was the regular disgorgement of raw sewage into the basement where county prisoners were jailed.

On those days — and this was one of those days — the stench of liquid shit wafted down Main Street, and when anybody in town would get a whiff, they'd repeat a phrase made socially acceptable by Whit Kelley, the town barber who'd been dead for thirty years: "Smells like a turd in the pool."

And when there was a turd in the pool, it was the sheriff's job to fish it out.

Trey Kerrigan slogged up the back steps in irrigation boots, a bandanna around his face and a bucket of nasty brown water in both hands. Morgan stood a safe distance away, in the shade of a gigantic cottonwood whose gnarled roots heaved the sidewalk.

"Figured I'd just wait out here for you," Morgan said.

The sheriff put down his buckets and stripped off his elbow-length rubber gloves. His uniform blouse and his badge were splattered with flecks of something Morgan didn't want to think about.

"You know, now I remember why I didn't want this job back," Kerrigan said.

"Hold it, let me take a picture of you for your re-election," Morgan said, painting an imaginary campaign poster in mid-air. "*Kerrigan Knows Shit.*"

The sheriff smiled lamely.

"Yeah, well, I think I saw some of yours down there, old buddy, and I'm thinking about locking you up for littering."

Morgan surrendered.

"Uncle," he laughed. "I'd pay any fine to avoid jail time."

Kerrigan blew a wad of stringy brown snot on the grass and wiped his nose on his soiled sleeve.

"So unless you're just loitering, I reckon you come down to see me about somethin'," he said. "And I think I know what it is."

"John Doe?"

"What about him?"

"Have you gotten any word from the FBI or ATF about his identity?"

"Should I?"

Morgan was puzzled. "You haven't heard anything?"

"Nope."

"You're not just shitting me, are you?"

Kerrigan opened his arms wide and looked innocent.

"Do I look like a shitter?"

"Well ... yeah."

"I ain't. What should I hear?"

Morgan studied his old friend's face, or more accurately, his mouth. They'd known each other since first grade, and when Trey was lying, the corner of his mouth pinched ever so slightly. Once Trey got wise to the tell, something like a poker player's twitch, he grew a prodigious mustache to cover his mouth and ran for sheriff. But now his walrus-like mustache was slicked back across his cheeks with sweat, and the corners of his mouth were exposed.

So Morgan could see he wasn't lying. Trey Kerrigan had no idea about John Doe.

"Trey, the FBI thinks John Doe is a missing federal agent named Gabriel Rodriguez," Morgan told him. "Disappeared a couple years ago while he was undercover for the ATF."

"No shit?"

Morgan peered down into the sheriff's honey pots.

"Well, there appears to be lots of shit ..."

"Those *federales* piss me off," Kerrigan seethed.

Kerrigan's front teeth and lower lip formed a long, exquisite "f" and a silent "uck".

"I guess they sorta look down their noses at the local cops, huh? Like you're an amateur. Gunther Toody. Barney Fife ..."

"Yeah, yeah, I get the idea, Jimmy Olsen" Kerrigan interrupted. "What else do you know about John Doe?"

"The usual stuff," Morgan lied. "But I'd hate for you to hear it all from me first. You can probably get the whole enchilada from your buddies in ATF. Then we can compare notes."

Kerrigan's foul buckets sloshed as he loped purposefully across the lawn toward the back door of his office. Morgan hollered after him.

"Hey wait, if you didn't know about John Doe, why were you expecting me?"

Kerrigan turned and walked backward with his slop pails hung out a safe distance from his lanky legs.

"I thought for sure you were coming to give me some shit about my newest case," Kerrigan said. "Some kid sent a threatening e-mail to the Mayor."

"How do you know it was a kid?'

"Cuz it started, 'Dear Dorkface.'"

"Well, that doesn't rule anybody out," Morgan quipped. "What did the e-mail say?"

"Said if the Mayor didn't release all the stray dogs in the pound, he'd blow up the town hall."

"It's a prank, for god sakes," Morgan laughed.

The sheriff shrugged, and his shit slopped.

"Yeah, prob'ly," Kerrigan said. "But you know law 'n' order Horace Thurlow. He sits on his fat seat of power, and he's intent on huntin' down the little perp and shootin' him, preferably in the town square."

"Where did it come from?"

"Funny thing. It came from the mayor's own e-mail address. As if he sent it to himself. Tricky little freak."

"Well, good luck. I'm afraid these little computer geeks are smarter than both of us put together."

"Hell, I think a re-boot is when you take off your ropers and put 'em back on your feet," Kerrigan said as he turned and walked away. "Why can't these kids just look at dirty pictures on the *Inner*-net like everybody else?"

Morgan punched a code into the keypad that opened the glass doors to Laurel Gardens' secure unit, and the intermingled odor of antiseptic and urine met him as he walked through. A teen-ager wearing headphones was mopping the tile floor and didn't look up.

All of the home's residents behind that glass posed some risk to themselves or others and required slightly more attention. Mostly, they'd simply wandered away from other caregivers in the past, and the locked doors kept them safely within the reach of the doctors, nurses and aides who took care of them.

To him, Rachel Morgan was still a misfit among the bingo players, the hand-wringers, the hooters, and the TV watchers. But it was getting harder to sustain his denial.

His mother's confusion became apparent the first day she spoke to her own reflection in the mirror. When the reflection wouldn't answer the question she asked, she grew petulant and pouted. In the coming days, she spoke to pictures over the fireplace mantel and finally swept them all off onto the floor when the people in them wouldn't answer.

He and Claire took her to the psychologist in Blackwater, the nearest town where one could be judged officially mentally ill. She gave her a barrage of clumsily named tests like the Pfeiffer Short Portable MSQ, Porteus Maze, Hooper Visual Organization Test, Boston Naming Test, Trail-Making Tests A and B, Wechsler Memory Scale Subtests, Familiar Faces Test, and the Geriatric Depression Scale. They simply tired her.

Later, in private, the doctor told them Rachel's test results suggested a primary progressive dementia, probably of the Alzheimer's type. Afterward, the doctor asked Rachel to come into the office. Rachel liked her very much, and when they closed the door, Morgan stood outside and listened. When she mentioned the word "Alzheimer's," there was a long silence.

"Oh," Rachel said with a dread a mother's voice almost never reveals. "I sure hope I don't have that. It'd be too hard on my family."

Now, Morgan walked past the rooms of others just like his mother, reading the names on the metal brackets outside each door.

In one, Shorty Puckett lay on his bed, curled in a pool of warm sunlight that streamed through the floor-to-ceiling west window. Morgan wondered what he might be dreaming. In another, Hanna Baker crocheted a small afghan, but he knew she hadn't spoken or smiled in years because she'd simply forgotten the process of making words.

Rachel Morgan sat in a wingback chair in her private room at the end of the air-conditioned hall. She brushed her hair back with her fingers incessantly and stared a thousand yards off toward something only she knew was there.

"Hello, Mom," Morgan said, kissing her on the forehead.

"Hello," she said. "Was the path muddy?"

He was accustomed to the peculiar questions that came from that strange, distant place only Rachel Morgan could see from where she sat.

"No, it was fine," he said.

"It filled my shoes. I had to sit here at the stream and wash my feet," she said, giggling at the cold water that she imagined flowing between her toes.

Morgan snugged her hospital slippers and smelled the oldness of her. She had always smelled of lilacs, had dreamed of living in the mountains of northern New Mexico, and had sung songs to him at bedtime. He ached deep down in the heart of his heart that it was all lost now, even if she were still here.

"How are you feeling, Mom?" he asked.

"I'm feeling so fine since my mother visited," she said. "It was so good to see her."

Jeff's grandmother had been dead for almost forty years, a farm wife who just sat down on her bed one day, and stopped. A faded, yellowing photo of her, when she was young, not old and tired, sat on Rachel's tiny dresser.

"Yes, Mother, I'm glad you saw her," he said, stroking her hair.

"Now you must get to work," she said, abruptly shifting her attention to her new visitor. "When you bring the cats in, please make sure the gate is closed. If they get out again, we'll never get them back. Come up to the church when you finish and I'll pay you. What was your name again?"

Morgan held her hand and cried, but she didn't see. She was someplace far away.

Crystal, *The Bullet*'s receptionist, was reading *Town and Country* magazine when Morgan got back to the newsroom. She handed him a handful of pink message slips and spoke without looking up.

"There's a turd in the pool," she said.

"Yeah, and I think we're going fishing," he said as he stopped at his rookie reporter's empty desk. "Where's

Josh?"

"Lunch."

Morgan glanced at the newsroom clock.

"Dammit, it's three o'clock."

Crystal licked her thumb and turned the page.

"Check his pockets."

Morgan stopped cold, his head cocked at a quizzical angle, as if he'd just slammed into the invisible wall separating reality from some other dimension.

"For what?"

"Butter."

"Butter?"

"Yeah. Butter. It's after three."

"What the hell ... *why* the hell..." Morgan stammered, not sure what the *real* question should be. But he was saved by the bell over *The Bullet*'s front door, as Josh walked in. The front pockets of his rumpled Dockers were bulging.

"Josh, where have you been?" Morgan asked him as the young reporter sauntered through the swinging gate that separated the newsroom from the foyer.

"Lunch."

"It's three o'clock."

"Well, you gotta admit," Josh said earnestly, "that's a little early for dinner."

Morgan shook his head and started to walk away, then turned for one last adventure in the Twilight Zone.

"Josh, what's in your pockets?"

The young reporter smiled big, exposing a set of ranch-boy teeth that had once-too-often met the dirt floor of a rodeo arena, but never an orthodontist. Whatever he had in his pockets tickled him.

"Butter. Want some?"

Morgan knew when to let well enough alone, and this was it. As he sat down at his cluttered desk, he tried to shake the mental image of a strung-out kid mainlining

Parkay in a grimy alley. It just didn't work.

"Josh, you got time to do a little legwork for a possible story ... or do you have to butter something?" he asked.

"Whatcha got, Chief?" Josh beamed.

"Don't call me Chief."

"OK ... Whatcha got, Coach?"

Morgan breathed deeply, just once.

"Some kid sent a threatening e-mail to the Mayor. That's a story, ten inches tomorrow morning. But while you're at Town Hall, compare all the recent stray-dog tickets to the computer data that was hacked. Look for names on both lists and see what comes up. And just for yucks, check to see whose dogs were picked up last week."

"Got it, Coach."

"Don't call me Coach, either."

"Got it, Boss-man."

Morgan squinted hard. "Git."

Josh's goofy smile crumpled. He didn't even stop to unload his pilfered polyunsaturates as he grabbed a notebook and hit the street.

That night, Morgan tried to write about Gabe Rodriguez, but he was still a body without a face, a life without a soul. He'd tap out a few lines on his word processor, then delete them, tap out a few more, delete. *Every death needs meaning, just as every life needs meaning ...*

He'd written about death before, in its every natural and unnatural shape. He had described the color of it, the smell of it, the cool, candle-wax feel of it. It was just a thing — a *thing* — to be described, explained, rationalized, given gravity, and gussied up for a family newspaper. Death was an event, a single moment of personal cataclysm that usually made good copy. Death was always news, and not just to the deceased, because humans have allowed endings to become the most important part of the story. Death is the banner headline, life is the footnote on the back page.

But life is the story. In the eulogy for a legendary Tribune editor, the preacher said of all the elegant words and dates that would be carved in his tombstone, the most important symbol would be the hyphen between the years of his birth and his death. That insignificant slice represented the span of his life.

There should be more, Morgan thought then.

And now.

Nothing can disappear without a trace. Not a head. Not a soul. Not a memory. Not a life. Nature doesn't practice emptiness, only transformation. Where does a man's story go when the man is dead? What does a good son or father or lover become when his heart stops?

The blinking cursor taunted him, so Morgan shut down his computer. The newsroom was dark.

He knew the house at Mount Eden was dark by now, too. Colter would be asleep, but Claire would be lying awake, waiting. In the dark, he would kiss his son, undress for bed, press himself against his wife and dream whatever absurd movie his fatigued brain was screening tonight.

As his jiggling headlights pushed aside the buggy veil of night, he wondered: *What becomes of dreams once dreamed?*

CHAPTER EIGHT

Morgan stood naked in his dark kitchen, staring at the nothingness beyond the back window.

The night was as black as an open grave, except for the faint, ancient starlight that had arrived, all but spent, in his backyard thirty million years after it first shined someplace far away.

The only light came from the green numerals on the microwave's digital clock: three-thirty-four.

His reflection was a ghost in the glass, nothing more. He hoisted a jelly glass of rye and toasted his other self, and promised to make no more promises to shadows, then smiled in the dark when he realized he'd made another promise to a shadow.

He sipped the rye he'd poured from a dusty fifth of Old Overholt, a rotgut whiskey said to be favored by the famous Wyoming ranch enforcer and killer Tom Horn. He liked it because he could tell a Tom Horn story when he poured it for friends and because it made him sweat.

Or maybe it was just the moonless, windless night. He'd tried sleeping, but the ghost of Gabe Rodriguez kept nudging him awake as he made mental lists of questions to ask and people to call. When it no longer distracted him to feel the sweat trickle down his side or to nuzzle a fresh, cool spot on his pillow, he got out of bed and went downstairs.

He heard a distant coyote howling, then another, in the dark pine forest beyond the back fence. He'd often listened to them on summer nights, their keening howls reassuring in an odd way. Life continued in the dark. But tonight, it was just part of the noise in his head.

Colter's little wooden baseball bat, bigger than he could swing but smaller than an official PeeWee baseball stick, leaned in the corner behind the front door. His leather mitt, warmed in sunlight and oiled on one of those father-son spring weekends that mothers never see or understand, was on the floor, a ball cupped in its web. Summer was almost a third over and there'd been no more of those father-son weekends beyond that first. Morgan slathered another heavy coat of guilt on himself.

Claire had fallen asleep hours ago, but she remained distant. He had gone into Colter's room when he got home and kissed his mouth, tasting his sweet breath.

This time of night, past last call at even the most decadent Wyoming roadhouse, had no soul. Even the creatures of the night had given up the hunt and gone to ground. It was a time of dew forming, when the warmth of the previous day had completely dissipated. It was a time when the winter stars actually came up in the summer sky and nobody cared. Even the crickets had gone to sleep. The only sounds he heard were the creaking of timbers as they cooled inside the walls of his old house and some horny coyotes hunting quick nocturnal couplings before dawn.

He had just raised his glass to the night when the phone rang. He fumbled around on the dark kitchen counter until he found the cordless phone behind the coffeemaker, where Claire had likely shoved it out of Colter's reach.

"Yeah?"

"You asleep?"

It was Cowper, and he sounded wide awake.

"At the moment? No. I was just waxing my car."

"Really?"

"Fuck you, Shawn. Why are you calling at three-thirty —" Morgan glanced at the microwave "— six?"

"Well, I was asleep four minutes ago. Dead to the world. I was dreaming about the night we sorta broke into the mortuary."

"Does that qualify as a wet dream for you forensic guys?"

"No, we have the same kind of wet dreams as everybody else," Cowper replied blithely, "except we wear rubber gloves."

Morgan stopped scratching himself and sighed.

"Yeah, so in your dream that woke both of us up . . ."

"Remember when we first went in and I told you I hated the smell of ether?"

"Yeah. So what?"

"Well, in my dream, I smelled it again. I don't normally believe in dreams. I mean, they're just random electrical impulses, and the brain is just doing its job by trying to make sense of all these illogical, unrelated miniature explosions, right?"

"Whatever you say."

"But sometimes . . . I mean, Jesus, sometimes it makes sense."

"It's now three-thirty eight."

"What are you, the atomic clock? Listen, this is weird shit. I dreamed of ether because we *smelled* ether at the mortuary."

"Dammit, go back to bed and dream of girls like everybody else," Morgan sniped, then added pointedly, "*other* girls, not Claire."

"Jeff, morticians don't need ether."

Whether it was the lateness of the hour or the ambiguity of Cowper's late-night epiphany didn't matter. Morgan was confused.

"And . . .?"

"Okay, ethers are organic derivatives of water, but they lack the labile negative-OH group. As a result, ethers, except for epoxides, are usually not very reactive and are often used as solvents for organic reactions . . ."

"Oh, Christ . . ."

"Yeah, I know. You're thinking, 'Isn't ether an anesthetic?'"

"No, I'm thinking I'm gonna hang up. Chemistry gives me a headache, especially when it's . . . three-forty in the morning."

"Well, they don't use ether as an anesthetic anymore because it tended to explode and induce peculiar side-effects like death."

"Okay, Doctor Know-it-all, what's it used for?"

"That's the thing. *Nothing* in a mortuary. They put it in starter fluid, in gasoline to boost the octane, use it as a solvent around machinery, and some *legitimate* labs use it."

His emphasis on the word *legitimate* piqued Morgan's enervated curiosity.

"It has *illegitimate* uses?"

"Yeah. A big one. Methamphetamine."

"Meth? Hold on. You think Carter McWayne is running a crank lab out of a funeral home? Did you close down the Buck Snort tonight? You didn't accidentally drink their Beaver Drool homebrew, did you?"

"There's only one way to find out. Meet me in the alley behind the mortuary in ten minutes."

"No way. No fucking way, Shawn. We can call the sheriff in the morning. I have no idea what we're looking for."

"I do."

"And what if you find it? What're you gonna do, huh? Roust Carter McWayne in the middle of the night and bore him into confessing with chemistry trivia? This is something for the cops."

A long silence.

"You trust these cops? You're not even curious?"

"We got no choice. You're a ghoul, and I'm a vulture. We can't just break and enter because we are curious."

"If you give this to the cops, you think you'll get the scoop? Bullshit, Jeff. Everybody in town will know more about it than you. And I'll never know what happened to Laddie or Rodriguez. Those country-club Gestapo boys from DCI will clamp the whole case shut."

Morgan sniggered, but he wasn't amused.

"How in the hell does this involve Laddie and Rodriguez? You need to take a deep breath, my friend."

"How the hell do you know it doesn't?"

Morgan said nothing.

"Okay," Cowper said. "I'm on my own. A man's gotta know his limitations. Sorry to wake you."

Cowper hung up, and Morgan threw the cordless on the counter, hard. The wood floor was cool on the soles of his feet. He cursed under his breath and threw back the last swallow of Old Overholt.

Then he snatched back the cordless and punched the redial button.

"I wasn't asleep. And I'll see you there in ten minutes," he growled and hung up.

A dog barked again as Morgan and Cowper crept down the alley behind the McWayne Funeral Home. They walked as lightly as they could, but the gravel still crunched beneath their feet like dry corn flakes.

Without a moon or even a streetlight, the way was dark. Morgan walked with one hand extended in front of him at crotch level, hoping to feel a garbage can before he stumbled into it and racked himself.

The mortuary's back door was, as always, unlocked.

Inside, Cowper gently closed it behind them and locked it. Morgan would have laughed at the irony of burglars locking themselves *in* if his gut wasn't already in a knot.

Cowper clicked on a small Mag-lite and took a deep breath through his nose. He smiled, as if he'd caught the faint, metallic-sweet, medicinal whiff of ether he'd come for.

But all Morgan smelled was death and cat piss. One was imaginary, the other wasn't.

"What are we looking for?" Morgan whispered.

"Look for some jars with a clear liquid over a whitish solid on the bottom. Look for anything marked 'iodine' or that has a dark red or metallic purple powder in it. Look for bottles labeled as sulfuric or hydrochloric acid."

Morgan deflated.

"More chemistry. Shit. This place is full of chemicals and substances I don't want to think about," Morgan said.

"Then look for propane tanks with fittings that have turned blue," Cowper said. "Beyond that, holler if you see bottles or jars with rubber tubing, glass cookware or frying pans with a powdery residue, a lot of cans of camping fuel, paint thinner, acetone, starter fluid, lye, drain cleaners or bottles of muriatic acid. Anything like that."

All Morgan knew about methamphetamine, or "crank," was that it was poor man's cocaine, cheap and easy to make. He first saw it as a cop reporter in Chicago, among the kids in the Projects. Now it was also the drug of choice among truckers, miners, oilfield roughnecks, bikers, railroaders, snowboarders and a cesspool full of social itinerants that clung to fringe of the dark.

He knew an investment of a few hundred dollars in over-the-counter medications and readily available chemicals could create thousands of dollars worth of the white, powdery crystals, which could be bought outside any truck stop or roadhouse for about twenty-five bucks for a quarter-gram, known as a "paper." Compared to its cuter, richer cousin, cocaine, that was a steal. In fact, on the street, cocaine was known as coke . . . crank was Pepsi.

In the early days, meth was a rural product, because the stench of cooking it was an unmistakable marker. So cookers moved to the countryside where nobody was around to whiff its stink.

Like every other drug, meth had its own argot: it was known variously as "annie," icee," "kryptonite" and "white bitch." A user was a "geek," "basehead" or "jibby." When he was loaded, a geek was "amping," "gakked" or "spun out."

There was no Colombian crank cartel, no global meth networks, no French ice connections. The raw material could be stolen off the shelves at supermarkets and auto stores. The crank economy was all small fish, small-time entrepreneurs making a buck off a cheap, potent, enslaving high.

A mom-and-pop meth "lab" could fit into a suitcase. Meth cooks loved small towns, where bumpkin lawmen were usually less sophisticated about drugs. Nonetheless, Wyoming cops had busted meth labs in barns, camp trailers, garages, porta-potties, root cellars, apartments, motel rooms, self-storage lockers, vacant outhouses and pickup trucks.

But a funeral home?

Cowper followed his nose to a carpeted, windowless hallway off the embalming lab. Morgan stayed closed behind.

The only other light came from a street lamp outside a bathroom window just past the embalming lab. Morgan could see only a stool and a sink, and he heard the constant drip of water from the spigot as they moved down the hall.

Several unlocked doors opened into cramped rooms.

One contained a dormant furnace, a clunky water-softener, some buckets and mops. One stored office supplies. One was festooned with plastic flowers and cheap suit coats, apparently for the unprepared and indigent customer, Morgan thought.

But one was locked. Not just securely latched, but padlocked.

Cowper lay down on the floor and sniffed the gap under the heavy door.

"This is it," he said. "Why do you think a guy who leaves the back door to his mortuary unlocked would lock a door inside? You got a bolt cutter?"

Morgan rolled his eyes. "No," he said, "and even if I did, I wouldn't cut that lock. Jesus, why don't we just leave a note that says, 'Hi. Just thought we'd drop in and burglarize your place.'"

Cowper was thinking, not listening.

"If he's cooking meth, he has to vent it either to the roof or out a window," Cowper said, his eyes and flashlight beam running the length of the low, shadowy ceiling. "Maybe he just runs it through his ventilation system from the embalming room, or maybe through the duct work from the furnace."

The game afoot, he pushed past Morgan, back up the hallway and went into the furnace cubby. Sure enough, a sheet-metal duct, no more than six inches in radius, had been spliced from the locked room into the main flue.

"What're you gonna do, crawl through that?" Morgan grumbled.

"Nope," Cowper said, "we're gonna crawl *over* it."

Cowper dragged an old Victorian chair, its upholstered seat worn through, from its hiding place behind the furnace. He shoved it against the wall and stood on it, pushing an acoustic tile into the false ceiling above. A fine mist of red brick dust filled the dead air, briefly obscuring the decaying brick wall that stood between them and the secret room next door. It was likely a wall in the original house, which had always been a mortuary in the McWayne family. At some point, one of the fussy McWaynes must have concealed the dirty brick wall behind sheet rock walls.

"Shit," Morgan cursed.

Cowper pounded the wall with the butt of his flashlight. More dust billowed, but a couple bricks flinched as chunks of mortar fell on the water-stained concrete floor.

"Looks aren't everything," the professor said. "It might be a brick wall, but it's probably only one brick thick and it's quickly turning to dust."

He pounded it a few more times and Morgan breathed in more dust.

"Give me a hand here," Cowper said. Morgan rummaged around the furnace room and found some wooden crates and empty buckets to stand on. With an old broom handle and the butt of an old two-by-four, they teetered on their rickety platforms and assaulted the wall. After a few minutes, they'd bored a hole in the wall large enough to peek into the next room. Pungent air, reeking of half-disinfected cat pee, surged through the breech, stinging Morgan's nostrils.

Borrowing the crate and buckets from Morgan, Cowper stacked himself a perch so he could shine his light into the room. After reaching through to remove acoustic tiles on the other side, he studied the room while Morgan stood in the dark below.

"I think we found ourselves a meth lab," he said, his head poked through the wall. "I'm going in . . . if I can just . . ."

Cowper pushed several bricks into the room beyond and enlarged the gap so he could squeeze through. Soon, all Morgan could see was fragments of the flashlight's beam between Cowper's legs as they disappeared into the other room.

"Oh man," Cowper's muffled voice came from the other side of the wall. "Jackpot."

Morgan clambered onto the rickety perch and looked inside. The stink of it was even stronger now. His friend's flashlight illuminated a small room packed with tanks, tubes, chemical vats, a variety of tools and several small propane tanks whose fitting were crusted with doughy blue chemical scabs.

He scuttled through the opening with a hand from Cowper.

On the floor, Cowper handed him a jar of some off-color liquid and smiled.

"So the cat piss isn't cat piss at all," Morgan said, examining the jug of ammonia.

"Nope. Man, this place is a mad scientist's dream. Look at this stuff," Cowper marveled.

The secret room was something out of an old Hollywood horror flick: burners and ovens, vats and tubes, peculiar flasks and jars marked with mysterious chemical hieroglyphs like HCL, PCl5, NaCN, HgCl2. And most featured a little skull-and-crossbones sticker.

"Don't touch anything unless you don't need your mucous membranes or a lung," Cowper warned. "There are more hazardous materials in here than down at the Crowbar. If it isn't corrosive, it's flammable. Some of these chemicals would explode if you simply poured in a drop of water."

Morgan imagined his eyes beginning to melt and the lining of his nostrils dissolving, but shook it off. He knew — well, hoped really — that Cowper was as knowledgeable about chemistry as he sounded. He glanced at a small Halon fire extinguisher on the wall and felt not at all comforted. Spitting on a big fire might be more effective.

"How the hell could McWayne get all this stuff and

nobody notice?" Morgan asked

"Who's gonna investigate an undertaker buying large amounts of chemicals and weird equipment? Who's gonna question strange smells from a mortuary? Who's gonna stand around and gawk while somebody loads a big box into a hearse? He's got the perfect cover."

"Hiding in plain sight."

"Exactly."

Still, McWayne didn't seem the type to Morgan. He was a small-town buffoon and pompous lard-ass, hardly a large-scale drug trafficker. Maybe he truly had the perfect cover after all, Morgan thought.

At one end of the narrow wooden workbench, Cowper's flashlight fell on a tangle of paper strips and some coffee filters with a white residue.

"And here's what we came for," he said. He dabbed his index finger in the dust and tasted it. "Oh baby, that's crank."

Cowper handed the flashlight to Morgan and stuffed the paper strips and coffee filters into a plastic grocery sack he found nearby. He wrapped it all up tightly and crammed the evidence in the back pocket of his jeans.

"He doesn't know it yet, but tomorrow, your buddy the sheriff is gonna have a big drug bust, and you're gonna have a big story," Cowper said.

A new smell enveloped them.

Gasoline.

Cowper swept his flashlight around the room and saw nothing. But Morgan saw flickering shadows and a dim light beneath the door. And gasoline was pooling in a widening circle over the threshold, inching toward them.

"Get out!" Morgan yelled.

Cowper dropped the flashlight as Morgan leaped up on the workbench. At best, he knew they had seconds to get back through the hole in the wall into the furnace room before the gasoline ignited. And it would be only the beginning of a larger, deadlier inferno when the combustible chemicals in the lab detonated.

The gasoline erupted in a ferocious whoosh and Morgan felt its searing heat against his legs as he hung through the cavity in the brick wall.

Then he felt Cowper shove him from below and he shot through the hole to the cool, safe room next door.

As he plunged from the ceiling to the floor below, his fall was broken only by the pile of boxes, chairs and buckets that had been his ladder. His shoulder collapsed in a sickening crunch as he hit the concrete floor, and electric pain coursed down his arm as he smothered his burning trouser leg with his bare hands.

Cowper was still somewhere inside the hellhole from which he had just fallen. Black smoke belched from the gap in the wall and Morgan could hear the angry flames beginning to growl.

Agonizing moments elapsed. Cowper made no sound, and more importantly, no appearance.

"Shawn!" Morgan yelled.

He heard nothing but the throaty thunder of the growing fire, glass breaking and lumber crackling.

There was no going back for Cowper. Impenetrable black smoke surged from the hole, filling the furnace room and Morgan's lungs. He covered his mouth and nose with the bottom of his sweatshirt, but the sooty toxic fumes seeped through.

An explosion rocked the walls and floor, then another, and another. Ceiling tiles and bricks began to fall around Morgan as he leaped out of the furnace room and ran down the hall to the padlocked door to the meth lab. Smoke seeped beneath it.

Summoning all his mass and determination, he hurled himself against it. Pain ripped through his injured shoulder and the blunt force of his collision with the heavy wooden door sliced a gash in his temple.

But the door held.

Once again, he threw himself against it, and he felt it give, but it remained steadfast.

Finally, in one last burst, it gave way and flames exploded into the hallway, searing Morgan and filling the hallway with choking smoke, but Morgan could see past the flames.

Cowper had collapsed in a far corner of the room, farthest from the flames and the flammable chemicals. He'd drawn a protective cordon around himself with the extinguisher, buying himself a few extra seconds.

But the heat and smoke had finally knocked him out. His mouth and nose were rimmed with black soot, and he slumped with his back to the wall, the tiny extinguisher spent in his hands. One sleeve had burned away, the other was aflame.

Two or three steps, Morgan's mind reeled, *that's all*.

Morgan sucked in and held a deep breath, heeled one step backward and then dashed through the wall of flames. He grabbed Cowper's legs and dragged him unconscious back through the fire into the hallway.

Suddenly, the whole room erupted, splintering walls and furniture. Morgan dragged Cowper toward the back door, where they were protected from flying debris and flames, briefly, around the corner from the embalming room.

Cowper needed a doctor, and the whole mortuary would soon be engulfed. Morgan left Cowper in the relative safety of the embalming room's doorway and rushed to the back door, knowing they'd locked it as they sneaked in, and knowing he'd have to unlock it before escaping.

He turned the knob. It was unlocked, but the door was jammed closed. Something blocked it from the outside. The narrow hall was filling with smoke, and he knew the flames were close behind.

With his hands, Morgan searched the opaque darkness around his feet. His eyes felt as if a hunting knife had been sliced across them, and his head was beginning to swirl from the inside. He pawed through broomsticks and snow shovels, plastic buckets and empty cardboard boxes before his throbbing hand scraped across a cinder block.

He gathered it in both arms and ran back down the windowless hall, to the little bathroom past the embalming lab. There, he heaved the cinder block through the little window and thrust his torso out, inhaling cool, fresh air that braised his lungs and set off a violent coughing spasm.

Filling himself with one last gasp of fresh air, he crouched and sprinted to Cowper and dragged him twenty feet toward the bathroom window, their last hope of escape.

Winchester's only ladder truck roared to a stop outside the McWayne Funeral Home just as Morgan shoved Cowper's limp body through the broken window frame. Two firefighters rushed to help drag Morgan and Cowper to safety, then turned to fighting the flames, which now licked the sky.

While paramedics tended to Cowper, who lay burned, blackened, suffocated, unconscious, concussed and slit — but alive — on old Doc Jackson's lawn across the street, Morgan tried to clear his brain. His shoulder pulsed with pain, but he followed some firefighters around the building, looking for a place to ram their way into the burning structure.

Just off the alley, Morgan stood among some gawkers who'd come out in their pajamas and slippers to stare at the flames that now swallowed the mortuary.

"Anybody inside, you think?" asked Lowell Tennyson, the local jeweler who dripped smarm and hair oil. He lived on the next street over, but had walked a block in his boxer shorts and huaraches to investigate the commotion.

"I don't think so," Morgan said, watching Winchester's volunteer firefighters — some only half-dressed in bunker gear, as if they'd rushed to the scene while still half-asleep — break windows and gather to storm the back door.

"No, I mean ... you know ... somebody *dead*," Lowell pressed. "That'd be a bad way to go."

The concept of death in a small town was sometimes as perverse as it was enigmatic, but still, Morgan still wondered how Lowell Tennyson could consider cremation worse than dying in the first place.

But when he turned to point out that Carter McWayne's "customers" were beyond caring, Tennyson was taking a snapshot with a little disposable camera from a drugstore checkout stand, its pathetic little flash no match for the dark and distance.

Morgan edged closer to the conflagration and watched Tubby Gertz, a volunteer firefighter who, by day, sold furnaces, swing his axe to knock free a short two-by-four that had been wedged beneath the backdoor's knob.

The shadowy arsonist who'd tried to kill them in McWayne's clandestine meth lab had escaped. He'd also hedged his bets by taking the extra trouble to make sure Morgan and Cowper wouldn't be so lucky.

"You're under arrest, my friend," said a familiar voice.

Trey Kerrigan stood in the dancing shadows beneath a juniper hedge, just behind Morgan. He already had his handcuffs out.

"For what?" Morgan asked.

Kerrigan pushed his cowboy hat back and his mouth

rumpled in an incredulous smile.

"Breakin' and enterin', for starters."

"Wait a minute . . . "

"Maybe burglary. Maybe arson. Maybe possession of a controlled substance."

Kerrigan pulled a crinkled plastic bag from his breast pocket. Morgan knew what it was.

"Your buddy had this in his pocket," Kerrigan said. "I ain't the smartest cop in the world, but I reckon there's a few hundred bucks worth of crank in here."

"It's evidence," Morgan insisted.

"Sure is," Kerrigan smiled.

"No, we found it. Inside."

"Uh-huh. I'm gonna ask you to put your left hand behind your back now, good buddy."

"Trey, honest to God ..."

"You have the right to remain silent, which I'm sure you can't or won't," Kerrigan said as he clapped the cuffs hard on Morgan's wrists, "and you have the right to an attorney, although you've pissed 'em all off, and anything you say can be used as evidence against you, so I'd suggest you tell me everything right now. And don't bullshit me, or I'll just shoot you."

Morgan was eager to talk, even though he knew Trey Kerrigan, like his father Deuce before him, was a sheriff who never carried a gun. Whether it was their homespun eloquence or their hair-trigger personalities that made them so convincing without forty-four magnum firepower, neither of them ever needed it.

"McWayne has a meth lab in there," Morgan said. "We saw it."

Kerrigan stared into the flames of the burning mortuary. Firefighters had lost the battle long before part of the embalming room's roof collapsed, spewing sparks into the pre-dawn darkness like dancing bits of star.

And Morgan watched any evidence of McWayne's

meth lab literally going up in smoke.

"This don't look good," the sheriff said, his dark eyes piercing Morgan's, even in the shadows.

"No, it doesn't," Morgan admitted. "And we shouldn't have been inside, but I'm telling you the truth. Somebody tried to kill us in there."

Kerrigan dismissed Morgan with an incredulous flip of his hand.

"You gotta be the dumbest-ass burglar I ever knew. You break into somebody's place, and *they* try to kill *you*. It's an occupational hazard. You're lucky you didn't get your ass shot off. Don't come whinin' to me."

Morgan's voice rose an octave.

"We weren't burglars, goddammit."

"No? Creepin' into somebody's business before the crack of sparrow fart — Jesus Christ, a *mortuary* — that ain't against the law? About the best explanation I got for that is that you're a sick puppy . . . What's your best explanation?"

Morgan was speechless and starting to feel the pre-dawn chill. Other than Cowper's suspicions about the meth lab, he wasn't exactly sure why a newspaper editor and a college professor might feel compelled to break into a funeral parlor in the middle of the night. It sounded more like a frat prank than a serious investigation.

"Trey, you know me. I'm no junkie or drug dealer."

"All I know is that you keep turnin' up in places you ain't supposed to be, and always about the time somethin' bad happens. You're a damned fine suspect, you know? Smart criminals usually run, but you hang around and make it easy for us cops."

"Listen to me. Cowper was suspicious of some stuff he saw when we were doing the autopsy on John Doe . . ."

"*We*? When did they open the damn morgue to reporters? John Doe is evidence and now you're lookin' up your own ass at a tamperin' charge. Maybe I'll just let those DCI boys eat you for lunch. Your hole is gettin' deeper, my friend. I suggest you stop diggin'."

Pain pulsed through Morgan's shoulder, coruscating down his arm like St. Elmo's fire. His scalded face felt badly sunburned. For the first time, he noticed his hands and arms had been scorched, and despite the horrendous assault on his nostrils, he was beginning to smell singed hair among the stench of burning chemicals on him and around him. He reeked like both an oil well hell-fighter and a burned shank of lamb.

"How's Shawn?"

Kerrigan showed no real compassion.

"I have no idea."

"Well, he's the guy who can tell you what we saw. Test that stuff in your pocket and you'll know. I'm telling you, somebody was cooking crank in there. While we were inside, somebody poured gas under the door and lit it. We barely got out."

"I'm sure a creative guy like you can come up with a better story than that."

Several small explosions sent forth yellow and green-ish blue plumes through the melting asphalt roof of McWayne's funeral home, and Morgan's heart fell. By dawn, his chance of proving his story was be a piled of wet ashes, melted debris and charred wood.

Kerrigan led Morgan to his Blazer in handcuffs. A few of the gawkers and firefighters watched, and Morgan knew the gossip would be flying all over town before the Griddle poured its first cup of oily coffee. And long before the ruins of McWayne's mortuary had cooled, Morgan would be tried and convicted, and his appropriate punishment discussed over most breakfast tables in town.

He sat in the silent Blazer, smelling his own rankness, while Kerrigan stood in the headlight arc between his vehicle and an infuriated Carter McWayne, who'd squealed into the crowd of firefighters and cops in his hearse, wearing only his pajama bottoms and a tee-shirt. Still deafened by the roar of the fire and the fury of explosions, Morgan couldn't hear what McWayne was saying, but he was clearly out of his mind with anger and fear.

The police radio was silent, except for some firefighting traffic that crackled like crushed aluminum foil over the air.

Kerrigan left his deputy in charge of Carter McWayne and settled into the driver's seat, his teeth clenched like a vise. Morgan could see the little muscles in his jaw pulsing. He turned down the scanner and started the Blazer.

"Do me a favor?" Morgan asked.

Kerrigan wasn't in the mood for special requests. He glared at his old friend, who was not a friend at the moment.

"You got a phone call coming to you. Ask somebody else for a favor. I'm a little pissed right now. No, a *lot* pissed."

"Okay, but only you can do this one," Morgan said. "Ask Tubby Gertz if the mortuary's back door was wedged closed from the outside when he got there. Why would we have blocked our only escape route?"

CHAPTER NINE

Claire Morgan bailed her husband out of the Perry County Jail as the sun peeked over the eastern edge of the vast, empty prairie grasslands that surrounded Winchester, Wyoming.

Morgan hadn't slept in more than a day, and although his body was drained, his bleary mind frothed and stewed like rancid meat in an unwashed stew pot. He was burned, arrested and humiliated in his town, and it was press day.

The jail nurse had already bandaged his burns and smeared some industrial-strength cortisone gel on his scarlet face, where small, watery blisters had already erupted. His shoulder throbbed, but X-rays would have to wait for more professional care than a seldom-used, small-town jail could provide.

Claire said almost nothing as they drove to the hospital to see Shawn Cowper. She only asked once, and in a small voice freighted with disappointment: "Why?"

He had no more and no better answers for his wife than he had for Trey Kerrigan, who had booked him on misdemeanor trespassing while he investigated charges of breaking and entering, and arson. Rather than say something stupid, he said nothing.

His arraignment was scheduled later in the day before Justice of the Peace Rayfield O'Brien, who loved to editorialize from the bench and who happened to be married — unfortunately for Morgan — to Carter McWayne's first cousin, Gwinny.

Morgan had been in courtrooms on a thousand days, but always as an observer, never in the dock. He'd often smirked when some skell had been laid raw by a judge's tongue-lashing, and now as an accused felon — not to mention an incisive editorial writer who had occasionally railed at and ridiculed certain injustices in the justice system — he would stand naked before the whip himself.

Morgan walked down the long, echoing hallway, past the nurses' station and radiology, to ICU. He had always hated the antiseptic smell of hospitals, where they tried to cover up the scent of illness and death, to wipe it away. Not like cemeteries, where the odor was more honest.

Shawn Cowper occupied a private room in the intensive care ward. His body was wrecked hamburger, chopped, sliced and braised, then sutured, stitched, glued and salved. He had drifted in and out of consciousness since he arrived a few hours before.

Dr. Ravi Pradesh, the new emergency doc, fingered the beeping, blinking machines connected to the wires and tubes that tapped into Cowper's nerves and veins, and tried to explain Cowper's condition in a hash of Indian accent and laborious terminology. Educated offshore like so many of the young doctors who came to small towns in the American hinterlands, he knew the words he'd read in medical textbooks, but not the words people needed to hear.

"The chemical burn to the airways has many, uh, manifestations. His mucosal irritation will continue, and he will develop bronchorrhea, so he will be, uh, coughing and expectorating," Dr. Pradesh said just as Cowper hacked a glob of sooty sputum into his mask.

"Bacteria are inside, and they are gathering . . . like a

team, yes? When his damaged mucosa becomes necrotic, it will fall off, and as his air pipe becomes inflamed, we will be watching very closely for the edema. That makes it very, very hard for him to breathe, which will make him fatigued and, how you'd say . . . not breathing easy."

"Will he be okay, doctor?" Morgan asked.

"The combination of the chemicals burning in his lungs and the fire on his body are, uh, very, very bad," the young doctor said in his chopped English. "If we can control the infection . . . maybe okay, maybe not. I'm sorry."

Morgan listened, but didn't need an interpretation of the ponderous, pidgin medico-speak: Shawn's lungs were baked from the inside out, flensed by the paring blades of chemicals and smoke. Except when coughing blackish goo, his weak, wounded breath heaved a vapor on the inside of his clear plastic oxygen mask, which dissipated every time he breathed in. Like doughboys who breathed mustard gas in World War I, the delicate sacs of his lungs had been melted and disfigured, and he would likely not take another painless breath for the rest of his life.

But he was alive.

Dr. Pradesh left the room, looking uncertain if he should or not. Morgan glanced at Cowper's chart, on which someone had noted that police were to be notified if and when he was conscious and speaking. Kerrigan hadn't posted any guards outside the room, so apparently he wasn't too worried his suspect would flee. And nobody stopped Morgan from going in, even though the town was most certainly abuzz by the time he arrived.

From Cowper's hospital room window on the second floor of the squat little hospital, Morgan could see a thin spiral of smoke coming from the tranquil, tree-lined neighborhood where McWayne's Funeral Home had stood less than twelve hours before. The fire had burned all night, booming and belching fire every time a vat or tank of some unknown chemical was consumed. By now, Morgan knew the state hazmat crews in their sealed space suits would be sampling the caustic air and sifting through the debris in the hot zone, hunting for remnant toxins.

In the daylight, it all seemed so absurd now.

A fantasy about a mythic outlaw's lover leads to an obsession about the identity of a mutilated corpse which leads to a sheriff's iniquitous hanging which leads to a nebulous drug conspiracy which leads to an ill-advised break-in which leads to jail.

Morgan would have laughed if the pain in his shoulder and his heart hadn't been so venomous. And he would have stayed right here in this room with his friend if he didn't suddenly realize that somebody out there was still trying to kill him.

The newsroom of the *Winchester Bullet* wasn't just Morgan's church. It was his obsession, his compulsion, his passion. And on Wednesdays, it was his sanctuary.

He went back there from the hospital, his clothes still pungent with smoke, sweat and shame. Half the morning was gone, deadline loomed, and he'd literally inhaled the biggest story of the week. He was more the story than the reporter now, but he must make a newspaper anyway, even if it was like writing his own obituary.

Morgan parked in the alley behind the *Bullet* and came in through the back door. Crows mocked him from the tall, ancient cottonwoods. The morning was already hot, and when he opened the heavy steel door, cool air rushed out to embrace him. The smell of ink hung like a vapor, not acrid and not sweet. It comforted him.

A safety bell, not unlike a short school bell or an apartment buzzer in a big city, rang on the press whenever the rollers inched forward for a new plate, warning anyone standing close enough that a finger, a tie, a sleeve might get snagged in the past week's news if proper care wasn't taken. As the plates came faster and the press deadline neared, the bell rang more insistently as the hulking black Goss press, smeared by years of inky hands, steeled itself for the task of spewing *The Bullet*.

Cal Nussbaum was preparing the press for the day's run.

At top speed, the week's full edition of two thousand papers would be printed in seven minutes, but Cal was a gentler printer than most. He treated the web of newsprint like a continuous sheet of tissue paper, protected from ripping by its uniform tautness from the half-ton rolls that fed each unit. As a pressman, Cal was a Sunday driver, a slow hand who preferred the low, rhythmic thrum of the machine to the speed of the journey.

Printing a newspaper was an art in itself for Cal Nussbaum, the beginning of the week, not the end. He was in no hurry, and the week's run of *The Bullet* might take more than a half hour to roll off the press.

Cal applied the ink in ethereal layers, rather than slathering it in thick, black gobs, because it was not only an expensive petroleum product he bought in fifty-five-gallon drums, but because he hated it when the Friday-night boys at the Elks Club complained about the inky residue it left on their wives' fingers. Every newspaper smudges, Cal told them, and he knew the man who invented a smudge-free newspaper ink would become a billionaire overnight, but he hated thinking of the gentle ladies of Winchester going to Wednesday night church with hands like auto mechanics in calico dresses. It was a point of pride for him to keep the smudging lady-like.

For Cal himself, the smudges on his fingers were permanent. The ink had seeped into every microscopic fissure and crevasse in his paw-like hands. Its distinctive tattoo could never be scrubbed off, even if he'd wanted to . . . and he didn't. The newspaper business had marked him indelibly for the rest of his life, and likely for the eternity of death.

Once, in an uncharacteristic moment of sentimentality abetted by several beers, Cal told Morgan he wished to be cremated after he died and some of his ashes stirred into the press's ink fountains. That way, he said, he'd truly become part of the weekly newspaper he'd printed since he was a kid back in the Forties. Morgan respected the simple charm of Cal's passion, and he fervently hoped he'd never have to explain someday to a state health inspector how a man's mortal remains had been thrown on every doorstep in town.

Cal was hunkered under the press unit, fastening a printing plate to the press, and looked up when he heard the back door close. He raised his chin toward his boss, more greeting than friendship. The best he could manage for Morgan was a crumpled smile, more pity than greeting.

"We're late," Cal grumbled.

"Yeah, sorry. What's still out?"

"Damn near everything. No sports, no living, no editorial, no front," the old pressman said, as if he'd said it a thousand times before. And he likely had. "Those damn kids don't know what to do without you ridin' herd."

The burns on Morgan's face tingled as the blood rose in him. He glanced at his watch: ten-thirty. A half-hour before the press was to start.

"Yeah, well, sorry," he said. "Let's see what we can do in the next two hours. If we can put it to bed by one, we'll still have time to get to the Post Office."

It would also allow Morgan an hour to find a lawyer for his two o'clock arraignment.

"Wouldn'ta happened with Old Bell," Cal

complained, as if invoking a saint. And to Cal, the old editor *was* a saint.

Morgan fixed a steely stare on Cal, who'd already turned back to his tinkering on the press.

No, it wouldn't, Morgan wanted to say out loud. *Old Bell wouldn't have been so stupid.*

The Bullet's three young reporters didn't look up when Morgan walked in, but they knew he was there. Although they should have been in the final, fervent moments before deadline, they simply tapped away at their keyboards with a logy distraction. Never mind their editor was now the topic of the police blotter as well as street-corner gossip. It wasn't their paper.

Morgan stopped beside Josh's cluttered desk. Josh kept his nose down.

"What do we have on the mortuary fire?" he asked the kid.

Josh flipped through his notebook.

"Uh. Started about four o'clock. No fatalities, dead or alive. Two injured, one critical. Arson suspected. Structure totally destroyed."

Morgan stopped being a suspect and started being an editor.

"Give me fifteen inches in twenty minutes," he said, "but it's 'deaths,' not fatalities. And dead people can't die again. And if something is destroyed, it's total. 'Totally destroyed' is redundant."

"Right, Chief," Josh said. "How am I supposed to handle your, um, well, you know."

"I was arrested at the scene. Get the sheriff's report and write it straight."

"No quote from you?"

"You have a question?"

Josh puzzled for a moment.

"Yeah," he said without looking at Morgan directly. "Did you do it?"

"No."

"Can I quote you?"

"You're a goddamned reporter, aren't you?"

Josh shrugged, and Morgan wondered if the biggest mistake he ever made was going into McWayne's mortuary in the dead of night with Shawn Cowper — or becoming an editor.

He settled into his own chair and booted up his computer. Exhausted, reeking of smoke, disgraced by his crime, and haunted by an invisible assassin, the last thing on his mind should have been journalism. But journalism was never far from any thought that passed through his brain.

He rubbed his burning, tired eyes. The caustic scent of his hand made his gut clench.

Morgan found Cowper's business card beneath the papers on his desk and called the pathology department at South Florida University, but nobody answered. It was two hours ahead, summer break and Cowper had advised his team to take a couple weeks off. He hung up, intending to find the university's main number, where he could at least deliver the news to someone who might contact Cowper's family, wherever they might be.

But when he looked up, Josh was standing beside the desk.

"So what did you want me to do with this dog-ticket list, Chief?"

"What?"

"You told me to compare the list of dog tickets with the hacked data in the city computer. And just for yucks, I looked to see whose dogs were impounded last week."

"I did?" Morgan vaguely remembered the assignment, but not the reason. "Why?"

"I don't know," Josh shrugged again.

THE OBITUARY

"You don't know why?"

"Hey, I just do what you told me, Chief."

"Yeah, right," Morgan huffed. "Okay, what'd you find?"

"Four names," Josh thumbed through his notebook and listed them off. "Evangeline Horner. Ray Pittman. Grady Stilwell. Eugene Peach."

"Who are they?"

"All of 'em had recent animal-control beefs. Runaways, chicken-killers, barkers, sidewalk-poopers and such. Nothing big."

Morgan's mind was still a swirl of smoke and flame, fingerprinting and the sobering antiseptic smell of a hospital. He couldn't think, and deadline was more pressing.

"OK, fine," he said. "Give me the list, get that fire story done, and stop calling me chief."

Josh ripped the narrow sheet from his reporter's pad and handed it to Morgan, who glanced at the names, all in Josh's infantile scrawl and all in fountain ink. It was a good thing Josh had read them off, for his handwriting would have been indecipherable if it weren't so illegible.

"You use a fountain pen?" Morgan asked.

"You bet, Chief," the kid said. "Graduation gift."

"Use a pencil. It won't ruin your shirts."

Then again, Morgan thought, this is a kid who smuggles butter in his pants. He looked at the list of names.

Evangeline Horner was ninety if she was a day, and timeless. When Morgan was just a kid in Winchester, Evangeline Horner was ninety, and her yappy Chihuahua was a noisy little sack of gristle. Without a doubt, Evangeline's equally immortal dog had survived two more generations of kids who tormented him by walking down the opposite side of the street.

But Evangeline was no hacker. She had nothing

more technical in her home than a pressure cooker.

Eugene Peach raised Bassett hounds in his enormous backyard. He was a much-decorated World War Two Marine, wounded at Tarawa and Guadalcanal, who came home to the inexorable quiet of Winchester and began to go slowly, steadily insane. He was always haunted by battle and by his left hand, which was missing. Everyone assumed it was a war wound, but he never talked about it.

Peach, the one-handed flag-bearer at the VFW, was no hacker either. It's more likely one of his bassets slipped his leash and wandered around the neighborhood, looking desperately sad and pissing on everything.

Ray Pittman, the north-county rancher and amateur paranoiac who decorated his ranch fenceposts with old boots, owned a perpetually hungry mutt he hated. He might imagine a grand conspiracy against ranch dogs, but it was doubtful he'd threaten municipal terrorism if the dog were jailed. He might celebrate by popping a Coors, but not by blowing up the Town Hall.

Morgan didn't know Grady Stillwell.

He picked up Winchester's thin phonebook — nobody in this town ever imagined how a child might be boosted at the dinner table by sitting on a phonebook — and leafed to the S's, which were on the same page as the Q's and the T's. He traced his index finger down to the four Stillwells.

No Grady.

But beneath the name of Willard Stillwell — a former classmate of Morgan's better known as "Speed" because he was always the first to arrive at the high school keggers — was another number at the same house: *children.*

Was Speed Stillwell's kid a dog-loving hacker who muddled the Town Hall computers?

It was a question that would have to wait until after deadline and, for Morgan, until after he was arraigned for arson and breaking-and-entering the McWayne Mortuary, now ashes.

Dode Hicks wasn't the most expensive lawyer in town, just the smartest. He didn't do much criminal work, but only because there weren't enough criminals in Winchester, Wyoming, to support a thriving practice. Mostly, Dode Hicks wrote wills and trusts, arranged land transactions, presided over the Rotary Club, and thought about running for the state Legislature someday. And everyone presumed he'd do it, too, maybe even be the governor, but his name was never actually on the ballot.

Now he was Morgan's lawyer.

Dode's office was tucked in a corner of the otherwise vacant floor above the First Wyoming Bank, an antique Main Street building put up in the Thirties with a magnificent brick façade and decorative tin ceilings. The bank downstairs had erased the historic charm by renovating with cubicles, glass walls and imported marble floors, but Dode's offices were still delightfully ancient, with ceiling fans, sagging bookshelves, braided rugs over worn wood floors, and the lofty pressed-tin ceilings of old.

Dode Hicks liked to refer to himself as a simple country lawyer, but he wasn't in some significant ways. True, he liked simple things, but he understood the country folk in his practice — and more importantly, on his occasional jury — better than any big-city barrister.

Like Morgan, he'd grown up in Winchester, the son of a bartender. And like Morgan, he ventured beyond the town limits after high school, eventually graduating near the top of his class at Pepperdine, the swank Malibu law school on the edge of the known world to most Wyomingites. He joined a silk-stocking Los Angeles firm, but Southern California wasn't his country, and he came home after a few years with more than enough money to rent a small space over a small-town bank, hire a secretary, join the Rotary Club, and hang his shingle.

Now in his late forties, he'd happily lost his shiny California plating, and the Wyoming boy underneath had emerged again. His close-cropped red hair was beginning to gray, making him look balder than he was. He'd thickened around the middle and had long ago forsaken four hundred dollar suits for golf shirts and rumpled khaki pants. But he kept an Italian suit pressed on the coat hook behind his office door for those days when court appearances really required court *appearances.*

He'd already agreed to represent Morgan and Cowper in a cursory telephone call that morning, but wanted to meet face-to-face before the arraignment. Now he sat at his unvarnished, scarred wooden desk, his back to the arched window that, if it hadn't been painted shut long ago, would have opened to the unhurried Main Street.

Blades of sunlight slashed across the hash of papers on top, reflecting off the screen of a dusty desktop computer in a roll top desk on the other side of the room.

"Okay, Jeff, you know the drill as well as I do," Dode said, leaning back in his squawking leather chair. "We go listen to that crusty old fart Rayfield rant for a couple minutes, hear the charges, set a date for the prelim, and go home. You've already got bond and I doubt you're a flight risk. So ten minutes and we're out. Painless . . . well, for me."

Morgan smiled and said nothing.

"Your buddy Trey did you a big favor," the lawyer said.

"How's that?"

"He only charged you with trespass. He could have held you on the felony counts and you'd have still been in jail until the arraignment. The misdemeanor let you make bail. They say the truth shall set you free, but sometimes truth isn't enough."

The lawyer's gentle attempt at humor wasn't lost on Morgan, just blunted by his exhaustion.

"Well, I could have used the sleep," Morgan said.

"Yeah, well, anything I need to know right off the bat?" his lawyer asked.

Hicks didn't care if his client was guilty or innocent, and Morgan knew it, but Morgan wanted to say something to somebody anyway.

"We were inside the mortuary. We shouldn't have been there, but we were. We didn't take anything, and we didn't start the fire. We think there is — was — a meth lab inside there. Somebody else was in there and I think he was trying to kill us. And I think whoever it was might want to finish the job."

Dode Hicks took some notes, nodding, but not smiling.

"Why didn't you just tell the cops your concerns?"

Morgan looked down at his shoes, blackened by dried soot and ash.

"I wish I knew. Honest to God, I wish I had."

Morgan tried to imagine how *that* answer would sound in court. It wasn't good.

"Well, we don't need to get our panties in a bunch quite yet," Hicks reassured Morgan. "Today is just a formality. No evidence. No testimony. No handcuffs. We'll know more if and when we get to the preliminary hearing."

"If?"

"You know a lot can slip between cup and lip. Charges get dropped as the investigation unfolds. We're still very early. Too early to start planning your prison wardrobe, my friend."

Morgan's blood went cold at the mention of the word "prison."

"Can we avoid the Big House?"

"Relax, Jeff," Dode said. His brown eyes were direct and heartening. "I think we can keep you out of prison. I'm more worried about the real arsonist. If you're right, if he was trying to get you, then that's a bigger problem for you. I think we should ask Trey Kerrigan to assign a patrol around your house, just to be safe."

"That'd be great, Dode. Just to watch the house, if nothing else. I thought about taking my family out of town for a while."

Hicks wrinkled his freckled nose.

"They can go," he said, "but you might have to stick around. The judge isn't going to let you go too far on these charges. I can ask, but I wouldn't hold my breath."

One more thing to worry about, Morgan thought. Claire wouldn't go if Jeff didn't go with her, not after what happened five years before in the Gilmartin case. She'd left town then, for her own protection, and never forgave herself for abandoning her husband just at the time she might never seem him alive again. No, she wouldn't leave alone. Even if she still wasn't speaking to him.

The light through the window dimmed as a cloud passed in front of the sun. A long gray silence enveloped the dowdy little office.

Dode Hicks tossed a pencil on the desk and spoke first.

"Don't sweat this, Jeff," he said. "It'll work out slick, you'll see."

Easy for him to say, Morgan thought. *He's not the one going to jail if he's wrong.*

"For once, and maybe the only time in my memory, I'm happy to see you in my court, Mr. Morgan," the wizened Judge Rayfield O'Brien bubbled from his perch.

His bald head, fringed by unruly white hair that

looked like ruffled feathers and road-mapped with tiny blue veins, reflected the humming fluorescent tubes overhead, but his eyes were little black holes that sucked in all available light.

His window-less Perry County courtroom had no oak panels, no polished wood bar, no lofty ceilings, no official seal hovering over the proceedings, Instead, it was no more imposing than a Sunday school classroom in a cheap church, with the teacher's desk at the front, a couple flags on cheap wooden poles, a small microphone stand between two laminate tables, and some folding chairs for whatever flock might be nosey enough to actually sit down.

Claire sat in the front row, just behind the defense table. So did *The Bullet*'s star reporter and butter thief, Josh.

Deputy Prosecutor Wallace Nixon fidgeted in his chair, but Morgan couldn't tell if it was because his polyester slacks were too tight around his plump midsection, or because the judge's scattershot rancor might, at any moment, be aimed his direction.

For the moment, it was aimed straight at Morgan.

"Now, some folks might say the press is superficial, biased, inadequate, sensational, inaccurate, unfair, misleading, irresponsible, and damned damaging to the public interest, but not me," Judge O'Brien lectured. "While I might admit to, oh, a certain disdain for the typical newspaperman's ignorance and insensitivity for the process of law, I ardently defend the freedom of speech, which has served me well. But in this court, Mr. Morgan, you will have no such freedom, and you'll keep your trap shut until I tell you. Understood?"

Dode Hicks rose to his feet. "Your Honor, I . . ."

"Stuff a sock in it, Dode," the judge growled. "You're just gonna have to sit down and shut up, too. Damn lawyers."

Hicks' jaw muscles pulsed a few times and he looked at some papers on the table in front of him while he formed his words.

"Your Honor, as to the charges against my clients . . ."

"You don't hear so good, do you, boy? I said sit down."

Hicks sat as the judge continued.

"Both your clients are being charged with breaking and entering, and as of a few minutes ago, first-degree arson. I'm fair certain they're gonna say they didn't do it, and we're gonna have to waste some taxpayer money to get to the bottom of it. That should make for a very eloquent editorial in next week's paper, eh, Mr. Morgan? I'll keep the bail at the current amount unless something more comes up, then I'll make sure Mr. Morgan awaits trial as a county guest. You got it?"

Hicks popped to his feet. "This is highly irregular, your Honor . . ."

The judge leveled his gavel at the lawyer, as if it were a gun.

"Another word, Dode, and you're in contempt. If anything is irregular here, it's the burning of a mortuary and a family's livelihood. But we're not here to hang Mr. Morgan just yet. I'm setting the preliminary hearing for September 15. Any objections?"

Both lawyers reached for calendars, but Judge Rayfield O'Brien rapped his gavel and disappeared from the bench in a flourish of black robes.

Claire reached forward and touched her husband on the shoulder. He bent his head back and sideways to kiss her hand.

The entire arraignment — an important step in a felony prosecution of a major crime against a well-known and solid local citizen — lasted four minutes, and the prosecutor never uttered a single word.

Morgan was running on fumes. He needed sleep and sanctuary, even if only for a few hours. His clothes still reeked, and the burns on his arms felt as if they were smoldering beneath the bandages, ready to catch fire again with the slightest breath of air.

But before he escaped his disgrace and the daylight altogether for a few hours, maybe the rest of the night, he wanted to see Cowper again.

And his mother.

They left Dode Hicks on the courthouse steps. Claire drove her husband back to the hospital, not because he couldn't drive, but because she wanted to be of aid in some way. On the way, she had reached across the seat and put her hand on his leg.

"I'm behind you, honey. Only you," she'd said. "I love you, and we'll get through this just fine."

For the first time in a day, since long before the fire, he felt comforted. She'd pierced the carapace of shit and shame that weighted him down.

Cowper's condition hadn't changed. He was paler. Some infection had erupted in a border of pus around some of his burns, and he continued to hack gray goo from his anguished lungs. He had regained consciousness, briefly, a few times, but he was still hovering on the razor's edge between living and dying.

They left their number at the nurses' station and walked two blocks to Laurel Gardens. The afternoon heat rippled off the blacktop, but the shady sidewalk was cool. The fresh air was windless, and he hurt when he breathed deeply, but the short walk revived Morgan in a small way. A longer walk might have been a problem.

The same teen-ager Morgan had seen mopping the floors at Laurel Gardens was now mowing the modest lawn in front of the nursing home. And he wore the same headphones as he bopped to some unheard beat, with a relentless bass line provided by Toro.

After the previous night's smells, Morgan now thought the air inside the home was refreshing, clean. Its artificial coolness soothed his scorched face, too.

A few residents sat in the hallway in wheelchairs, some played cards or watched the soundless CNN picture on the lounge TV as he and Claire passed through the main wing, where the elderly residents who had comparatively complete control of their senses lived. They could come and go as they pleased because they knew the way home, they could count their own money, could recognize their friends and family, and knew the time and the day — unlike his mother and most of the other confused residents in her locked wing.

A frail old couple, easily in their eighties, sat at one of the tables in the day room, sharing a cup of coffee and holding hands. Morgan hoped wherever he might be near the end of his life, Claire would be there, holding his hand.

He pecked out the security code and they entered the secure area. An aide in a blue smock, a young girl he didn't recognize, passed with a cart of empty lunch plates and smiled. They walked down the long, polished hall to his mother's room, but she wasn't there.

She wasn't in the day room at the other end of the wing, either. Claire checked the bathrooms while Morgan wandered the halls, peeking into each room as he went. Rachel Morgan had once fallen asleep on the floor in another room, and it was possible she'd simply strayed in her confusion.

But they didn't find her.

"Have you seen my mother, Rachel Morgan?" he asked a passing aide who was carrying soiled towels to the laundry room.

"This morning," she said, "before the doctor came."

"What doctor?"

"I dunno," the girl shrugged. "I'm kinda new here. He signed her out before lunch."

"She's gone?"

"Yeah, I guess. He said he needed to take her for tests."

Morgan double-timed to the nurses' station, across from the day room. A dumpy nurse with thin glasses perched on her nose played solitaire on the computer. Morgan didn't know her, but her name tag said "Peggy."

"I'm looking for Rachel Morgan. I'm her son," he said, a little out of breath.

A little embarrassed to be caught playing instead of working, Peggy quickly closed the game screen. She spun around in her chair and flipped through some pages on a clipboard.

"Checked out for medical tests," she said, without any hint of urgency. "Eleven-oh-nine. Wasn't one of the local docs."

"You let her go without my approval?"

"He said he was a specialist from out of town. Dressed like a doctor. And everybody knew you were . . . well, in jail or something. Let's see, his name is Doctor . . . I can't make out the signature . . . Comeaux?"

Morgan's blood turned to ice. The mere mention of the name forced cold blood into hidden places inside him.

But P.D. Comeaux, the serial killer, cannibal and patron saint of every delusional, disaffected domestic terrorist who ever ventured beyond the lunatic fringe, was a dead man walking.

While still on the crime beat at the Chicago *Tribune*, Morgan had used a small laptop computer and thousands of public records to help the FBI identify Comeaux, the long-haul trucker and radical militiaman who was killing women along the slender blue highways between Illinois and Washington State.

If not for Morgan's work, Comeaux might still be cruising for victims out there. Since 1993, Comeaux had been on Death Row in South Dakota, where he'd raped and murdered and literally eaten Sandra Tarrant, a former high school homecoming queen who became a prostitute to maintain her $1,000-a-week cocaine habit.

She was just one of Phineas Dwight Comeaux's fourteen known victims. Nobody who knew him believed that was all.

In the intervening years, he'd become the martyr, a symbol of the government's malicious intent.

At the time of P.D. Comeaux's arrest in 1993, the Fourth Sign wasn't even a blip on the government's radical-right radar screen. Mostly, it was just a small, secret society of angry Bible-Belt farmers on the verge of bankruptcy, seeking conspiracies that weren't there, rationalizing their plights irrationally, and peddling a poor man's gospel. They believed the government was engaged in a global and domestic conspiracy to create a "New World Order" that would enslave ordinary citizens by taking away their means to revolt, namely their land and their guns. And when they searched their Bibles for answers, they came to believe even more fervently that one-world government was the last prophesied sign from God before Armageddon, the "fourth sign."

Nobody cared. The Christian Identity movement hadn't yet bubbled to the surface of the national consciousness. Radicals hadn't yet begun to call themselves "constitutionalists."

Its followers considered themselves soldiers in a war against the United States government, practicing an Aryan theology that saw racial minorities as sub-human "mud people," Jews as Satan's children, and a New World Order as a precursor to tyranny.

At its core, the Fourth Sign was among scores of

obscure and loosely organized Christian Identity bands mixing ultra-fundamentalist zealots and anti-government paranoiacs in a combustible, fuming frenzy that produced more smoke than fire.

But Comeaux was the spark that ignited a wildfire.

Before his arrest, he'd attended a few secret meetings at a small church near Dixon, Illinois, but he mostly kept to the back pews. He put his faith in violence and fear, not talk. His heart burned with a savagery far more advanced than anyone had dreamed.

Once he was jailed, the word went out. To the Fourth Sign's believers, he was no serial killer but a casualty of a government conspiracy designed to uproot true patriots. Even if Comeaux were truly guilty, some said, he should be sainted for exterminating the vermin whores that dragged America toward Hell by its private parts. Offshoots of the Fourth Sign sprung up all across the forgotten interior, its demented gospel spread via the Internet and rallied by the whispered name of P.D. Comeaux.

On the day of closing arguments in Comeaux's South Dakota trial, a sophisticated pipe-bomb filled with roofing tacks and packed in a shoebox between two plastic bags of human feces, was mailed to the county prosecutor's office. When it exploded, it decapitated a legal secretary and badly mutilated a law-school intern, whose wounds became lethally infected by the excrement and dirty shrapnel blasted deep into him. The day before the student died in excruciating pain, an anonymous caller with a Western accent told a sheriff's dispatcher that the bomb had been sent by the Fourth Sign.

"And the shit inside came right out of the ass of Saint P.D. hisself. Consider yourself baptized," he cackled, then hung up.

Nobody was ever arrested, nor was it ever known if P.D. Comeaux had actually smuggled his own waste out of the county jail, but the Fourth Sign was quickly added to the feds' short list of America's most deadly domestic terror groups.

The heart of the Fourth Sign beat somewhere in the Midwest, Morgan knew from his follow-up investigation in Comeaux, but its leadership was shadowy. It gathered money from its far-flung members through a series of drop-boxes rented by mysterious groups with names like The Millennium Institute and The Rapture Forum, most of the money going to an ever-expanding arsenal of legal and illegal weaponry. ATF intelligence suggested the organization's more militant factions — radicals for whom the old-school Order and the Aryan Nations were not radical enough — financed themselves by declaring their own war on drugs, robbing and murdering dealers from Tulsa to Detroit.

Sometime in the late Nineties, the Fourth Sign's soldiers branched out into piracy. Not on the seas, but on American highways. Eighteen-wheelers were lumbering, easy targets, and they carried large amounts of goods — from guns to pharmaceuticals to vehicles — that could be quickly and quietly converted to cash.

Over the past ten years, the FBI and ATF estimated the Fourth Sign and its revolutionary offshoots had grown from penny-ante militants to a cancerous cartel more heavily armed and with better intelligence resources than most National Guard units.

Was Comeaux out? Not likely.

But was his name invoked by a sympathizer, someone who might have been connected to the fire at McWayne's mortuary, someone who wanted Morgan dead?

That was chillingly possible, Morgan knew.

"Can I use your phone?" he asked Peggy. She shoved it across the desk.

He called the Perry County Sheriff's Office and told Trey Kerrigan everything, how Rachel Morgan had disappeared mysteriously five hours before, how he thought it was linked to the fire, how he should post a guard at Cowper's hospital room.

And the abductor's only message, one intentional and personal name: *Comeaux*.

CHAPTER TEN

The blood-smeared western sky spilled along the brink of the horizon, seeping slowly beneath the earth where it peeled back at the edges. A summer sunset in Wyoming was silently violent, a death that could not be prevented.

Morgan sat alone and quiet on the back porch at Mount Eden, the cordless phone, a bottle of Percocet pain-killers, and his mother's fading wedding portrait spread across his lap. His body wanted to sleep, but his fevered brain — abetted by his troubled heart — conspired to keep him awake, if not alert.

Rain was coming. He could smell it, but the unseen storm hadn't yet gathered. When he was a kid, his father told him how to know it would soon rain. Crickets chirped louder, the leaves on trees moved even if no breeze blew, chickweed closed up. But tonight he knew it because he could smell the impending freshness of it.

He'd showered when he got home and changed out of his smoky clothes, but his nerves remained raw. He called *The Bullet* to make sure it had beaten the Post Office deadline, and it did, barely. The afternoon had been filled with the usual press-day nuisances, like Bob Buck of Bob Buck Buick, who always wanted to change his ad two minutes *after* it went to press and peevishly announced he would not pay for any outdated advertisements.

Sitting now on the wide porch, barefoot and indolent, Morgan had only enough vigor to keep his eyes open, to watch the sun collapse behind an unseen ocean, and to imagine the unimaginable heartbreak the dark might bring.

But he couldn't fall asleep.

After supper, Claire and Colter had gone up into Mount Eden's tower, where Old Bell Cockins had so often sought refuge with his books and his endless horizons. Claire understood, without a word, that her husband wanted to be alone. The tower was cooler in summer because its open windows channeled the gentler upper winds unroiled by the surrounding forest. It also seemed safer, a sanctuary with a view for miles in every direction. Maybe they'd sleep when the sun went down, and dream pleasant dreams.

Having grown up in such twilight, walking in forests and vast mountain meadows where only a few square feet of soil had ever been touched by a human sole, Morgan knew the tragic rhythms of this place, where majesty and menace inhabited the same landscape. Places where a little boy could be alone with his dreams were also places where he could be lost forever, never found.

You can't step in the same river twice, his father once told him when he was very young, *and you can't stop, or even slow down, a sunset.*

Morgan couldn't get his mind around the inevitability of sundown, then or now. Or fathers and mothers who must eventually die. It was certainly foreseeable as long as there was an Earth to rotate itself away from the sun, and it was undeniably recurrent. What Morgan couldn't imagine was something else, something like being dead, where sunsets and sunrises and the smell of fresh-turned earth no longer existed. Those things just stopped in a very intimate way for the unlucky dead, and were therefore not inevitable forever, just inevitable for now.

His mother has disappeared.

He stood accused of a crime he couldn't deny.

Someone wanted him dead, and his friend already lay near death.

He was haunted by a murderous ghost.

His faith had evaporated, in his wife and whatever affable spirit created sunsets.

His beloved son hadn't heard his father laugh in days.

And now his braised skin smoldered as the pain pills wore off, so he glided his sweaty, ice-filled glass of Jack Daniels across his cheek.

Sheriff Trey Kerrigan, once Morgan's best friend and now his tormentor, had deputies scouring the county for Rachel Morgan. But her abductor had a three-hour head start, and they might have crossed any number of borders by now. Not just county and state lines, but . . . Morgan didn't want to think how far it might have gone. His imagination was unnecessary; in twenty years on the Chicago crime beat, he'd seen what happened when desperate, sick men crossed certain thresholds.

The bloody, guttering light of the dying day had saturated the ground beneath his feet, and he was sinking. He only wanted to sleep, to escape the inferno in his brain and on his skin.

Blood chugged behind his eyes and deep in his ears, roaring like a locomotive under steam. He popped two Percocets and washed them down with whiskey to anaesthetize the ache of it, but it stung his raw lips.

The phone chirped in his lap and he snatched it up quickly.

"Morgan," he answered.

"Jeff, this is Trey." The sheriff's voice betrayed no urgency or good tidings. "Just checking in. We've got nothing right now. We have a witness who thinks your mother might have gotten into a green SUV with a man, but she's not sure. We're alerting surrounding counties and states, but . . . well, I'll keep you posted. Meantime, keep this line open in case the kidnapper tries to call."

"So you got nothing?"

"For now."

"Fuck."

"Jeff, you need some sleep. It's been a long day. It might be a long night. I've got Cecil Box watching your place all night, so Claire and Colter will be safe. I'll call in the morning if something doesn't break tonight."

"Thanks."

"Jeff?"

"Yeah?"

"Don't worry," Kerrigan said. "If she's out there, we'll find her. Be with Claire and Colter tonight, and be safe."

Morgan didn't say goodbye. He just clicked off and closed his eyes. *If she's out there.* He knew she was out there, and Kerrigan knew it, too. What the sheriff really meant was *if she's still alive*.

The thin light passing through the veil of his eyelids swirled as tears spilled into that airless space between his eyes and the rest of the world.

The bleeding sky drained to corpse blue, then decomposed to black while Morgan slept.

When he awoke sometime near midnight, disoriented and bleary, it was as moonless and silent as a grave. The only light shone from the Milky Way. Sleep had made him groggier, uncertain for a moment where he was.

The absence of wind left him cold. He'd grown so accustomed to the soughing of the trees and the tinkle of wind bells at night that the quiet made him uncomfortable.

No lights shone in the house, either. Through the veil of waking, he could make out a glittering swath of stars above the silhouette of forest to the west, away from the lights of town.

Then a star, tiny and blue, jiggled below the ragged shadows of the pine forest. Less than a hundred yards away, just this side of the woods, it quivered for a second, changed direction, then disappeared again. Morgan rubbed the fog of sleep from his eyes, but the light — too low, too blue and too erratic to be a star — had vanished.

He watched the spot for a minute, maybe two, never blinking. His skin prickled as he leaned forward across the porch's whitewashed baluster, bracing his chin against his forearm, trying to peer inside the bowels of night. The dry air stung his wide eyes, but he dared not miss the ghostly light if it appeared again.

Instead, the light found him.

Not the blue light, but a pinpoint of laser-red that flitted like a neon mosquito across the back of his hand and seemed to disappear beneath his chin.

Morgan lurched sideways along the rail, spilling out of his chair as the garden window behind him disintegrated, a split second before he heard the muffled *fup* of a high-powered rifle. He scrambled on his belly along the porch, desperately seeking cover, but redwood chaise lounges and clay flower pots hadn't been placed there to save his life. He dove off the decking and crouched behind a rain barrel, his hands and knees bloodied by slivers of broken glass.

The second and third shots thumped close together into the water-logged oak staves, and Morgan heard water trickling fast from the other side of his hiding place. When he saw the deadly speck of the laser sight dart across the dark opposite wall, he knew the shooter must have a night-vision scope with laser targeting, mounted on a semi-automatic sniper rifle.

Whatever it was, and whoever was shooting at him, it was no deer rifle, no midnight plinker spotlighting skunks.

Then he heard the screech of the screen door at the far end of the porch. It was too dark to see anything, too quiet to know if there was anything to be seen.

An anxious moment passed and then Morgan froze.

"Daddy?"

It was Colter's voice.

"Go back, baby!" Morgan shouted.

Colter whimpered. Morgan could make out a ghostly outline of his six-year-old son in the doorway, stock still.

"Go to Mommy! Go!"

But Colter didn't move. Those three, maybe four seconds, were a slow nightmare.

Suddenly, the flimsy screen-door frame ruptured into flying splinters, and Colter screamed, frozen in place colder than a fawn in an open-season crossfire. The sniper had turned his attention to the child.

As if the dream had suddenly flown into hyper-speed, Morgan flew across the deck, crouched low. He lunged at least a body length, his torso between his son and the assassin. His desperate momentum carried them both back into the house, sliding across the kitchen's tile floor until they collided with the refrigerator.

Colter wanted to scream in horror but he couldn't catch his breath. Morgan quickly ran his hands over the child's trembling body, praying his fingers wouldn't slide into the warm, slick wetness of an open wound, or the nauseating softness of torn flesh. There in the dark, lying on the cold, safe floor with Colter, Morgan could see the boy's wide eyes, frightened and pooled with tears. He was unhurt.

He scooped Colter to his chest, and keeping below the level of the windows, he carried him quickly to the tower. Claire met them halfway up the shadowy stairway, half-asleep and scared.

"What's going on?" she whimpered as Colter fell

into her arms and clung to her. "I heard Colter crying and . . . oh my God!"

"Go back upstairs and lock the door," Morgan demanded. "Don't turn on the lights."

"They don't work. I already tried. Power's out."

"Shit. Just get down in the window box, behind the couch, anything. Don't open the door for anyone except me. Go!"

"Jeff . . ."

"Go!"

Back downstairs, Morgan picked up the hallway phone, but it was dead. He slumped against the wall. Blood pulsed through every part of him, and he felt the prickling sting of glass shards in his bare feet and between his fingers. He tried to remember where he'd left his cell phone. The bedroom dresser? The bathroom counter? The kitchen table? The car? His mind raced but went nowhere.

His father's guns were under the bed upstairs, but were of no use. Even before Colter was born, he'd locked all their triggers, wrapped them in old sheets, and hidden a few boxes of ammunition inside the trapdoor that led through the closet ceiling into the attic, well above the reach of most curious children. He prized his father's guns and hoped to teach Colter to shoot them one day, but right now, there was no time to arm himself, even if he could find the tiny brass keys to the goddamned trigger locks.

And the kitchen, with its wide windows and floor covered in broken glass, might as well have been a thousand miles away. Knives or cleavers were too far.

He cursed his vulnerability.

The dark enveloped Morgan. No starlight, no moonlight, not even the pathetic luminosity from the distant lights of Winchester helped him see what might be at arm's reach, what benign household item might become a defensive weapon against a relentless and invisible sniper with night-vision. A table leg? Colter's bronzed baby shoes on the mantel? A dead phone?

Fuck.

His breaths shortened, quick and insufficient, as he slid along the oak floor to the hallway, close to the front door. The cold tile just inside the door, where snow boots and muddy shoes were always shed, was empty — except for Colter's baseball bat, still waiting for the moment Dad would suggest a game of catch in the yard. In Morgan's hand, it was light enough to slap one-handed, soft-rubber grounders to a six-year-old, but much heftier than a blackjack.

Then, over the sound of his own breaths, Morgan heard the tinkle of a wind chime on the back porch. In a windless night, it could only mean someone was close. Morgan was in a kill zone that had suddenly shrunk from a hundred meters to ten.

Morgan scuttled through the dark hall and backed up against the wall beside the kitchen door, bat high, back elbow up, ready to swing for the fences. Both hands wrapped around the bat's handle until his sweaty fingers overlapped. He held his breath and felt the cool trickle of sweat down his spine.

What was left of the splintered screen door creaked. Slow, deliberate footfalls crunched across the broken glass on the smooth tile. They came closer to Morgan's hiding place . . . then stopped.

Morgan's eyes were buggy, snagging every ion of light from the dark room, focused on the opening inches away. Sweat began to dribble down his neck, and his scalp was taut and alive. Blood thumped in his ears.

With one more glass-grinding step, a shadow of a shadow stirred somewhere in the periphery of Morgan's murky vision. He swung the bat and connected with something metal and leaden, not flesh nor bone. It clattered heavily to the floor.

Morgan's would-be assailant cursed aloud in the dark, his voice injured . . . and familiar.

Before Morgan could cock the bat back for another swing, his front door imploded and several dark figures spilled into the house in ricochets of flashing light and shouting. Morgan was momentarily blinded by a powerful beam shining directly at his head from the gunsights of an M16 assault rifle.

"Police! Get down! Now!"

Startled but half-relieved, Morgan threw his bat into a dark corner of the room and held his hands high. The lead cop, who wore a flak vest over a pajama top, slung Morgan to the floor, smashing his face against the hardwood. Kneeling hard in the small of his back, his rifle was aimed directly at the back of Morgan's head, ready to fire.

Prone and pinned to the floor, with his arms cuffed behind his back, Morgan saw a police service revolver beneath Claire's favorite wingback chair. He knew it at a glance: It was Deuce Kerrigan's antique Colt.

The Tac squad swept the rest of the house, finding Claire and Colter hidden in the tower, finally declaring the place clear.

Another cop stepped over him into the kitchen, where he knelt on the floor beside Sheriff Trey Kerrigan, who cradled a bloodied right hand tightly against his chest and clearly harbored no small amount of anger toward Morgan.

With only the light of small, fragrant candles between them, the Morgans sat on the leather sofa in their uprooted living room. Trey Kerrigan stood, checking on his investigators and still fuming nearly a half hour after the place was secured.

"I'm sorry, but I didn't know it was you," Morgan told him.

Secretly, Morgan wondered why he was apologizing for walloping a mysterious intruder moments after his family was nearly wiped out by an assassin.

But Claire sat safely close, embracing a still-whimpering Colter, whose delicate face was streaked with tears. And he wanted to ask when Trey had started carrying a gun again. Like his father before him, Deuce Kerrigan, he'd never felt the need to be armed. But as hard as it was to keep from asking, Morgan didn't want to ratchet up the friction between himself and his one-time best friend, not at this moment.

"And I didn't know if you were still alive, goddammit," the sheriff said, rubbing his forearm to get feeling back in an injured hand smashed between Morgan's bat and his own gun. Blood seeped through the gauze where his skin had been split open by the blow.

Kerrigan's hand had been bandaged by paramedics while his investigators taped off the kitchen and back porch. They worked quietly in bright pools of artificial light, powered by portable generators. Power wouldn't be returned to Mount Eden until the power company could repair a sabotaged transformer on a pole a mile away.

Claire clutched her husband's arm as if she'd just realized how wrong things might have gone while she hid with Colter in the tower's window box. The silence was sobering.

"Your deputy, Cecil, is he . . . ?" Morgan asked quietly. He'd heard some of the cops talking in subdued tones. He knew how it sounded when a cop was down, how the usual dark humor at a crime scene turned to silence. One of the cops had called the dispatcher from the front porch but walked off into the night when he realized paramedics were treating Morgan's flayed hands and feet just inside the door.

Kerrigan just shook his head and looked at the floor. Morgan glanced at Claire, who bundled Colter tighter in his blanket and took him upstairs to his bedroom. She touched her husband's cheek as she passed. Nobody said anything until she and the child were out of the room.

"Shift changed at midnight," Kerrigan said without looking up. "His relief radioed but couldn't raise him. We tried his cell phone, too. They, uh, found him out at the end of the road. One shot to the right temple. Whoever it was shot him through the open passenger window, probably crept up on that side of the car. Still had a cup of coffee between his legs. Didn't spill a drop. Never knew what hit him."

"I'm sorry," Morgan apologized again.

"You didn't hear any shots before he started shooting at you?"

Morgan shook his head. "None. And hardly then. The gun was silenced somehow. And far. The bullets hit first, then I heard this sort of muted thump. I think so, anyway. I don't know."

"Long shot," Kerrigan said.

"Long and bad," a third voice spoke.

Morgan turned to see Leigh Moody, the monolithic Perry County deputy who was leading the investigation.

Six-foot-four and as serious as a heart attack, a fighter jet could land on the former Marine gunnery sergeant's gray-fringed flat-top. His beat was three thousand square miles populated only by rattlesnakes, oilfield roughnecks, lonesome cowboys, hopped-up long-haul truckers, and pig-ugly roadhouse tarts in the north county, and he patrolled it alone. He was so tough and so prone to growling that the younger deputies and most of the townsfolk just called him "Gunny," a nickname that suited him better than the feminine spelling of Lee.

Between his two beefy fingers he held two small

metal slugs as if they were sixteenth-century porcelain teacups.

"These come out of the rain barrel," he said, unsmiling. "Pristine. Looks to be a .300 Mag, so I'd guess our boy's shooting an M24, standard U.S. Army sniper weapon. Won't know much until we run 'em through ballistics."

Morgan piped up.

"So you think this guy is former military?"

Finally, Deputy Moody smiled, his lips curling slyly beneath his white cookie-duster mustache. He knew guns, and he knew what it took to make a kill from a half-mile away, and everybody knew why: he'd been a Marine scout and sniper in Vietnam. Eighty-eight confirmed kills.

"No, sir. If he was military, you and your little guy would be dead now. Graduates of the U.S. Army's sniper school are expected to achieve 90 percent first-round hits at 600 meters with an M24; one shot, one kill. But that's just the Army . . . Marines have higher standards. No, if our shooter was military, even Army, he wouldn't have missed five shots. He'da gotcha dead center . . . emphasis on 'dead.' But he emptied his magazine and missed every time."

"He had a laser sight. I saw the red point on my hand."

Gunny did a quick calculation.

"Coulda been up to eight hundred yards out. He had good weaponry, but not a good eye."

"So how does a civilian get a military sniper rifle?" Morgan asked.

Kerrigan shrugged, not because he didn't care, but because it was fruitless to care. Gunny just smiled his cynical smile as he dropped his two slugs into a plastic evidence pouch.

"Inner-net. Gun shows. Black market. They're out

there. Like the man said, only outlaws got the big guns now."

"Or he's been a cop," Gunny said. "M24's one of the preferred long-shot weapons in most police SWAT arsenals. We got one ourselves. But, hell, he might be a guy who works at Wal-Mart and just *thinks* he's a damn good shot."

"A guy with access to military or law enforcement hardware," Morgan pointed out.

"There's lots of them," Kerrigan said, not at all reassuring.

Morgan took a deep breath.

"What about my mom?"

"Nothing yet. It's still my first priority."

"You think this shooting could be related to my mother's disappearance?"

Kerrigan glanced uncomfortably at Gunny, then at Morgan.

"I don't know, Jeff," he said. "But it's damned suspicious. I just can't put it all together yet."

"At least you believe me now that we didn't start the fire at McWayne's mortuary? Right? Some homicidal nut is out there and doesn't like what we found."

The sheriff held his hands up in a beatific shrug, neither confirming nor denying whether he believed Morgan. He had no answer.

Morgan pursed his lips.

"Fine. What now?"

"Can't stay here, that's for sure," Kerrigan said. "And you can't leave the county. You got some place local you can hide out for a while?"

There was only one place he felt safe.

The sedative smell of press-day ink had settled in *The Bullet*'s newsroom. To Morgan, it was better than any pain pill. Or any stimulant, for that matter. He was wide awake at four a.m. and, for the first moment in a long night, finally felt some small measure of control over his fate. Here, in this place, he knew what had to be done.

Claire and Colter had hastily packed some clothes and toys before Trey Kerrigan drove them to a safe house over in Blackwater. Two deputies would be posted outside the house around the clock, and Morgan would be allowed to come and go as he needed. But he already knew he'd land nowhere for very long, coming and going quickly, without notice. A moving target was harder to hit.

Morgan left the overhead lights off. Instead, while his computer booted up, he turned on a small desk lamp and thumbed through the small pile of pink message slips Crystal had left for him the previous afternoon: Bob Buck. His lawyer, Dode Hicks. Bob Buck. An insurance salesman who wanted to write a weekly Christian fishing column. Bob Buck. Three complaints about lost quarters in newsstands. Two cancellations over a letter-to-the-editor from a local Baptist minister who zealously believed Mormons and Catholics weren't real Christians but, in fact, cults. Bob Buck. And Bob Buck.

Too early to return any of them, he knew. He tossed the messages beside his computer and logged onto the Internet. The local internet service provider, *BarbedWire.com*, operated in the back room of Gizmos, a combination electronics and auto parts shop. Signing on usually took two or three tries. The mom-and-pop ISP maintained an cyber-pipeline as ample as a soda straw, but it was Winchester's only connection to the ethereal Web world.

When the buck-snorting, bandy-legged pony on *BarbedWire.com* home page appeared, a digitized voice signaled the presence of new e-mail by hollering, "Yee-haw!"

Morgan's box was filled with the usual spam: mortgage offers, porn-for-pay sites, business opportunities for lazy people, prescription drugs for self-medicators, web cams showing college girls with names like Amber and Chelsea in the sorority shower (sometimes together), and enough penis-enlargement pitches that, if answered by any one man, might make him a freakish rival for the Alaska Pipeline.

But his eyes were stopped cold by an e-mail address strangely out of place, a name and a time that didn't fit together, and a slug-line that chilled. Morgan clicked on it.

>   Subj: *A good day to die*
>   Date: *7/1/2003   2:04:46 AM Mountain Daylight Time*
>   From: *Shawn.Cowper@BarbedWire.com*
>   To: *BulletEditor@BarbedWire.com*
>
>   *I'm next. Save me.*

Morgan felt a sudden cold. He snatched up his phone and dialed the nursing station. At first, the duty nurse refused to give out any information, but rather than risking a long debate in the wee hours, she relented. She told him Cowper had had no visitors and had not yet regained consciousness. Then she hung up.

Turning back to his computer, Morgan pecked out a reply to his mysterious e-mail correspondent: *"Who are you?"*

Sitting in dark silence, waiting for a ghost to speak, a man's voice startled him. It was the chirpy, disembodied drawl from his computer.

"Yee-haw!"

Morgan opened his e-mailbox again. Its single entry

came from MAILER-DAEMON . . . his reply had been returned, undeliverable. An e-mail address that had been used only two hours before no longer existed. He cursed under his breath.

It felt like a trap.

A trap that had been laid in plain sight before him.

A trap he could not avoid stepping into.

A trap that might kill him.

The next morning, before Winchester's dowdy but dogged Main Street began to show signs of life, gray light spilled through the big front window of *The Bullet*. It was a little after six a.m. and rain had moved in.

His two hours of sleep had been fitful, but even the filtered greyness of day comforted Morgan when he awoke in his chair, still sitting at his desk. He didn't dream, or didn't remember dreaming, but the vague anxiety of the long night still clung to his mind, the same way the dull ache of his wounds clung to his skin and bones.

The newsroom was cool. He tried to stretch, but his shoulder was stiff, bruised. His hands prickled with tiny slices and microscopic shards of glass. The skin on his face and arms still felt brittle and warm, as if badly sunburned and unsalved. He tapped two more Percocets out of the little pill bottle and looked for something to wash them down, cold coffee, lukewarm water, anything at hand.

He opened a warm diet soda he found in his desk drawer, and it promptly surged down the sides of the can faster than he could suck it in. He cleared a spot on his desk amid the litter of old newspapers, letters and photographs and plopped the wet can on a loose scrap from a reporter's notebook, although the antique wooden desktop was already lacquered with more interlocking brown rings than a rusty chain.

A few words — no, some scribbled names written in fountain ink — began to bleed as the soda soaked into the leaf of paper. Morgan quickly realized they were Josh's pool of suspects in the City Hall hacking. He rescued the stained piece of paper and wrote, in pencil, in the margin: *call these people and see if they know anything.*

As he laid the note on Josh's chair, where he'd surely see it, a different idea took root in Morgan's foggy brain. Instead, he folded up the damp scrap, stuffed it in his shirt pocket and hurried out the back door of *The Bullet* into a clammy morning that had held no promise until thirty seconds before.

Speed Stillwell and his four kids lived on the other side of the train tracks, on Buford Street, in that part of town where his ancestor railroaders and everybody's poorer relations tended to settle. Their little white house, a Sears & Roebuck kit house pasted together on this spot before 1920, seemed to be rotting from the ground up. Its clapboards hadn't been painted in years, and what few pickets remained on its fence had been gnawed by weather and neglect. The brilliant red paint on every window shutter was flaking as the weathered wood beneath cracked and warped. A "Beware of Dog" sign hung cockeyed by a single nail from the gate.

Speed's wife had died three years ago when her SUV rolled off an icy bridge. He retreated into boozing and the long nights when he was aboard some bootlegger or highball — trains not drinks — somewhere. He never gave up the thought of her, but he tried to wipe away the constant memory of her with liquor and railroading, and he still spent most nights every month between mythical railroad stops like Edgemont, South Dakota, and Honeyville, Utah. Anywhere but home.

Morgan didn't know Speed's kids well, only that there were four of them. His youngest was Colter's age, and by virtue of being the only kindergartner ever ejected from a Winchester youth-league soccer game for fighting, she was also apparently the toughest.

The Stillwell kids, according to the other soccer parents who knew them better, were left on their own for the most part, but they stayed out of trouble and did well in school. They didn't complain and they didn't act out, except for the occasional soccer scrap. Somebody besides their father was feeding them, doing their laundry, helping with homework and keeping the peace.

Morgan sat across Buford Street in his rattletrap Ford Escort, waiting for the Stillwell kids to come out to play. Speed's 1976 Ford pickup was gone, so Morgan assumed he was out working the board. Again.

He sipped convenience-store coffee from a steaming paper cup and listened to the execrable Curtis and The Bug on KROK's morning radio show, finally back after a few days of dead air. He hated their poop-and-boobs humor, especially so early, but they always broke for a network news segment at the top of the hour. Unfortunately, he was a few minutes early.

"So did your mom kiss you goodbye this morning, Bug?" Curtis asked, ever the straight-man.

"Oh, dude, did she ever," The Bug replied lasciviously.

"Cool," said Curtis. "Did she slip you the tongue?"

The two of them cackled as the image sunk in. Morgan grimaced as the inane electronic banter continued.

"So let's give away a date with your mom to the seventh caller, dude," Curtis said.

"Yeah, if we still got seven listeners out there."

"OK, maybe a date with your mom and this new Dixie Chicks CD the Boss won't let us play anymore."

"Yeah, they suck the big one, especially the chubby one."

"Dude, you don't even have a big one."

"Shut up! Looky here —" a zipper sound effect rolls "— that bad boy is a good seven . . . Caller, you're on the air, dude."

A smaller, familiar voice spoke.

"Hi."

"Hey, dude," The Bug said. "Who's this — as if we didn't know?"

"It's Grady," all three said at the same time.

"Grady-dude, you gotta let somebody else dial. Get a life, little dude. "Don't you ever go to school?"

"It's summer."

"Oh yeah. OK, well, you come by the studio and pick up your Dixie Chicks CD and Roxanne will give you The Bug's Mom's measurements. We gotta get to the news, dude."

So much for segues. One of those solemnly familiar network-news themes popped up, followed by a solemnly familiar voice from New York or Los Angeles delivering a solemnly familiar account of yesterday's news. The world in sixty seconds.

But before Curtis and The Bug's truncated broadcast had ended, the front door of the Stillwells' miserable bungalow flew open. A little after eight a.m., the Stillwell kids came out of the house together. An older boy spoke earnestly to each of them before the three younger ones spilled out the crooked gate and ran down the slick street, off to whatever summer-morning adventures beckoned.

The older boy rolled his mountain bike from beside the house, where it must have spent the night unchained. Except for a thin, dirty-blond rat-tail that hung over the back of his collar, he looked to Morgan like every other seventh-grader in Winchester: winter-pale skin, Walkman earphones, too-short black jeans, mud-caked Reeboks, Broncos cap with a brim rolled nearly into a tube, a denim jacket with some colorful logo, and a slightly nerdy countenance that suggested he had no idea there was a bigger, badder world out there. And didn't care.

Morgan got out of his Escort and crossed the street. The drizzle had faded to a nearly invisible mist that condensed on his shirt in minute droplets. As he got closer, he saw the embroidered logo on the kid's jacket: KROK-FM.

One of many prizes, no doubt.

"Grady?"

The kid didn't hear. His Walkman was turned up. Morgan touched his shoulder and the boy jumped.

"Sorry," Morgan apologized as the kid sheepishly hung the earphones around his neck, revealing two hearing aids wrapped behind his ears.

"Are you Grady?"

"Yeah."

"Hi. I'm Jeff Morgan, editor of *The Bullet*. I knew your dad back when we were your age."

Grady fiddled nervously with the zipper pull on his jacket and kept his eyes on the cracked sidewalk. "He's, like, working."

"Yeah, I figured. But I wanted to talk to you."

Grady shrugged.

"Broncos fan?"

"Sorta. Yeah."

"Who's your favorite player?"

"McCaffrey. He's cool."

"Yeah, Eddie's cool. Tough, too. You gonna play next fall?"

"Football? Nah. Don't like the program. It's a waste of bandwidth."

Morgan briefly wondered what kind of "program" a junior high school might have, but he wasn't here to talk X's and O's.

"So, you planning to join the computer club?"

"They don't have a computer club. It's called Tech Habitat, and I was in it last year after school."

"Cool name. What happens in Tech Habitat?"

"You know, computer stuff. Like, writing our own programs and stuff. And games and stuff."

"You like computers?"

Grady shrugged.

"Yeah, I guess."

"I bet you know some cool stuff, huh?"

"Yeah, I guess."

"You got your own computer?"

Now in comfortable territory, Grady started to warm up a little. He even smiled a little, showing his braces.

"Yeah, custom kluge. It's got, like, a dual processor, overclocked to one-point-two gigs each side, and a gig of RAM. Starbuster three-D graphics accelerator. Firenze audio and awesome VoxPop speakers. It's like pretty awesome, but one of my friends has this new rig with a hyper-threaded Pentium Four running three-point-oh-six gigs. It's so sweet, you know?"

Morgan didn't. He responded with one of the few technical computer terms he knew.

"Windows?"

Grady was insulted.

"Pffft. Too primitive. I have better. Linux. Like, waaay better. Waaay cooler. It's like, whoa."

He said it with such sly pride, Morgan knew the kid was a desperado geek, just who and what he was looking for.

"Hey, I bet you could help me down at the paper. I have some viruses in my e-mail. You think you could disinfect my computers?"

"No sweat. Prolly just a Klez worm, or Bugbear."

"Probably won't take a computer whiz like you long at all to fix it, huh? And I could pay you."

"Cool."

"If you could do it today, that'd be great."
Grady shrugged.
"Whatever."
"Where you headed now?"
"Library."

Morgan handed Grady his card. On his way out of the yard, he paused at the broken-down gate and its dangling dog sign.

"You got a dog?"
"Did."
"What happened to him?"
"Dorkfaces busted him. Got wedged in puppy jail. Then deleted."

Morgan was sympathetic. He also knew who had hacked the City Hall computer, delivered an e-mail bomb threat to the "dorkface" mayor, and scrambled KROK's programming. On that basis alone, the hacker couldn't be all bad. And Grady Stillwell — a pale, intelligent, scruffy, intense and abstracted kid who took his job as a surrogate father seriously, disliked authority, was slightly deaf, and preferred to spend summer days in the library instead of the sandlot — was a budding hacker.

"Sorry," Morgan said. "It happens."

Without a word, Grady Stillwell pedaled off down empty Buford Street. He was high-tech *wetware* — geek-slang for the human brain and nervous system, and the only real bit of computer lingo Morgan understood — in a low-tech town.

Morgan's life had dissolved into vapors, and he was risking the feeble remnants of his career and reputation - hell, his life — on a thirteen-year-old vapor-pirate.

Rachel Morgan remained a shadow.

Nearly a full day since she disappeared into thin air, the Perry County Sheriff's Office still had no news either about her or her abductor. No ransom notes, no tips and no corpse. Law enforcement agencies in three states were watching for her, but it was as if she had crossed the electronic borders of Laurel Gardens and melted into the vast, enigmatic Wyoming landscape.

Dr. Shawn Cowper was still suspended in the twilight between living and dying. Trey Kerrigan had posted a guard outside his hospital room, not because he worried the professor would escape, but because of the real possibility he was being targeted by killers with unfinished business.

Claire and Colter were safely concealed far away, in the next county, without an address or a telephone. They had survived a dangerous night and when they awoke, a deputy would deliver Morgan's only message that morning: *I am safe. I love you both.*

But before he hung up, the deputy shared another troubling bit of news, another invisible shadow.

Nobody had seen Carter McWayne in almost twenty-four hours, since the morning after the fire reduced his mortuary to ashes. A state arson investigator interviewed him at his home shortly after six a.m., but when he returned with some follow-up questions three hours later, the mortician had vanished.

CHAPTER ELEVEN

The kid was good.
Instead of a computer kit that looked like the product of a cybersex affair between Bill Gates and Mrs. Goodwrench, thirteen-year-old Grady Stillwell carried only a Leatherman tool — he called it his "geek toolbox" — and a bootable CD with all his disinfectant software in his backpack. Hackers traveled light.

He settled into Morgan's squeaky chair, this slight kid whose feet barely touched the floor, and got to work.

As Morgan watched the kid navigate *The Bullet*'s computers, it occurred to him that he had invited a fox into the henhouse. But he had a feeling that if this young ether-ninja wanted to be inside the newspaper's computers, he didn't need to be sitting in Morgan's chair.

Up to his elbows in DOS prompts, Grady was in his country. He wasn't big on conversation, but Morgan wasn't sure if it was the nature of computer geeks, kids in general, or a little boy who'd grown up straining to hear what anybody said to him and just finally drifted away from human sounds altogether.

"Finding anything?" Morgan asked him.

"Uh, the usual stuff. A couple little, like, Klez worms, and I fixed a couple back doors you left wide open."

"Kill 'em?"

"Oh yeah. Dead. You're virgin again."

"Where did they come from?"

"E-mail usually."

"Yeah, I got a strange e-mail last night. It supposedly came from somebody I know, but they didn't really send it. Is that possible? I mean, maybe it had a virus, huh?"

"Yeah. Easy."

"Probably not a way to figure out where it really came from though, huh? Somebody like that, well, he's probably a pretty smart guy."

Morgan hoped Grady couldn't resist the temptation to show how much smarter he was than some moronic e-mail ghost. And he was right: Grady's eyes brightened at the challenge.

"Local server?"

"Yeah, *BarbedWire.com*."

"Not so smart. There's a back door."

"Show me."

Grady inserted his CD, punched a few keys and, in a matter of seconds, was inside *BarbedWire.com*'s main e-mail server. He'd clearly been there before. A few more seconds, and he'd found the only local file to arrive in Morgan's box in the past twelve hours, the mysterious e-mail from a Shawn Cowper impostor.

"That's it," Morgan said, putting his finger on the screen over Cowper's name. "How'd you do that?"

"Magic," the kid said. "And lazy admins. This guy uses Telnet to log-in as root, so I just set up a sniffer and nabbed his password. Cake. I go there all the time. It's fun to see what people are talking about. Mail servers are easy."

Morgan studied the hash of codes and words on the screen. They meant as much to him as Grady's geek-speak.

"So if it didn't really come from Shawn Cowper, can you find out who sent it?"

Grady pursed his thin lips and rubbed an invisible

spot on his jeans. He suddenly seemed nervous.

"What's wrong?" Morgan asked.

Grady shrugged.

It was all wrong, Morgan knew. Grady now knew it, too. What he might do in the dark seclusion of his own room on his own computer when nobody was watching was one thing. Acting it out for someone else was more daunting. A joy ride through cyberspace was harmless, but even Morgan knew a deliberate back-door assault was sounding more ominous to the seventh-grader, whose only security so far had been in his obscurity.

Morgan surrendered his charade. He looked around the mostly empty newsroom and pulled a chair up close.

"Grady, some bad things have happened. People have been hurt. I need your help. I know about the City Hall computer and the e-mail to the mayor. But I'm not a cop. I'm not gonna bust you or narc on you. I know you're a good kid, a smart kid, and I'm sure there's a way we can work it out. Maybe you can volunteer for some computer work down at City Hall. Payback, you know? They don't have to know. But right now, I need your help. It might save somebody's life."

Grady said nothing. He kept his head down, his magical, skinny fingers tracing uneasy, pointless circles on his trousers. Suddenly, he was just a kid again. A scared kid.

And Morgan had morphed into a father.

"Grady," Morgan said, leaning closer to the boy, "if you can't do it, it's okay. I understand. I won't say anything."

Grady tried to hide the tears welling up in his eyes, but couldn't. They trickled down his smooth cheek.

"My dad would kill me," he said softly.

Morgan knew the fear a son had for his father. And the respect. Especially when little-boy secrets might be exposed. He put his hand on Grady's trembling shoulder.

"Look, Grady, I . . . We don't need to do this."

But Grady wiped his eyes and sat up straight in the chair.

"It's okay. I can do it. But not here. I need my stuff."

"You sure?" Morgan asked.

"I don't want anybody else to die," the scared little boy not-so-deep inside the hacker said. "I miss my mom . . ."

Except for the dirty underwear on the floor, Grady Stillwell's tiny bedroom was more like a wired prison cell than the place where a little boy slept and dreamed.

Where Morgan had tacked posters of Farrah Fawcett, Barbarella, Bob Dylan and "Easy Rider" in his room, Grady's walls were plain and empty. No model airplanes, no anime posters, no Star Wars or Star Trek action figures. The room's single window, facing the shady north side of the house, was made even darker by an ordinary white pull-down shade.

It was a cave with four white walls, an unmade bed and a machine.

In the far corner of the room, on a rudimentary but sturdy table, sat an oversized flat monitor, a scanner, printer, and a few computer modules laced together by a web of power and audio cords. A prodigious stack of home-burned CDs — games, music and software Morgan didn't recognize — were stacked neatly in a metal stand.

A red KROK-FM sweatshirt was draped on the arm of an overstuffed leather office chair, plusher than Morgan's ass had ever known in more than 25 years in newsrooms and probably costing more than almost any other piece of furniture in Speed Stillwell's frowzy little house. No desk lamp, no phone, no photographs — only three empty Mountain Dew cans. More were stashed in a black plastic trash bag on the floor.

It was as if Grady's personal tastes in clothing and accessories — and probably religion and social status, too, Morgan figured — held a much maligned priority in his online world. He staked everything on his skills in the cyber world, where he was esteemed for different talents than the jocks or the skaters in his school. Grady's computer was his great equalizer, and he had built it with his own hands.

Going online for the first time is not unlike being born: you start naked and alone. But as you mature, so do your experiences and knowledge — and avatars. Grady could fashion himself as a D-Day survivor as easily as he could cloak himself as an Oklahoma City librarian with a slutty streak.

To Grady, worrying about how anyone looked on the outside was something only the uninformed did. It was a game he'd always lose, so he elected not to play. Online, he was more. Better. Smarter.

Free.

To Grady, it was more important to have a good chair than a good bed. Better to be a mountain in an artificial world of electrons than a shadow in the messier one he inhabited outside this room.

And this assembly of silicon and sparks on the table before them was the equalizing gateway through which Grady Stillwell passed.

"Where did you get all this stuff?" Morgan asked.

"Here and there. My dad gave me the money," he said. "I help him when he's, like, gone and stuff."

"With your brother and sisters?"

"I guess. Whatever."

"I'm sure he is grateful."

Grady smiled nervously and turned away.

"You're not gonna tell him, are you? About the mayor guy?"

Morgan shook his head.

"And the radio station?"

Morgan was startled.

"What about the radio station?"

"Never mind."

"Too late," Morgan scolded him gently. "What did you do to the radio station?"

"Well, uh, I phreaked."

"Got scared? Why"

"No, dude. Phreaking is like breaking into the phone system. I just busted into the Wyoming Power & Light PBX and, when the radio guys have a contest and stuff, I just flood the switchboard with calls, see? Right before the contest, the deejay usually puts a hold on all the lines into the station so my computer goes to active wait. And so when he takes off the hold, I send about forty calls to his phone. They're all me. Cool, huh?"

"So you win every time."

Grady just smiled, his face as bright as his braces.

"And the other thing I didn't tell you about before. Where I scrambled up their programming computer and stuff. That was a kick."

"You did that?"

Grady smiled even bigger.

"Okay, I promised I wasn't gonna bust you, but it really wouldn't be a good idea for you to do it again," Morgan said sternly. "It's just not right."

"So you won't tell my dad?"

"No, Grady. I won't tell. But maybe you and I can make it right. He doesn't have to know. Nobody does."

"Thanks."

Grady sat down in his extraordinary chair and began to tap his keyboard. In a few moments, he was back inside *BarbedWire.com*'s e-mail server. Morgan watched closely, but he couldn't follow the alternating screens and rapid-fire commands that flew from Grady's fingers. In less than four minutes, he had an answer:

Cowper's putative e-mail had been sent, in fact, from another server.

"What was it?" Morgan asked, a little impatient.

Grady punched a few more keys.

"Oh dude!"

"What?"

Grady giggled, partly out of a sense of accomplishment, partly out of a teen-age boy's scatological sense of humor. He couldn't say it out loud, so he just pointed.

Morgan squinted.

"*TittiesofDeath.com*? What the . . ."

Grady started to type the web address, but the father in Morgan leapt out again. "Hold on. Better let me do this, just in case . . ."

"I've seen 'em before."

"This site?"

"No," Grady said, rolling his eyes. "You know. *Them.*"

Morgan was mildly embarrassed. About discussing breasts with a teen-age boy. About his technical inferiority. About contributing to the delinquency of a minor. About not being able to speak English to a kid, for God's sake.

"Yeah, well, maybe. This is . . . you're just a . . . your dad would kill *me*."

"I've seen lots worse, dude," Grady smirked.

In fact, he probably hadn't.

The home page for *TittiesofDeath.com* promised the best necrophilia and slab photos on the Web — for $39.95 a month. For about the same cost as cable TV, perverts on the farthest edge of sanity could get their still-living rocks off on pictures of dead women, and worse.

"Dead end," Morgan said. "Literally."

"Maybe not," said Grady. "There's always a back door to, like, get inside without paying. Easy. Watch."

Morgan and Grady traded places again. The kid

found an open proxy server and ran an exploit. Within seconds, he was inside an electronic chamber of horrors. On the Chicago cop beat, Morgan had watched autopsies, seen faces peeled back from skulls, observed medical examiners probing knife and bullet wounds with their fingers, even and witnessed the reconstruction of dismembered children as each piece of meat and bone was laid in its approximate living position. He'd come to be able to laugh at the gallows humor in morgues, and hold a conversation about a Cubs double-header over a corpse. He had eaten dinner after visiting a triple murder scene, had never cried about a stranger's death, and had only puked once.

Early on, he learned not to look into the eyes. It was as if the eyes tripped the shutter of his mind's camera, and the image would be burned in his memory forever, a grotesque snapshot he didn't want to see again, ever.

He wasn't callous or pitiless about the dead. Nor was he comfortable with them. He'd simply believed that although it was among the most personal, intimate acts in a human's life, death initiated certain protocols among the living, such as continuing with life.

But this web site took it too far. Various pages featured sex scenes with cadavers, nude and lewdly posed corpses of young women on stainless steel mortuary tables, extraordinarily grisly crime- and accident-scene pictures, and the fleshy, contorted mess found at dozens of suicides.

Although Internet necrophilia salon featured necro-porn, cannibalism, a tribute to Jeffrey Dahmer, torture, snuff videos and mock-murder, *TittiesofDeath.com* carried its own uniquely pleasant disclaimer:

"This site promotes healthy illustrations of sexual intimacy in a loving relationship by exploring fetishes and fantasies that can keep intimacy alive through understanding and accepting private sexual feelings for

THE OBITUARY

the dead as being part of who you are, dead or alive."

"Who'd pay for this shit?" Morgan blurted.

A few more key strokes, a couple administrative screens, and Grady pulled up a list of 2,587 paying customers. Morgan did the math in his head: If each one paid $39.95, that was more than $100,000. In one month. In the anonymous world of online fetishes, death had become a profitable commodity.

The exploitation sickened Morgan more than the stink or the decay of any human carcass.

"Where does this originate, Grady?" he asked.

Grady's little fingers flew. Using Traceroute, he found the IP address, which he ran through something called *arin.net*, which cheerily revealed that the server was in Winchester, Wyoming.

Morgan was startled.

"So can we tell who runs it or who wrote the e-mail I got last night?" he asked, trying to control his breathing.

Grady smirked again, clicked his mouse a couple times, then set loose his password sniffer. Within a few minutes, he had the code name of the server's administrator: *Horus*.

"Isn't he the Egyptian god of death?" Morgan asked.

"Uh, actually, no," Grady responded smugly. "Horus was the son of Isis. She got like pregnant with, uh you know, the *spunkum* from a dead guy. That's like, whoa."

How quaint, Morgan thought, an erudite pornographer.

"How on earth do you know that? Surely they don't talk about spunkum in school."

"Pffft. Nope. He's a good guy in this cool online game I play, called Pharaoh. God of the sky and stuff."

"Okay, so this *Horus*" — Morgan tapped the screen — "he runs a porn site. What do we know about that e-mail?"

Grady flipped to a new screen, typed some codes, and a ledger of *Horus*'s e-mail transmissions appeared.

Many were from customers, but a few were not.

"Does he know we're snooping in here?" Morgan wondered.

"No. I daisy-chained like three different servers. If this guy had any magic, he'd think somebody from the University of Perth was hitting him up."

"Australia?"

"Yeah. Cool, huh? I'd like to go to college there and stuff. But this guy's like a poseur. He knows some stuff, but not as much as me."

"So if a hacker can use different servers anywhere in the world, how do we know if this guy sent that e-mail to me last might?"

Grady plunged into his hard drive for something new and then turned back to the screen and ran through a complicated sequence of codes Morgan couldn't follow. He was completely lost.

Finally, he ran his finger down a screen full of encrypted data. It was incomprehensible . . . but not for long.

Suddenly, the characters on the screen transmuted into plain text and made sense.

"*Horus* logged onto the barbed wire.com server at one-forty-nine a.m.," Grady read. "He created a new screen name for shawn-dot-cowper at one-fifty-eight. He composed an e-mail and sent it at two-oh-four. He deleted the screen name at two-oh-six and slipped out the back door."

Morgan studied the monitor, but his low-tech brain was playing out scenarios. Grady, again, was way ahead of him, already prying into *Horus*'s e-mail.

"And lookie here, dude, he's meeting somebody named Klassen from *QuikSilver.com*, I dunno, someplace in Denver today. He rented an I-Haul truck online. And here's like his flight schedule. Dude's going to Mexico City tonight. United 4767. Leaves 8:27 p.m. Arrives . .

. whoa, at 3:50 a.m. Cool."

"When's he coming back?"

"Um, let's see," Grady said, squinting. "He's not. One-way."

To Morgan, Grady was a true wizard, in a frightening way. *Horus*, by comparison, was a newbie, but who was he?

The kid paged back through the *TittiesofDeath. com* site, skipping the dirty pictures and scrolling the administrative pages nobody ever sees. Then he stopped.

Without saying a word, he just put his finger on a name — plus numbers and passwords for his credit-cards, Social Security, banks and his mother's maiden name — that appeared in a registration page for the server.

Morgan leaned closer. His blood ran cold as he read the name.

Carter McWayne.

On the phone, Morgan explained it all to Trey Kerrigan. The sheriff wondered out loud how Morgan could know such details, but there wasn't time for an interrogation.

"I'll tell you everything on the way," Morgan promised.

"On the way where?"

"To Denver."

"You ain't goin' to Denver, no way, no how, good buddy," Kerrigan snarled. "This is police business, and your nose is stuck in it too far already. You're still a goddam suspect!"

"You need me, Trey, and you haven't got time to bitch about it. I've got his addresses, names, flight times, everything."

Kerrigan cursed. "Meet me at the truck stop in fifteen minutes," he growled. "If you ain't there, tough shit."

Then he hung up.

Shortly after one p.m., armed with Morgan's intelligence, Kerrigan phoned the Division of Criminal Investigation's headquarters in Cheyenne for help. He summarized the problem, but Director Jim Talbott was unenthusiastic.

"Oh, so now you need our help, huh?" Talbot asked snidely.

"That's what you do, Jim," Kerrigan responded. "We have a potential witness on the lam. We're on the way, but your guys are closer. We just need to talk to this guy."

"You've got jurisdiction issues," Talbot warned.

"Fuck that. Make a couple calls. I don't care if we get a little help from the Denver cops, or not. But we gotta get our hands on this guy."

"I want Halstead and Pickard on this. This is our investigation and we get credit for any bust. And I don't want any more shit from you, Kerrigan. Got it?"

Kerrigan hated bureaucrats and he especially hated the DCI's cop bureaucrats, but there wasn't time to make a deal, only a threat.

"If your guys aren't there and this guy flies, there's gonna be a storm of shit, my friend," Kerrigan said, and hung up.

McWayne had some questions to answer.

About the porn site.

About the e-mail.

About the meth lab.

About his rush to get out of Winchester.

About a murder.

Long before midsummer, drought had sucked most of the moisture from the Colorado plains, and the South Platte River had all but evaporated. What remained in the river bottom was a slow-moving, greenish-brown liquid that was too thick to drink and too thin to plow. Its muddy banks reeked with rot, and in the heat of high noon, it hung in the claustrophobic air like a putrid vapor.

While Carter McWayne waited behind the abandoned warehouse on Denver's South Lipan Street, the river's stink embraced him. He inhaled the aroma of motel soap on his pale skin to distract himself from the earthy stench of the desiccated river. It might have seemed odd to anyone else, but not to Carter McWayne, that he'd find the odor of a sick river worse than the odor of a decomposing corpse.

But McWayne's senses were on high alert. His old life was over. In a way, he'd died. He was suspended between Heaven and Hell, and the last thing he wanted was to be exposed, for any price.

A rented black Buick eased slowly through the front gate of the old warehouse and parked outside a side door. A man in a dark suit stepped from the air-conditioned comfort of his sedan into the stifling, fetid air of the warehouse district. Carter waited in the shade.

"Mr. McWayne?" the man said.

Old habits are hard to break. The mortician sized him up immediately — slight of build, bony, maybe in his forties, not at all the international man of mystery he'd imagined. McWayne smiled his perfunctory funeral-director smile, stuck his hand out and just nodded.

"I'm Klassen from *QuikSilver*," the broker said. "Ready to do our little deal?"

"Truck's inside."

"Good. Let's get started and get you on your way."

Inside, Klassen set up his laptop on an overturned box, while McWayne opened the back of his rented truck and, with considerable effort, hefted his ample body inside.

He peeled back an Army surplus canvas tarp and

exposed his cargo: three large wooden crates, sealed with padlocked latches.

Inside, the start of his new life.

One hundred silver bars. Nearly a half million dollars worth of ancient silver. Each bar weighed about eighty-five pounds and was the size of a VCR. The truck had nearly cratered after all four tons of it were loaded, just over the rental company's maximum load limits, but McWayne took it slow.

It came from Laddie's crypt, where it had been hidden within the stone crypt and the coffin itself.

The rest, two hundred more bars worth a million dollars at today's prices, remained safely hidden in sixteen paupers' graves at Pine Lawn Cemetery in Winchester, all buried at night under simple metal markers with the names of old outlaws like Ben Kilpatrick, Bill Carver, Harry Tracy and Harvey Logan. And all were in that part of the graveyard where nobody ever lingers long. Better than a Swiss bank, except for the interest, and the security guards were ghosts. It had been Laddie's idea.

In life, Laddie Granbouche always feared the silver's existence would solve the mystery she tended so diligently. She wanted to be the woman who *might* be Etta Place, because she knew it was better to leave something to the imagination.

In death, she didn't care anymore. The silver was meaningless to a corpse, but she didn't see why anybody else should have it either. It would become just another mystery associated with Butch and Sundance, which was far more valuable to her than money.

And McWayne's father, old Derealous, became her co-conspirator, too moral to reveal Laddie's story after she died. He didn't know if Laddie's legend was authentic, but he buried her silver — every ounce — in seventeen different graves. After all, he'd buried people for more than forty years and all went to their final judgments wearing the diamond rings, gold watches and other precious items. He never took anything from a corpse except its vital fluids. He was too honest.

But Carter wasn't.

Klassen climbed in and helped McWayne open the crates of silver. For an hour, he inventoried the contents on his clipboard, closely examining hallmarks on random bars taken from deep in the boxes. It didn't much matter where it came from, only that it was pure silver and he'd soon draw a fair commission for the trouble of flying to Denver from Los Angeles.

When he finished, they locked everything up, and Klassen went back to his laptop. Connecting to the Internet through a wireless network, he dialed into the server at an off-shore bank in Latvia and logged on. With a few keystrokes, he transferred $416,700 into one special account, and his ten percent commission of $46,300 to another, his own.

"Here's your totally anonymous debit card. It's just a number," Klassen said, handing McWayne what first looked like a common credit card with a shiny silver design, and then several pages to seal the deal. "And here are your receipt, passwords and instructions for accessing your account. Okay, now you're rich, my friend. Go ahead and check."

McWayne looked long at the papers, tapped out a few codes on his Palm Pilot and, sure enough, he was indeed rich. At least, he was rich somewhere out there in the ionosphere.

"Latvia is safe?" he asked. "I mean, I hear the Russian mob is involved."

Klassen smiled.

"It's like the Wild West, my friend," the broker said as he packed his gear. "Where there are few laws and a lot of people willing to take risks, there are profits. Rest assured, they're very discreet."

Then Klassen handed McWayne the keys to the Buick.

"Just go to the nearest ATM and see for yourself," he said. "Try not to spend it all in one place, Mr. McWayne."

Klassen shook his hand, then clambered into the rental truck's cab and it roared to life. Fat and low to the ground under its load, the truck pulled out into the unblinking sun, following the potholed pavement back to the interstate. Its belly nearly scraped the asphalt.

McWayne walked down to the stinking river bank. He waded through muddy beer bottles and dead weeds to an eroded ledge. He reached in his trousers and withdrew a gold pocketwatch on a tarnished chain.

He flicked open the bezel and studied the hands frozen in another time. He wound it a little and listened, but it no longer worked.

So he closed it and wrapped the fob tightly around it, then tossed it into the river. It plunked into the muddy water and was gone.

Bit by bit, Carter McWayne was exorcising Laddie's ghost, which had haunted him for too long.

With half of a day to kill before his flight, he stood alone beside a reeking river, sweaty and rich.

And less haunted.

CHAPTER TWELVE

Morgan hadn't eaten since the day before, and the smell of fat, juicy hot dogs twirling on heated rollers at Motortown Truck Stop's convenience store drew him like a siren's song.

The lunch rush, such as it is at a truck stop, had passed. The dogs were a little forlorn and wrinkled, but Morgan was hungry. With a pair of greasy tongs, he plucked the plumpest bratwurst and laid it across a crumpled bun. He slathered it in mustard, ketchup and relish, the way he ate ballpark dogs.

The Tolbert girl, Robin, was working the day shift at the counter. Today she was reading the autobiography of Bertrand Russell, but when she looked up, her dark eyes flickered with recognition.

"Oh hi," she said to Morgan, far friendlier than the night Cowper had flirted with her. She smiled and was even prettier than she'd seemed that night. "You're the newspaper guy, right? I hear you and your friend got into some bad business the other night. Is he okay?"

"He's gonna make it, but he's not too good right now."

Robin sagged a little.

"Oh."

"But I'm sure he'd be pleased to know you asked about him."

"Well, maybe I could visit sometime?"

Morgan marveled at the complexities of women.

"Sure," he said. "Shawn would like that."

"Shawn," she said, rolling it around in her mouth for a delicious moment. "I didn't know his name. That's nice."

She rang up his hot dog and slid the change across the well-worn glass counter. Morgan headed outside to wait for Trey Kerrigan, and was nearly to the door when Robin called after him.

"Oh, and how's your mom?"

Morgan turned to say something but didn't know exactly what to say.

"I mean, I heard she was sick or something. Somebody was asking me about her a few days ago. Wanted to know what nursing home she was in. I didn't know."

Morgan came back to the counter.

"She's, um, missing. Who asked?"

Robin closed her eyes, as if the darkness might help her remember.

"Gosh, it was . . . sorry, I don't recall. Nobody local, or I'd know right off."

"When did this person ask?"

"I haven't worked since, oh, the graveyard shift Monday night, so it was sometime overnight Monday."

Morgan froze. His mother was stolen from Laurel Gardens on Tuesday.

"It's important. Are you sure you don't know who asked?"

She shrugged and looked a little sad. "No. Sorry."

Morgan pulled a business card from his wallet and left it on the counter, in case she remembered. He thanked her and turned toward the door again.

But he didn't even get past the little chocolate donut rack when Robin hooted.

"Oh, it was the preacher. The guy in the RV. He was hanging around here one night, talking about Jesus and sinning and all that, but not like he really believed it deep down, you know? Wondered if I knew anything about your mom and where she lived. Said he wanted to visit her and pray. Freaky guy. Kind went off the deep end, considering . . ."

"Considering what?"

"Oh, I thought he was just horny, you know? He just doesn't seem like a real preacher. Lots of guys, they . . . well, he said he used to be a cop or something."

Morgan left his hot dog on the counter and sprinted out the front door.

The preacher was taking a dump out back.

Or rather, a flexible hose drained the Reverend Pridrick Leighton's unholy excrement from his gaudy Winnebago's septic tank into the truck stop's waste hole. His RV's internal pump purred with relief.

Morgan came up behind him, out of breath.

"Rev, we need to talk."

Leighton looked up at Morgan through his mirrored sunglasses. Sweat had seeped through the band around his crumpled Cubs cap.

"Hey there, son," he said, as at ease in the heat and odor as only a Texan could be. "Kinda caught me in a little bit of a sacrilegious position here, but I s'pose the Lord had something wise in mind when He created the crapper."

Morgan cut to the chase, literally.

"The clerk inside says you were asking about my mom the night before she disappeared. What was that about?"

"Disappeared? Son, I . . . "

"Do I know you? How would you know anything

about my mother?"

"Hold on a second, son. Lots of folks know you around here. I got ears. I was just asking, that's all. I don't know nothin' about your mama bein' disappeared."

"Why did you care at all?"

"It's just my job."

Morgan wasn't in the habit of calling preachers liars, but he was perilously close.

"Were you ever a cop?"

Leighton drained the last swallows from a diet soda can and crushed the can beneath a black shoe. He said nothing.

"You ever shoot at somebody, Rev?" Morgan persisted.

Leighton looked up.

"I done a lot I ain't gonna confess to you, son. Not here. Not anywhere. Now, I'm sure your mama is somewhere in the Lord's view, and He'll keep an eye on her. She's safe. And if I was you, I'd let the cops do their work, and I'd keep my nose out of that, too. That's their job, and you already done enough. Now, I hope you find whatever or whoever you're lookin' for, son, but it ain't me."

Morgan's jaw tightened. Leighton knew more than he was letting on.

"You ever heard of the Fourth Sign, Rev?"

Leighton looked Morgan in the eye for a long moment before he spoke. His sun-baked face was taut and unforgiving.

"Heard of 'em."

"A bunch of radical religious nuts, you know?" Morgan said. "Got their hands in a lot of bad stuff. Drug deals, gun-running, terrorism. Got people all over. Scouts, mules, runners. Watchers."

Leighton's septic pump ran clear, but he ignored it. Instead, he stopped close enough to Morgan to whisper.

His breath was day-old coffee and sour creamer.

"You've got your hot head up your ass, son."

Trey Kerrigan's Bronco, trailing a slight blue haze, glided around the corner of the truck stop's café and rolled to a stop beside Morgan and Leighton. The sheriff leaned out his window.

"You comin' or are you just breathin' hard? Let's hit the road. McWayne ain't gonna wait at the gate for us to give him a farewell party."

Morgan stared hard at Leighton, but all he saw was his own reflection. The preacher's eyes remained hidden, inaccessible, behind his mirrored lenses.

"'The terror you inspire and the pride of your heart have deceived you, you who live in the clefts of the rocks, who occupy the heights of the hill. Though you build your nest as high as the eagle's, from there I will bring you down,'" the Reverend Pridrick Leighton quoted the Bible softly, ominously.

Morgan recognized the words from the Book of Jeremiah. The serial killer P.D. Comeaux had written them in a letter to Morgan after Comeaux was condemned to die more than ten years earlier. They still chilled Morgan.

Reverend Leighton smiled and waved as Morgan backed away slowly.

"Y'all travel safe now, y'hear?" the preacher smirked. "The Lord is watchin' over ya."

Speed limits are irrelevant to Wyoming highways. No place is close, and going faster only makes the driver feel he is winning some esoteric battle against time and distance. It's an illusion.

Even in a speeding police vehicle, the journey from Winchester to Denver is long. Six hours, give or take the ten or twelve minutes gained by hurtling fifteen miles over the speed limit through blustering headwinds on narrow, decaying, deer-infested state roads.

On the way, Morgan laid it all out for the sheriff. What if McWayne was boldly cooking methamphetamine and shipping it — not to mention running an online necrophilia salon — from a place that nobody cared to linger, a mortuary? What if he had tried to kill Morgan and Cowper to cover up the discovery of the meth operation? What if he had abducted Rachel Morgan as a bargaining chip? And what if, like nothing less than a common grave-robber, he had likely stolen a million-dollar cache of silver from a casket? And what if he replaced it with the headless corpse of a federal agent, who was investigating McWayne's crank lab? And what if Morgan and Cowper had accidentally exposed McWayne, and he was now running?

Kerrigan just listened, but he was dubious, and Morgan knew it. Morgan's theory rested on the literally fantastic theory that Laddie Granbouche had, in fact, been the mythic outlaw Etta Place.

But the hardest thing to believe was that the verbose, slightly nervous Carter McWayne was a murderer, a major-league grave-robber, a drug kingpin, a kinky cyber-pornographer and a kidnapper of senile old women.

"He's in the Rotary Club, for God's sake," was all Kerrigan could say, as if he'd never known a Rotarian to show up late for lunch, much less break the law.

They hit Denver at rush hour. A tanker roll-over had constipated the interstate leading to Denver International Airport, and neither Morgan nor Kerrigan knew the city well enough to navigate the surface streets, so they waited and fumed in four lanes of traffic at a dead stop. Even though his asshole had puckered on the hell-bent drive, Morgan understood the vagaries and vicissitudes of the big city; Kerrigan despised them.

The sun was settling behind the wall of the Rocky

Mountains on the western edge of Denver when traffic started moving again, albeit slowly. It was nearly seven p.m. Kerrigan flipped on his vector lights and scooted around the amoebic mass of commuter traffic on the shoulder.

Denver International wasn't just on the other side of the city. Its circus-tent roof — a white-canvas simulacrum of the snow-covered Rockies — rose from the plains more than twenty miles northeast of Denver's downtown, a crystal garden of high-rise offices, stadiums and skyscrapers utterly that always seemed to Morgan to be misplaced at the edge of the windswept western prairie. It always seemed odd to Morgan that the airport, splattered over fifty-three square miles of former buffalo range, was the tenth largest in the *world*, yet it existed in the least populous corridor of the United States, the Mountain West.

Denver was an island of self-conscious urbanity surrounded by a sea of cow shit and rattlesnakes. Thirty miles from the penthouse suites, artist lofts and overpriced fashion malls — and as far as the eye could see — were ranches still run by families that had homesteaded this country.

Kerrigan parked at the far end of the passenger drop-off zone. A badge-heavy traffic cop challenged him, but Kerrigan whipped out his badge and the cop let them pass. Inside the terminal, they checked the departure screen. McWayne's flight was leaving in ninety minutes from Gate B37, a concourse reached only by the airport's subway train. If he was already there, they could talk to him; if not, they'd wait.

But the airport's security screeners saw it differently. Since September 11, nobody got a free pass, especially if they were carrying guns instead of tickets. At Kerrigan's request, a uniformed technician with a hand-held metal detector radioed for two of the airport's main security officers, moonlighting city cops who hustled Morgan and Kerrigan into a small, airless room.

They listened to Kerrigan's story, but a Wyoming sheriff, far from his home and legal jurisdiction, had little stroke and less respect among the sleek and cocky Denver cops. They seemed amused by the ancient Colt revolver he slung on his hip, like he was Matt Dillon or something. His emergency was not theirs.

It was seven-fifty-five p.m. McWayne's plane would board in a few minutes. Time was running out.

Finally, the airport cops got clearance to escort Kerrigan to the gate.

But not Morgan. He wasn't a law enforcement officer, and the courtesy would not extend to him. He'd have to wait outside the security gates in the main terminal.

The three cops finally rushed down to the subway platform, skipping escalator steps as they ran, Kerrigan in the lead.

The brief train ride through the airport's concrete bowels dumped them at the B concourse, where they scrambled up the moving stairs past other passengers toward Gate 37. On the way, Kerrigan heard an announcement for the flight's first-class ticket-holders to prepare to board. His lope quickened to a sprint through the sparsely crowded concourse, the two cops close behind.

Passengers had already queued up at the door to the jet way when Kerrigan and his escorts arrived at the gate.

McWayne wasn't among them.

They milled around the boarding area. Kerrigan watched for McWayne, and the cops watched Kerrigan. Passengers quietly hovered, impatiently waiting for the invitation to economy boarding. Gate clerks checked boarding passes, plucking the random passenger from line for another security screening. Nothing seemed amiss.

Except that Carter McWayne was not there.

At the gate, an appealing redhead with a pleasant smile and tired eyes checked her computer for Kerrigan, then spoke to a flight attendant by phone. McWayne was indeed booked on the flight, she told him, and he had checked his baggage at the main ticket counter, but the first-class passenger who had been assigned Seat 1B had not yet boarded.

Morgan stood outside a Seattle's Best coffee stall and watched the stream of anonymous travelers float past. He checked his watch every few minutes until McWayne's flight to Mexico should have been pushing away from the gate.

Maybe it had been a trick. McWayne didn't seem to be the kind to set up an elaborate diversion, but maybe Morgan had underestimated him. Maybe he was skipping to France, not Mexico. Maybe he caught an earlier flight. Maybe nothing was as it seemed. Maybe Grady Stillwell was playing another practical joke with a computer. Maybe McWayne was taking an innocent vacation after his family business was destroyed. Maybe this was all a wild goose chase. Maybe Morgan was wrong about everything.

Anything was possible.

The only thing that seemed utterly *impossible* at that moment was that the tubby Carter McWayne would suddenly appear in the swarm of people.

But he did.

McWayne emerged from the subway platform in precisely the spot where Morgan's eye had lingered. He carried no luggage. His white shirt was damp with sweat and wrinkled, his porky face pale and drawn, like he was about to cry. He seemed not to move under his own power but by some magnetic force field that drew him forward against his will.

Then Morgan saw why: McWayne was flanked by DCI agents Halstead and Pickard, both tanned and dressed as if they'd been working undercover in the Professional Golfers Association.

They were moving fast toward the baggage claim area and the parking garage beyond. Morgan started toward them, but he was swimming upstream in the surge of people, rolling suitcases and skycap carts. He kept looking for Kerrigan and the two airport cops, but they weren't with McWayne and the DCI guys.

DCI is trying to hijack this bust, Morgan thought. *Those pricks.*

By the time Morgan had picked his way through the mass, they had disappeared around the corner, toward the stainless-steel ranks of carousels where bags were squirted out of the labyrinthine bowels of DIA's infamous state-of-the-art baggage system.

Morgan scanned the baggage-claim area, but his targets had blended into the crowd. White shirts, pudgy men and razor-cut pretty boys abounded, all moving in different speeds and directions among the throng. If nothing else, he'd slow them down until Kerrigan showed up — if he could find them.

Then he saw them at the far end of the mall. McWayne was balking at an automatic doorway into the passenger pick-up lanes and the dark parking garage beyond. Pickard and Halstead had grabbed him by each arm, trying discreetly to usher him out into the night.

Morgan dashed toward them. Within hailing distance, he shouted to get their attention over the din of gray-noise.

"Pickard! Halstead! Wait up!"

Pickard looked toward him, and so did McWayne,

who stiffened his legs and tried to wrench himself free of the two agents.

"Jeff! Help me!" McWayne screamed.

Morgan froze in his tracks as the attention of passengers within the sound of McWayne's voice suddenly focused on the frightened little man and the two strapping men struggling with him.

Then Halstead drew his Glock from a shoulder holster beneath his wind-breaker. He drew a bead on Morgan, who raised his hands as passengers screamed and ducked behind any cover they could find, including suitcases.

"Not another step, mister," he barked. "This is police business. Back off! Now!"

McWayne cried out as Pickard wrestled him through the door.

"They're gonna kill me! They're gonna . . ."

Pickard, who'd pulled his own gun, pistol-whipped McWayne with a single blow to the head, then dragged him out the sliding glass. Halstead backed slowly through the door after them, then disappeared into the dark night beyond the fluorescent reflections in the glass.

Nobody moved for several seconds.

Where were Kerrigan and the cops? Morgan wondered, even before he began to breathe again. A baby began to cry and then another, until the enormous space had fallen into chaos. They weren't detaining McWayne, or even arresting him. This looked more like an abduction.

Morgan was on his own, and he couldn't let them get away. He ducked out a different door into the street where cars were jockeying for position, stopping and going, seeking purchase at the curb to pick up passengers and then get the hell out. Half a block away, he caught a glimpse of Pickard and Halstead hauling the dazed McWayne into the shadows of the parking garage. Edgy drivers honked as he threaded his way among the cars and the reunions and the loose luggage to the other side of the busy four-lane street, then another, and followed them into the darkness.

Squealing tires, distant voices and car horns echoed through the concrete warren of the parking garage. Morgan plunged deeper into the maze, but they had simply melted into the dead air, shadows and steel. Morgan's curse reverberated in the concrete cave.

And so did a whimper.

Morgan followed the sound. He couldn't be sure where it had come from as noise bounced in every direction.

He heard it again off to his left, beyond the elevator shaft, in a murky corner of the garage, near an enormous black Suburban with impenetrably tinted windows. Or perhaps inside it.

Crouched low, Morgan moved closer, keeping a safe distance and using other cars for cover.

Suddenly, McWayne cried out.

"Jeff! Help me!"

The sound came from the other side of the Suburban, not inside. Morgan felt a cold rush of blood beneath his skin. He peered along the pavement and saw McWayne on his hands and knees on the far side of the vehicle. Alone.

He ran to help. McWayne was there, crying, down all fours like a whining, overfed dog — and Pickard sat in the open door of the passenger seat, his feet on the running board, his gun to the back of McWayne's head.

"Took you long enough," the agent said.

Adrenaline spurted into Morgan's bloodstream, but before he could run, he felt the cold barrel of Halstead's Glock behind his ear. He raised his hands, palms open.

"Couldn't have worked out better, eh, Scott?" Halstead said to Pickard. "Two fish on one hook."

"Perfect, Eric," Pickard responded by kicking McWayne in the ribs. "I'm glad we missed him the other night. This is much better. You da man."

Morgan was ensnared in something he didn't quite understand.

"Hey, I'm unarmed. I'm on your side."

Halstead laughed menacingly as he frisked Morgan.

"Our side, huh? That's a good one, you fuckin' pencil-dick. Okay, we're ready here."

"Ready for what?" Morgan asked.

Pickard chuckled as he helped McWayne to his unsteady feet.

"Why, you're gonna be a fucking hero, Morgan," he said. "See, we're detaining Mr. McWayne here for questioning, just like your piss-ant sheriff buddy requested. But Mr. McWayne here is gonna grab my gun while I'm helping him into our vehicle. He's gonna shoot, and you're gonna take a bullet for my partner. Then my partner is gonna shoot your assailant, Mr. McWayne, dead. And we're gonna try — unsuccessfully, I'm afraid — to save your life. Kinda sucks, don't it?"

Morgan couldn't speak, but Halstead could.

"Don't worry," he said, "we'll tell all your media pals how you died bravely. Just try not to piss your pants. It doesn't look good on the evening news."

"Okay, who gets it first?" Pickard asked. "Maybe the paperboy should watch. Fat-boy here got to watch the last one and he didn't seem real appreciative."

Pressed into the dark, empty space between the Suburban and the wall with a gun to his head, the terrified McWayne did just that. A damp, pungent stain spread across his groin, and trickled around his shoes.

"You chickenshit bastard," Pickard snarled. Again, he pistol-whipped McWayne, who dropped to his knees, stunned.

"Fuck him. Just do it," Halstead commanded, and

Pickard raised his handgun. He aimed it at Morgan's chest.

The air exploded. The roar of a gunshot pierced the garage's stagnant air and ricocheted through Morgan's skull. Before he could open his eyes to see what killed him, he was hurled to the pavement hard, laying raw the flesh of his arm and face.

Is this how it is to be shot? his brain asked him. *Shouldn't it hurt more? How does it end, this story? How does it start? Will someone tell Claire? Colter ... Bridger ...*

Blackness seeped in around the edges.

Dying wasn't so hard.

CHAPTER THIRTEEN

Funerals are for the living, not the dead.
It had rained the night before, a warm July rain, pregnant with distant thunder. The earth of Pine Lawn Cemetery was soft and the air scented with new-mown wet grass, because it was Monday and the caretaker always mowed on Monday, come rain or shine. The customers didn't care.

And if the cemetery had its peculiar rhythms, so did dying in Winchester, Wyoming. The church service would begin at ten a.m. on burying days, be finished by eleven, and then a cortege of working-men's pickups and Sunday sedans would meander slowly to Pine Lawn Cemetery for a brief graveside service. Come rain or shine.

The mourners' faces might be re-arranged in church and in the small circle gathered around the grave, but they remained essentially the same. Death was a community event. Any loss in a small town sent out its dreadful ripples, and few were untouched by it. Saying goodbye at the cemetery was as natural as saying hello in the park on a Saturday.

Today, the young widow and her child sat tearfully while pallbearers placed the coffin on its bier. The sun was high overhead, the shadows on the ground dispersed.

They all prayed, and the words drifted on the breeze.

The Lord is my shepherd, I shall not want ... green pastures ... quiet waters ... although I walk through the valley of the shadow of death, I will fear no evil, for you are with me ...

The Reverend Joel Wright, the Presbyterian pastor in town, said a few more words before the casket was lowered into the damp ground.

"He had a passion for what he did," the preacher said, "and he died doing it. He put himself in harm's way so that we would be secure and warm. He died as he lived, knowing his presence made us safer, and it made us better. May he continue to watch over us."

A bagpipe played an ancient Scottish dirge and a squad of Perry County deputies fired a salute to a man who died protecting another.

And Cecil James Box, who'd only been a deputy for three years, was laid to rest forever in the town where he was born twenty-four years before, and never left.

And never would.

After the service, Morgan visited Laddie Granbouche's empty grave one last time.

After a long hug and a kiss from her husband, Claire took Colter and Rachel Morgan back to Laurel Gardens, where she had miraculously re-appeared after news of Pickard's death and Halstead's arrest in Denver. Nobody knew who brought her, and the Perry County Sheriff's Office — that is to say, its six remaining patrolmen and investigators — was focused intently on the biggest crime it had ever worked. And every hour, it was getting bigger.

But she was home and safe. She had no memory or awareness of what had happened, but had apparently been treated well. She kept talking about the sea and sunflowers.

After the press ran on Wednesday, Morgan, Claire and Colter planned to take a long weekend. They were going camping together in Montana, which seemed far enough away to Morgan to be close to his wife and child again. Maybe he'd show his son how to shoot one of his grandfather's guns.

Morgan resolved it would be the first a many more days when he would walk away from the newspaper long enough to take his son fishing or make love to his wife without the haunt of his work.

Tomorrow, the state crime lab and the county commissioners would remove the crumbling old crypt for good, giving Laddie's memory a fresh start and a fresh memorial in another part of the cemetery. And gravediggers would begin exhuming the rest of Laddie's silver from other graves, each one an alias for Laddie's grand joke. Who owned it now? Nobody knew, but that's why God made lawyers.

Morgan merely contemplated the life, the death and the mystery of Laddie Granbouche. Her ghost had turned out to be the wind generated by a butterfly's wing, moving the water and, somewhere beyond the horizon, creating a tempest.

Carter McWayne had stolen some of Laddie's silver, which she had stolen from Pancho Villa, which he had stolen from Wells Fargo. Or maybe the truth was not so romantic. Morgan didn't know and, for the moment, he didn't care as he traced Laddie's epitaph with his finger: *Yesterday is history, tomorrow is mystery.*

"That's evidence there, friend," said a voice behind him.

It was Sheriff Trey Kerrigan, in a full dress uniform he never wore. A small black band of electrical tape wrapped his badge.

Morgan nodded.

"Trey, I'm sorry about Cecil. I feel guilty."

Trey put his good hand on Morgan's shoulder.

"Wasn't your fault. He was doing his job. You gonna be okay?"

"Yeah. Eventually. Shawn doing okay this morning?"

Kerrigan shrugged.

"Takin' it pretty hard about his students. I still got a guard up there, just in case. South Dakota found the vans yesterday. McWayne told us what happened. The doc was supposed to be the real target, but he stayed here. They was just kids."

Morgan was silent for a moment. He'd already been told about the attack on the USF vans. Of all the players in this tragedy, they were the most innocent.

"McWayne, is he talking?"

Kerrigan smiled wryly.

"He's singin' like a meadowlark. And you wouldn't believe the song."

"Try me."

"Pickard and Halstead were on Fourth Sign payroll, just like the mob. Scouts. They mostly just looked for opportunities and kept the wolves away from the door, you know? Well, they apparently got wind of McWayne's little web site. Suddenly, they had the poor guy in a pickle. He could help them, or he could go to jail, plain and simple."

"Blackmail?"

"You got it."

"So they built the meth lab in McWayne's parlor?"

"Damn straight," Kerrigan said. "Who's gonna raise a stink about queer smells comin' from a mortuary? Big ol' barrels of chemicals comin' and goin' all the time. Big boxes bein' carried away . . ."

"So Shawn Cowper was right," Morgan said.

"Yeah, and since he woke up, he's remindin' me of that fact on a regular schedule. And that lab was a big-ass operation, too. FBI guys are still checkin' but we know it distributed all the way down to Arizona and out to Oregon."

"Who was cooking the crank?"

"They sent guys in. McWayne just had to keep his mouth shut. Pickard and Halstead were just the enforcers, like hit men. They were watching everybody, and they knew who was watching."

"Rodriguez."

"Yeah, Rodriguez. He'd got inside, like he was some cocky ex-con. ATF gave him a whole fake prison record for drug-running and murder and everything the Fourth Sign desired in an employee. He was trying to follow the money all the way to the fuckin' heart of the Fourth Sign, but he screwed up by trying to turn McWayne. Pickard and Halstead got him one night . . ."

Kerrigan choked up. He had just buried a cop, and the wound was still too fresh. But he steeled himself and continued.

"They took him back to the mortuary and . . . they made McWayne watch. And they told him that's what would happen to him if he got stupid. They handed him Rodriguez's head, just . . . Well, McWayne wasn't gonna talk. He kept the body in his winter salt bin in the basement until he come up with a plan to escape."

"Is that when he started stealing Laddie's silver?"

"Yeah. When the county come up with the idea to move the crypt, McWayne saw his chance. He reckoned he could steal the silver and dump Rodriguez's body where it'd be found, I guess."

"That's bullshit, Trey," Morgan fumed. "If he wanted the cops to know about Rodriguez, he could have propped him up on Main Street and left a note."

"He was scared shitless, Jeff. Still is. I guess him and Rodriguez had got to be friends. He felt some responsibility, I s'pose. People do dumb things when they're scared."

"So it was McWayne who tried to kill us and burned down the mortuary?"

"Nope. It was Pickard. Or at least that's what Halstead is sayin'. Once you and the doc got on the scent, they started followin' you. When you busted into McWayne's, they knew the jig was up. And you give 'em a damn fine chance to kill all the birds with one stone. Clean as a whistle."

Morgan shook his head.

"And the sniper?"

"Pickard again. But I suspect it was a team effort. But while they was shootin' at you, they lost track of McWayne. He took off that same night."

"Has he explained the e-mail he sent to me, under Cowper's name?" Morgan asked.

"Carter says it was his way of warning you and protecting the doc. He figured we'd put a guard on him. He just didn't want anybody to know it was him. He was high-tailing it out of town, and those DCI guys just lost him."

"Lost him?"

"Yep, but thanks to you, they found him again. Once their meth lab burned down, they didn't need him anymore. He was a liability, not an asset. I guess the plan was to snatch him before he got on the plane and take him out somewheres and whack him. I guess they planned to say he was resisting arrest and tried to escape."

"But I got in the way."

"Yep."

"Shit."

"Lucky for you, the ATF was there, huh? I still don't know how they knew it was going down, but they had a tip. They'da preferred to arrest Pickard and Halstead, but they saved your life instead."

"I don't remember any of it until the ambulance was there. Just Pickard . . ."

THE OBITUARY

Kerrigan squeezed Morgan's shoulder, still a little sore from the night in the mortuary.

"ATF sniper took him out, and Halstead freaked. The ATF guys come down fast on him, and I guess you got roughed up a little. Nothing personal. I'm sure you'd rather be bruised and alive than perfectly dead, huh?"

Morgan touched the bandage that covered twelve stitches on his flayed jaw. "Yeah, I guess it is," he said.

"Well, we got plenty of loose ends to tie up, my friend. McWayne is likely to do some time, and DCI is damn sure gonna get more credit for this fiasco than it wanted. I best get back to it," the sheriff said, expending his good left hand to Morgan, who squeezed it with his own uninjured left hand. "Glad you're off the hook."

"Was Hi Goldsmith involved in all this?" Morgan asked, almost an afterthought.

Kerrigan looked around, as if to keep the secret.

"It's lookin' like an accident, pure and simple," Kerrigan said. "We found some stuff at his house that suggests he'd done it before and was into that stuff. Just miscalculated, I guess."

The mourners had dispersed, except for a few who lingered at Cecil's grave while the casket was lowered. Morgan watched it disappear and said a little prayer, thanking the Lord it wasn't him in that box.

Morgan looked up into the ancient cottonwoods. The sky was azure, uncluttered by clouds and without the promise of more rain. If there was a Heaven up there, he imagined he could see the bottom floor.

But he didn't see the man who came up behind him.

"Mr. Morgan?"

Startled, he turned.

It was Pridrick Leighton, the truck-stop preacher. *A loose end.* Morgan stiffened.

"I just wanted to say how sorry I am about your friend," Leighton said. "It's hard to know exactly what to say at times like this."

Morgan pursed his lips.

"But that's your job, isn't it, rev? To know what to say?"

Leighton looked off into the distance, across the stone garden of the cemetery, and smiled. Then he took off his mirrored sunglasses and wiped them with a greasy finger.

"Well, not really," he said. "Seein' as how this thing has sorta wrapped up, I guess I oughta introduce myself."

He extended his hand to Morgan, who was reluctant to take it.

"Name's Grant Dreyer. ATF."

Morgan's jaw dropped.

"I worked with Gabe Rodriguez. Good cop. I appreciate what you did for him and his family. Anyway, after he was . . . well, we couldn't lose this investigation. We knew they had somebody inside, probably a cop on the take, but we didn't know exactly who it was. We were close, but you were closer."

"You're ATF?"

"Yeah. I've been inside the Fourth Sign as a scout goin' on three years. A truck stop preacher talks to a lot of people, you know? Good cover. Didn't save any souls, but I'd tell them about loads that were left unattended, or pass on delivery information. Most of the time it was a set-up. Halstead's bust opened the floodgate. As of today, we've popped a couple dozen guys in six states, all major league busts, and there'll be lots more. Drugs. Guns. Murder. Interstate piracy. Racketeering. They're going down hard and long."

Morgan was speechless. If Leighton, or Dreyer, was telling the truth, the Fourth Sign's back would soon be broken. All he could manage was a flabbergasted smile.

"Yeah, Jerry Overton said you'd be pleased. It's your scoop, if you want it. He says to call him when you need a good quote for your story. This was his baby before he retired, you know?"

"He knew?"

"Yeah, he knew all along. And when the shit started to come down — Jesus Christ, it's good to be able to cuss out loud again! Anyway, when the shit started coming down, Overton pulled some strings to get your mom out of there, for her safety. You were next, but you moved too damn fast."

"You took my mom? You're 'Comeaux'?"

"Yeah, she was with me the whole time. Overton said if you didn't know the Fourth Sign was involved, that name would wake you up, you know? She's a nice lady, and I wish I'd have known her before. Anyway, we lost McWayne until you and the sheriff came by to see me. We made a call to see where he was going and the rest was easy. ATF had guys there hours before you. Halstead and Pickard were under surveillance all afternoon. We had a nice, quiet arrest planned until you showed up."

Morgan scuffed the wet grass. He didn't know what to say.

"The Lord — and the U.S. government — work in mysterious ways," Dreyer said.

Then he smiled and walked away.

Laddie Granbouche would remain a mystery.

As Morgan stood at the crypt, Old Bell's obituary bubbled up through the years. *Did she truly ride with and love mythic outlaws ... or was she merely a lonely woman who yearned for a history more romantic than her own? Have we missed our chance to know her? To know ourselves? The river flows on.*

Maybe Laddie's mystery made life more interesting, Morgan thought. No legend worth his — or her — salt ever died. They cheated death.

Does it matter if Laddie Granbouche carried Etta's true memories inside her, or if she just snatched a mythic life for herself? Does it matter if the shootout at the OK Corral was a mythic struggle between good and evil — or a gang rumble in a manure patch? History was funny that way. People shaped it more than it shaped people, Morgan thought.

Even if Cowper and his team had proven Laddie Granbouche was, in fact, Etta Place — or not — the argument wouldn't have died. They never do.

Morgan smiled. Even though mysteries beg to be solved, he knew the best ones never are.

Jefferson Morgan inhaled, and wondered if particles of death floated on the cemetery air.

After a night of rain, the graveyard smells like sweet resurrection. The morning sun draws out the damp, the dark and the ferment, and they mingle as they rise on the warming air.

The long-dead floated in the July morning, cleansed by the clay and concealment in Wyoming's ancient soil.

The living simply had to breathe.

Have you read the first book in the
Jefferson Morgan Mystery series?
The DEADLINE

"A brilliant and engaging blend of fast-paced suspense, painstaking prose and characters so real they could drive down southbound I-25." —**DENVER POST**

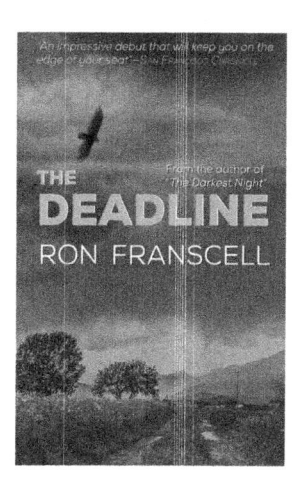

A dying convict's last request thrusts small-town newspaperman Jefferson Morgan into a deadly maelstrom as he explores a fifty-year-old case of child murder — a wound his town still isn't ready to scrape open. Under the heaviest deadline of his life, and amid threats from unexpected foes, Morgan must struggle with his own conscience to tell a story no matter the consequences, dig deep into the town's past, and unveil a killer who's managed to remain hidden in plain sight for almost 50 years. Before CJ Box and Craig Johnson mined mysteries from the Wyoming landscape, national bestselling author Ron Franscell introduced crime fiction fans to Jefferson Morgan and the Winchester Bullet in **THE DEADLINE** and now in its exciting sequel, **THE OBITUARY**.

Learn more about THE DEADLINE
and how to order the book at:
http://wildbluepress.com/obit-deadline

RON FRANSCELL

MORE BOOKS BY RON FRANSCELL

Nonfiction

EVIL AT THE FRONT DOOR (2014)
THE SOURTOE COCKTAIL CLUB (2012)
DELIVERED FROM EVIL (2011)
THE DARKEST NIGHT (2008)

Fiction

ANGEL FIRE (1998)
THE DEADLINE (1999)
THE OBITUARY (2003)

Crime Buff's Guides

Crime Buff's Guide to the Outlaw Southwest (2014)
Crime Buff's Guide to Outlaw New Mexico (2014)
Crime Buff's Guide to Outlaw Arizona (2014)
Crime Buff's Guide to Outlaw Pennsylvania (2013)
Crime Buff's Guide to Outlaw Washington DC (2012)
Crime Buff's Guide to the Outlaw Rockies (2011)
Crime Buff's Guide to Outlaw Texas (2010)

NOW FOR THE FIRST TIME AS AN EBOOK AND AUDIO BOOK!

NO STONE UNTURNED: The True Story Of The World's Premiere Forensics Investigators

"A fascinating journey into the trenches of crime [investigation]"
--Lowell Cauffiel, New York Times bestselling author of House of Secrets

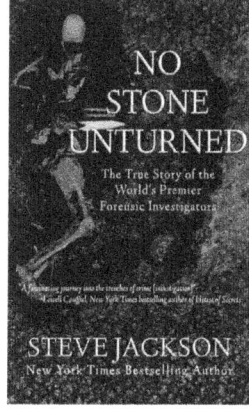

Order Your Updated Copy of NO STONE UNTURNED at **wildbluepress.com/ NSU-BM**

NO STONE UNTURNED recreates the genesis of NecroSearch International as a small eclectic group of scientists and law enforcement officer who volunteer their services to help locate the clandestine graves of murder victims and recover the remains and evidence to assist with the apprehension and conviction of the killers. Known early on as "The Pig People" because of their experiments in locating graves using the carcasses of pigs (because of their similarities to human bodies), NecroSearch has evolved and expanded into one of the most respected forensic investigation teams in the world. In NO STONE UNTURNED, New York Times bestselling author Steve Jackson, the author of **BOGEYMAN** and MONSTER, vividly tells the story of this incredible group and recounts some of their most memorable early cases that if taken separately would each make great true crime books.

See the Next Page for More about No Stone Unturned

"The book covers the group's quirky beginnings and digs into its most important cases suspensefully; Jackson's sharp eye misses nothing in the painstakingly rendered details. A must-have for true crime fans, it should also be of great interest to anyone fascinated with the practical applications of science."
—Publisher's Weekly (Starred Review)

"A fascinating account of a group of extraordinary people who volunteer their time and expertise to locate hidden murder victims for the police and prosecutors. ... Recommended for public and academic libraries."
—Library Journal

"No Stone Unturned" delves into cases that would make good novels, but they're real. Furthermore, he describes a group of uncommon people performing uncommon tasks, and he does it with respect, accuracy and genuine style."
—Ron Franscell, bestselling author of The Darkest Night.

Order Your Updated Copy
of NO STONE UNTURNED at
wildbluepress.com/NSU-BM

WILDBLUE PRESS

Check out more True CRIME and Crime Fiction from WildBlue Press
www.WildBluePress.com

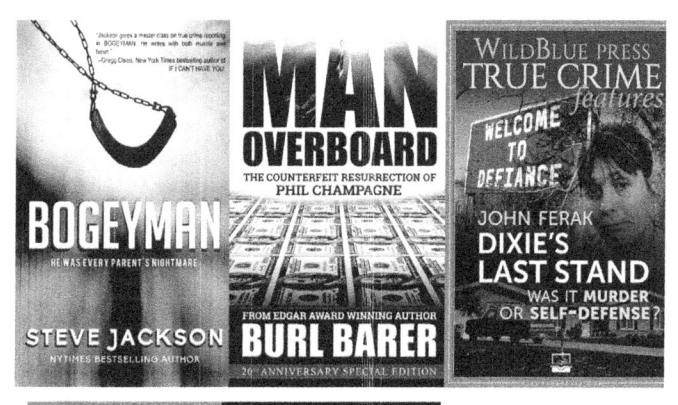

Go to WildBluePress.com to sign up for our newsletter! By subscribing to our newsletter you'll get *advance notice* of all new releases as well as notifications of all special offers. And you'll be registered for our monthly chance to win a **FREE collection of our eBooks and/or audio books** to some lucky fan who has posted an honest review of our one of our books/eBooks/audio books on Amazon, Itunes and GoodReads.

Made in the USA
Coppell, TX
07 December 2020